D1556127

BODY ON THE ROCKS

RACHEL GREEN

ALSO BY RACHEL GREEN

Body on the Rocks

Five Dead Men

Body on the Rocks
Copyright © Rachel Green 2021

The right of Rachel Green to be identified as the author of this work has been
asserted in accordance with the Copyright, Designs and Patents Act 1988.

All rights reserved. No part of this publication may be reproduced, stored in or
transmitted into any retrieval system, in any form, or by any means (electronic,
mechanical, photocopying, recording or otherwise) without the prior written
permission of the publisher. Any person who does any unauthorised act in
relation to this publication may be liable to criminal prosecution and civil
claims for damages.

This is a work of fiction. Names, characters, businesses, places, events and
incidents are either the products of the author's imagination or used in a
fictitious manner. Any resemblance to actual persons, living or dead, or actual
events is purely coincidental.

To find out more about Rachel Green visit: www.rachelgreenauthor.com

1

Margot was coming back from the cove, picking her way along the rocky headland path, when the shout came down from the street. Fifty metres away, a small group of men were running along Rue Voltaire, heading towards the harbour.

It was seven a.m. and the town was slowly waking up. Keen to see what the commotion was, Margot hastened up the last few steps to the street. With her Speedo still damp beneath her beach sarong she would normally go straight home to change, but instead she followed the hurrying figures into the harbour where a small crowd had gathered beside the concrete wall.

The fortified harbour dominated the little town of Argents-sur-Mer. An ancient stone turret stood sentry at its mouth while beyond it the bright blue waters of the Mediterranean sparkled in golden sunshine. Margot searched the crowd for a familiar face but failed to spot anyone she knew. Most of them were fishermen, and they were speaking in Catalan, though she knew enough to get the gist:

"Someone saw a boat out last night."

"There was fog on the côte."

"They won't reach it across the rocks. Fetch François. He'll need to get a boat out."

Margot weaved between the gathered bodies to find a space by the wall. On the other side of the concrete barrier a beach of rocks sloped down to the sea. It was so steep and littered with such large boulders that no one would normally go out that way, but now two boys were heading in the direction of the water, leaping between the rocks like a pair of human fleas. Margot shielded her eyes from the dazzling sun. It wasn't obvious what they were up to. Picking up on her confusion, the man at her side leaned in. "Down there. See?" He nudged her arm.

He was pointing at a formless object just visible at the bottom of the beach, seemingly morphed into one of the big brown rocks. At first Margot couldn't believe it actually was what it appeared to be, but as the teenagers honed in on it she realised it couldn't be anything else: a small brown body, face down on a boulder.

The first boy to reach it paused on the edge of an adjoining rock, as still as a statue. Despite his initial bravado he now seemed unsure and waited for his friend to catch up. After a brief exchange of words, the first boy hopped to the body and crouched beside it. He gave it a brief examination, his actions mechanical. A hush descended upon the crowd as he stood up straight and looked back at the harbour. Cupping his hands to his mouth, he cried:

"*Il est mort!*"

And several people gasped.

———

The route over the rocks was too perilous to bring in the body so François, the harbourmaster, instructed two of the fishermen to launch the RIB. Once they were on their way Margot moved further along the wall for a better view. The RIB turned sharply as it emerged from the harbour and then slowed to edge its way along the beach of rocks. It was a tricky landing, and when one of the fishermen jumped out he slipped and almost fell. They passed the body between them and loaded into the back of the RIB where it was quickly covered with a tarpaulin. The teenage boys looked on as the boat powered away.

Margot took the shortcut to the jetty by going down the old stone steps and joined the smaller group that stood waiting. François had made a barrier out of rope and was urging people to stand back. By the time the RIB came in many hands were ready and waiting to help, but the body was so small it didn't take much lifting. After removing the tarpaulin, two men swung it up onto the jetty and laid it flat on its back. And suddenly before them on the wooden planks lay the lifeless figure of a small boy, no more than six or seven years of age.

His eyes were still open and his face bloated, his little body naked apart from a pair of blue and red football shorts. A long moment of stunned surprise passed before someone thought to cover him up. But the hush was rudely broken by a *tut* and a *plop*. Margot turned sharply: a few metres away an elderly man had just spat into the water.

"*Migrants,*" he muttered, and headed off with an indifferent shrug of his shoulders.

Margot's eyes bored holes into the back of his head.

2
———————

News of the discovery spread quickly through the town. When Margot went to buy cigarettes later that morning everyone she encountered was talking about it. Then, in the boucherie, the owner's young assistant came in to announce that a second body had been found, this one down by the old fort.

"He was just lying there, dead on the beach," she declared, breathless and excited, as she knotted the strings of her apron.

It was the body of an adult male, similar ethnicity to the boy, spotted by a dog-walker. The assumption was that they were migrants from North Africa, washed up after an accident at sea, and everyone seemed to be an expert on the subject despite the fact that the washing up of bodies in a town like Argents-sur-Mer was far from an everyday occurrence. Margot bought some duck comfit and a coil of Toulouse sausage and headed home.

She took Rue Voltaire back to the harbour and turned right into the lane that led to her cottage. A multi-coloured row with hers at the centre, pretty as a picture with its yellow-washed walls and painted blue shutters. She unlocked the gate to the covered passageway and went through to the courtyard at the rear from where she entered the kitchen via a pair of glazed doors. And then, because it was Friday, she opened a bottle of champagne.

She unpacked her shopping and then gathered the ingredients for her cassoulet. It was a winter dish really but making one usually cheered her up.

The house had been her and Hugo's holiday retreat for the past five years – their escape from the pressures of his job in the Paris police. In two years, when Hugo would have turned fifty-five, the plan had been to move here full time; in reality, here she was alone, having to make a fresh start. Friends had advised her to establish a new routine, decide what was most important in her life and build her day around that. And so, in the three months she'd been down here, Margot had begun every morning with a swim in the sea, regardless of the weather. Afterwards, she would have breakfast at Le Paname, maybe treat herself to an éclair. Or two. Did it matter if she put on a few extra few pounds? When the tourists started to arrive, she would wander up Rue Voltaire and lose herself in the steep narrow laneways of the old quarter. Look in on the galleries; she'd always wanted to paint. But finding motivation had not proved easy.

She took some salt pork from the fridge and started cubing it with Hugo's sushi knife. In Paris, this had been one of their little traditions, a dinner they'd prepared together when the nights started to draw in. They each had their roles: Hugo would chop the vegetables while Margot prepared the meat. In his youth, he'd trained as a chef and would always get tetchy whenever she touched one of his precious knives. He would watch anxiously from the corners of his eyes, *tut* irritably over how long it was taking, and then finally take over. "No, like this," he would say, taking the knife from her. The onion she'd been methodically slicing would be reduced to a thousand tiny pieces in a blur of motion. "Not that I don't trust you with a knife in your hand," he would smile slyly.

Margot would playfully throw something at him.

"No one wants to be the unarmed man in a street-fight," she'd responded.

Words that would come back to haunt her.

Dear Hugo.

One of the first things she'd done after moving down here was place a photograph of him in every room. Here, on the shelf above the cooker, was one from a Christmas night out at Chez Raspoutine. Hugo had been into vintage clothing at the time and looked quite the Al Capone in his dark brown trilby and wool blend suit. They'd danced until two in the morning and walked home in falling snow. But the image they brought back never lasted long; it would soon be replaced by another: a scene-of-crime photo taken on the night her husband had been murdered. She wasn't supposed to have seen it. When they'd called her in the early hours to break the news, Pierre, Hugo's friend and colleague, had collected her from the apartment and driven her back to the station. The office had been in turmoil. Hugo had been a respected and well-liked member of the force, and everyone was breaking a limb to track down his killers. Pierre was so busy he'd left her unattended, and Margot had drifted across to his desk where she'd found the image staring back at her from the screen of his computer: a man lying dead in an alley, face and torso latticed with knife wounds. It had taken her several long seconds to realise it was Hugo. She had no idea how long she'd stood there, transfixed, before someone had drawn her away.

He was on his way home, he hadn't needed to attend. A report had come through of an incident at a hotel near Stras-bourg-Saint-Denis. Three masked men, armed with knives and a machete, had forced their way into the owner's room, killing a man and maiming a child. An armed response unit had been sent, but being only minutes from the scene Hugo and Pierre had pursued the three men on foot. They'd chased them into a maze of streets in Petites Écuries. Briefly losing touch, Hugo had ordered Pierre to wait at an intersection, ready to guide in the armed officers, while he went on alone. By the time the squad had caught up, Hugo was lying dead in the alley, a pool of his blood spreading across the cobbles.

He hadn't stood a chance. Camera footage showed him being ambushed by the men who'd set upon him with their knives and the machete. Had they not been disturbed by a passer-by they would probably have turned him to mincemeat. The pathologist's report detailed a total of fifty-seven injuries, any one of which could have killed him. The face Margot had seen in the photograph bore little resemblance to her husband, the man she'd loved for all those years.

Margot looked up from the chopping board. Had the room turned a little bit darker?

She went on chopping the salt pork. She tossed the cubes into the hot pan and watched the fatty edges sizzle, and then stared down at the sharp knife in her hand. At once an innocent tool and a terrible weapon. One capable of inflicting an unimaginable degree of pain.

She laid her left hand flat on the board and held the knife over it with her right. What did it feel like to have a blade cut into you? How much pain would fire through your body when that slither of metal sliced open your skin? She imagined drawing the knife over her hand right now, the silky sharp steel cutting into her flesh, through veins and cartilage, until it got right down to the bone. Blood would puddle in the gaps between her fingers before dripping onto the floor. The human body was such a fragile thing. What thoughts had gone through Hugo's mind as he'd lain in that alley, watching his killers lay into him? A person you'd loved for the better part of your adult life could be gone like that, and all it took was a knife like this.

Margot bit her lip, tormented by the horrible images, the knife blade hovering close to her hand. But then she forced the bad thoughts from her mind and cast down the knife in disgust.

Leaving the cassoulet unfinished, she took the photo of her Al Capone down from the shelf and went out into the courtyard in search of solace. She sat at her wrought-iron table, surrounded by her window boxes and her pot plants, and struck a match. She smoked her cigarette with her face tilted to the sun, enjoying the heat. No one had been brought to justice for her husband's killing. The police had rounded up a small army of gang members from across the district, but none of them had admitted to knowing anything. For over nine months now the case had gone unsolved.

Margot heaved a sad sigh. She balanced her cigarette in the groove on the ashtray and then laid her fingertips onto the lips of the man in the photograph.

Poor Hugo.

3

The only sandy beach in town was on the north side of the harbour, and in summer it would be crammed with tourists. Even now, on a chilly Saturday morning in April, a dozen hardy souls were out walking the sands. Margot avoided it by taking the concrete walkway that skirted its edge and then followed the narrow path around the headland. The beach in the next cove was rocky and wild and screened by tall cliffs, and the path to it was steep, treacherous in places, meaning she could usually count on having the place to herself.

She worked her way over the rocks to get down to the narrow band of shingle and then stripped down to her Speedo. She packed her clothes away into her bag and put on her bathing cap, tucking in strands of loose hair. When the water fizzed up over her feet Margot wiggled her toes. She waded in until she was waist deep, and then threw herself onto the waves. That first rush of adrenaline as the water enveloped her was intoxicating. And then it was just her and the sea and a feeling of freedom that few things could beat. Head down, Margot swam with vigour.

She liked to swim a long way out. It was invigorating to see how far she could go. Sometimes she would venture out several kilometres and drift in the current, imagine herself being swept away into the ocean. After twenty minutes she paused for a breather, bobbing in a slight swell. To the south, the lighthouse on the tip of Cap Béar blinked away, warning of the cliffs of the Spanish coast while inland, craggy green hills rose up above the town before merging into the mountains, their tips shrouded in haze. Despite the fact she'd swam in this water hundreds of times, today something felt different. So far, only two bodies had been washed up but there must have been more of them on the boat. There could be dozens of corpses floating around in the water beneath her feet. Now she was out here it felt like disturbing a watery grave.

Margot kicked away, tempted to go back in. Wasn't drowning the worst way you could go? She'd always loved to swim in open water but she never underestimated the dangers. When she was little, her parents had taken her on holidays to Scotland, and as soon as she was old enough she would swim in the lochs. She would dive in from the bank and head straight for the middle. "Don't go out too far," Dad would call out, watching anxiously from the shore. "It's deeper than it looks."

But it was the depth that excited her most. She'd read somewhere that the volume of Loch Ness was so great you could drown the entire population of the world ten times over and still have room to spare. Sometimes she tested how far down she could go. She would pinch her nose and let herself sink, dare herself to get close to the point of no return. As the pressure built, her lungs would come under such strain that she would be forced to open her airways and let them fill up with water. One time she'd stayed down so long she'd almost blacked out. Kicking furiously to get back to the surface, she'd emerged with her oxygen-starved mind seemingly tuned to an altered reality: the trees had turned orange, the sky gone yellow. Dad had had to wade in to rescue her. There was no harm done, but they'd never gone on holiday to Scotland again.

The current was pushing her south towards the harbour but Margot dug in deep and focussed on the headland to the north. She was in the mood for something more energetic today and gave herself the target of making it to the next bay, determined to work off those extra few pounds. But after a couple of hundred metres the muscles in her calf started to cramp and her energy faded, forcing her to give in.

She swam back to the cove and emerged on the beach, breathless and drained. Tugging off her bathing cap, she sat down on a rock, slumping her shoulders in frustration. Sometimes she forgot she was no longer twenty.

The sound of voices made her perk up. A couple of fishermen had appeared on the path and were making their way towards the tip of the headland, laden with tackle. Margot retrieved her swimming bag and pulled out her towel, drying herself quickly. She'd just finished putting on her sarong when a flash of colour caught her eye. She stopped what she was doing and moved for a closer look. An item of clothing was snagged on a sharp edge of rock. Picking it up, she found that it was a football shirt, garnet and blue – the same colours as the shorts the boy on the rocks had been wearing.

———

The gendarmerie was located at the top of Rue Voltaire, next to the Office du Tourism. It was an old two-storey building with thick stone walls and heavy timber doors. Each of its sixteen windows was flanked by louvred shutters, and the window-boxes overflowed with red and orange blooms. A blue enamel plaque next to the front door stated that the building dated back to the 19th Century, making it one of the oldest in the region. If the façade was anything to go by, little had changed in the ensuing hundred years.

The front door was locked so Margot knocked and waited. When no one answered, she found herself peering through a small glass panel into a gloomy lobby. She knocked again and waited a full minute for a light to come on. A figure appeared from a shadowy doorway and then a man's face came looming up to the glass, prompting Margot to take a step back. His expression wasn't welcoming.

"Yes?"

"Can I come in?"

"It's eight-forty-six, Madame," he said, showing her the dial of his wristwatch as if to prove it.

"And?"

He appeared to tut. "The gendarmerie doesn't open until nine on Saturdays."

Margot rolled her eyes. Did criminals around here restrict themselves to office hours?

"Could I come in and wait?"

The man smoothed down his jet-black hair. His fringe was so shiny it looked like it had been finished with boot polish. "I'm not fully dressed," he said, though when Margot glanced down she saw that he was wearing trousers and a shirt, albeit only half buttoned-up. She produced a smile.

"I promise not to look."

It didn't amuse him. "Is it an emergency?"

"Not as such."

"Then you'll have to wait."

He turned to go, but Margot knocked again. He shot her a look of irritation which she returned in full.

"I've just found this." She held the football shirt up to the glass. "I thought it might be important."

The gendarme came back to the door and stooped to peer

through the glass, his face contorting like a gargoyle. Not once had he offered even the suggestion of a smile. After taking a cursory look at the shirt he gave a little shake of his head. "The lost property box is next door."

"It's not lost property. I found it on the beach in the cove. I think it might belong to the little boy that was found by the harbour."

His eyebrows pinched as he appeared to ruminate. He took another look at the shirt, and then glanced again at his wrist-watch. Finally, he bent down and noisily slid back the bolts. "Wait here," he said and then exited through an opening on the other side of the lobby, closing the door firmly behind him.

Margot stepped into the dimly-lit space. It felt strange to be back in a police station, although this was a world away from Hugo's office in Paris. Apart from the two plastic seats bolted to the floor there was little that was modern. Everything appeared to be made from either stone or dark brown wood – even the ceiling was painted a chalky brown. Many of the papers on the noticeboard were curled and yellowed, and a flyer for last year's summer festival still held pride of place. A ceiling lantern gave out light of a quality that seemed to belong to a different century. The place looked like it hadn't been redecorated since the 1950s.

One of the seats had a horrible stain on it and the other was covered in graffiti so Margot remained standing. The blind was down on the glazed screen but the slats in one corner were damaged and by stooping she could just about see through it. On the other side of the screen lay a tidy office: a wooden desk piled neatly with papers, a pair of filing cabinets. Next to the cabinets, a half-open door connected to the inner room into which the gendarme had gone. Margot could hear him moving around in there. She shifted her posi-tion and managed to catch sight of him, albeit his reflection in a full-length mahogany mirror. He appeared to be alone, though he wasn't hurrying himself. He raised one foot onto a wooden stool in order to polish his already shiny boots. Despite being tall and otherwise slim he had a pot belly that hung over his waistband like a cantaloupe in a stocking. When he put on his tunic, he buffed each of the buttons with a soft white cloth and then primped his epaulettes with a stiff brush. He was clearly a man who took pride in wearing his uniform.

A few minutes later he came into the office via the connecting door and Margot took a step back, pretending she hadn't been watching. As the church bells were striking nine, he raised the blind and greeted her with what appeared to be a smile. It clearly was not an expression that came naturally to him.

"Bonjour, Madame. I am Captain Bouchard of the Gendarmerie de Argents-sur-Mer. How may I help?"

Margot narrowed her eyes. What a strange man. She stepped back to the screen. "I was swimming in the cove a few minutes ago. When I came out I found this." She showed him the football shirt once again.

The captain seemed unimpressed. "What makes you think it belongs to the migrant boy?"

"It's the same colour as the shorts he was wearing. Don't you see?"

"It's an FC Barcelona strip, Madame."

"And?"

"They're very common here."

"But the name and number on the back …" Margot turned the shirt around. "Dembélé. That might be the boy's name."

Captain Bouchard's mouth twitched. It was hard to imagine how he could appear more supercilious but he managed it somehow. "I hardly think so."

"Why not? Don't boys often have their names printed on their shirts?"

"Yes, they do, but Dembélé plays for FC Barcelona. He's one of their most famous players."

"Is he?"

The captain nodded.

Margot flushed. She had no interest in football but she should have checked. She felt foolish but resisted the urge to look away. She wasn't going to give him the satisfaction. "Even so, it must still belong to him."

"It's of no use to him now."

Margot's eyes widened, blood beginning to simmer. "Shouldn't you have it analysed?"

"If it's been in the water that long it's hardly going to reveal anything."

"It's still evidence," Margot persisted. "It needs to be properly examined and recorded."

After a pause he conceded a small nod. He fetched an evidence bag from a drawer and opened a panel next to the screen so she could pass it through. He started bagging it up, but Margot didn't celebrate the small victory just yet.

"Has there been any progress with the investigation?"

"It's too soon to say."

"I heard a man was found down by the fort. Was there any clue to his identity?"

The captain shook his head and carried on bagging up the shirt. He seemed to have lost all interest in the conversation.

"Were they both on the same boat?"

"It would seem logical."

Margot clenched her jaw. "There must have been more than two of them. What happened to the others?"

"Someone reported seeing some shady types sneaking through the town around dawn."

"Did you catch any of them?"

The captain looked at her as if she'd said something stupid. "They'll be long gone by now. They soon slip through the cracks." He tossed the evidence bag into a box on the desk and then looked at her as if he expected her to leave. Margot wasn't done yet, however.

"How did the shirt find its way into the cove if the body was washed up at the harbour?"

"The current must have taken it."

"That's highly unlikely. The current flows southwest; the cove is north of the harbour."

"Is that a fact?"

"Yes, it is. I swim in it every day."

"So your point would be ...?"

Margot had to work to control her temper. "My point is, he must have been on the beach in the cove at some point before he died. Which means he didn't just fall off a boat and drown."

The captain took a form from below the desk and placed it on the counter between them. "Could I have your name, please?"

Margot wasn't letting it drop. "Don't you think that's a possibility?"

He looked blankly back at her. "Your name."

"Will you search the cove?"

"Possibly."

"If his shirt was there there might be other evidence."

"Perhaps."

"The longer you leave it the less use it will be."

"I am aware of that. Now, your name, *please*."

The captain's face hardened but Margot continued to look him in the eye, unwilling to back down. She couldn't understand why he was being so uncooperative and had half a mind to remain there all morning, making life difficult for him. But common sense prevailed. She looked away and let out a sigh.

"Margot Renard."

He began to write it down but paused mid-stroke, his head tilting upwards. "The police inspector's widow?"

Margot fixed him with another stare. Was that how she was going to be known from now on? She could barely walk to the end of her lane without thinking that people were looking at her, muttering behind her back: *there goes Madame Renard, the police inspector's widow.* The lack of anonymity here was proving hard to get used to.

The captain lowered his pen. There was at last a note of compassion in his voice when he said, "I'd heard you'd moved to the town. I'm sorry for your loss."

Margot bit her bottom lip. This man wasn't half the police officer Hugo had been. "So am I, Monsieur," she said, and quietly left the building.

4

After the chilly start, the day quickly warmed up and bright sunshine bathed the town in a rich golden glow. But Margot was in no mood to enjoy the fine weather and bought herself a bottle of cognac on her way home. Madame Barbier from the house at the end of the row paused the tending of her window boxes and tried to engage her in chat, but Margot feigned a headache and walked swiftly by, pushing the bottle of cognac to the bottom of her bag.

After locking the gate and closing the shutters, she took off her beach sarong and her swimsuit and then, because the court-yard wasn't in any way overlooked, braved the lukewarm water of the outdoor shower. Whenever they'd come down here in summer, Margot would usually shower outside and often walk naked around the house, glad of the way it had made Hugo smile. She put on a robe and poured herself a large cognac, and then sat on the settee, smoking in silence. The air had a stillness to it. Sometimes the quiet of the house felt like a physical thing, holding her in.

Bookshelves filled the walls on either side of the fireplace; she'd arranged them exactly as they'd been in their sitting room in Paris. The one on the left housed Hugo's record collection, the one on the right her favourite books. On the middle shelf was her pride and joy – the Riverside edition of the *Complete Works of Shakespeare* (which she'd read before the age of twelve, beating her father by five years who hadn't read them all until he was seventeen). Below it was the first edition *Alice Through the Looking-Glass* that he'd read to her whenever she was ill. She took her tin of family photos down from the top shelf and sat on the floor in front of the log-burner, the bottle of cognac by her side. On top of the pile sat Hugo's medal – a posthumous award for his final act of bravery. Margot set it against the books on the bottom shelf and stared at it while she drank her brandy. To say she was proud of him would be the understatement of the century but it was hard being a hero's widow. She'd had an on-off career herself: gained a first-class law degree from UCL, had an offer of tenancy at a top London chambers, was forecast a glittering career in the judiciary – her peers had even opened up a book on her becoming a judge by the time she was thirty.

But life wasn't like one of Hugo's LPs – the needle didn't always stay in the groove. Sometimes it got knocked, and you found yourself following a completely different track. Losing a child was a pretty big jolt. All she'd wanted to do in those first few months was wrap herself up in something soft, hide away. At times it had come back to haunt her and caused her to have a little relapse. In the first few years of their marriage, weeks had often gone by without her leaving the apartment. Other times she would go out and not come back for days. Sometimes she just needed space.

Hugo had understood.

It was cold with the shutters closed so she went up to the little spare room in the attic where the warmth of the morning had started to accumulate. She leaned into the dormer window and peered out across the terracotta rooftops. You could see the sea from here, and part of the harbour, the Catalonian flag flying from a pole on the turret. All traces of yesterday's grim discovery had gone and now the tourists were back in force, sitting in the shade of the palm trees, or ambling around the harbour. The day after the funeral she'd resolved to make a fresh start and move here full time; another three or four months went by before she'd sorted through their belongings and shipped everything she'd wanted to keep. Every night of the first few weeks she'd sat at this window and cried. At times the emptiness of the house had been really quite shocking. Then she'd taken to going out in the dead of night and wandering the streets, just to see who was about. Now she could sit here and not shed a single tear, but the emptiness hadn't gone away.

She drew in a sharp breath, coming back to the present. It was almost noon so she went downstairs to make a cup of coffee. When she checked her phone, one voicemail was waiting:

"Margot. It's Pierre. Please call me as soon as you get this."

It was unlike him to call on a Saturday morning so Margot called him straight back. "Pierre – I'm not disturbing you, am I?"

"No. It's fine." He sounded tired.

"You asked me to call."

He paused. "I have some news."

Margot waited. At the other end of the line Pierre took a few moments to clear his throat. "We've made some arrests."

She swallowed. "Hugo?"

She imagined him nod. "I'm coming down to see you."

———

After her swim the next morning, Margot took her binoculars and went for a walk along the coastal path. She took the route south where the path climbed high over the rocky bluffs and the coastline turned wild. She stopped at every viewpoint, and scanned every beach and cove, but there were no abandoned boats, no more washed-up bodies. The sea glistened in the sun, looking calm and innocent.

Pierre was coming down on the midday train and wouldn't be here until seven so after her walk Margot went to the shops. She bought herself a new madeleine pan from the homeware store and a bag of fresh apricots from the indoor market – after the cassoulet she was going to serve madeleines with honey-glazed apricots and vanilla ice cream. In Cave Saint Joan, she bought two bottles of La Grande Dame Veuve Clicquot and a bottle of fortified sweet Muscat, then called in at the tabac to stock up on Gitanes. In Paris, the three of them had enjoyed so many boozy nights together.

Pierre arrived on time, clad in his policeman's raincoat. Paris born and bred, he didn't seem to get that the weather elsewhere could be anything other than grey skies and drizzle.

"Good trip?" She hugged him tight and gave him a kiss on both cheeks.

"Not bad. I had a little sleep on the train. I certainly needed it."

She hung up his coat and led him through to the kitchen. He was looking a little peaky, overworked no doubt. Hugo had always said the boy would work himself into an early grave.

"I hope you're hungry."

"I'm starving, as usual."

"We're having cassoulet for dinner, and for afters—" Margot pulled back the tea towel and proudly revealed the madeleines she'd baked. "Voila!"

Pierre grinned. "The queen of desserts, just like old times."

He gave her another peck on the cheek.

At thirty years of age Pierre was nineteen years younger than Margot and she'd always treated him like a son. Eight months ago he'd come round to the apartment to announce that his wife was pregnant, and Margot had been so surprised she hadn't believed it for weeks. She'd never pictured him as a father.

She opened one of the bottles of champagne while Pierre made himself comfortable at the kitchen table. "How's Camille?"

"She sends her love."

"And the baby?"

Pierre looked up with a twinkle in his eye. "She's fine. I have some pictures on my phone." He reached into pocket. "Would you like to see?"

"You have to ask?"

"I wasn't sure—"

Margot tutted. "It's perfectly all right, Pierre."

She finished pouring the champagne and then took the glasses to the table. Pierre angled the phone between them so they could both see. Noémie was a bright-eyed six-week-old with curly black hair and a dimple in her chin. "Aww, she's so cute," Margot cooed.

"Not so at three o'clock in the morning, trust me."

Margot smiled wistfully. Being a parent must be so exhausting. All those middle-of-the-night feeds and nappy-changing. The woes of teething. The constant fear you might not be looking after them properly and they would fall ill. Was it all worth it? A wave of sadness crept up on her and she couldn't stop her face from dropping.

Pierre immediately picked up on it and switched off his phone. "I'm sorry. I shouldn't have ..."

Margot inhaled deeply, putting a lid on the rising emotion. "It was a long time ago."

"Even so—"

"Don't be silly." She put the smile back on her face and reached for his hand. "Come on. Let's put some music on."

They left the dinner heating up and took the champagne

through to the sitting room. Pierre went straight to the far book-case where he greedily looked through Hugo's record collection – he was as much into collecting vinyl as Hugo had been. He made his selection and carefully extracted the LP from its sleeve, then laid it on the turntable. The Beatles: *Yesterday and Today* – Hugo had a rare first pressing featuring the infamous "butcher" cover.

Margot sat down on her little settee and patted the space beside her. "You will stay the night, won't you? I've made up the spare bed."

Pierre sank heavily into the cushions and rubbed his eyes. "I'd give anything for a good night's sleep."

She retrieved her Gitanes from the table and offered him one. Pierre resisted, but then caved in. "You're such a bad influence."

"Where would we be without bad influences?"

Margot struck a match.

They talked about old times. It was nice to catch up, but she couldn't stop her mind coming back to the reason that had prompted his visit.

"So who was he?"

Pierre was in the middle of drawing on his cigarette and seemed in no rush to reply. He held the smoke in his lungs while he stared into the air, and then released it slowly as he put down his glass. He lowered the volume on the record player.

"We've made three arrests. We can't say for certain which of them delivered the fatal blow but they'll all be prosecuted for murder."

"Which gang were they in?"

"They had no affiliations. They were just hired guns. They'd been sent to the hotel to teach the owner a lesson."

"Have they shown any remorse?"

Pierre shook his head. "They were just kids. One nineteen

and two eighteen-year-olds. They hadn't even bothered to get rid of their weapons; they'd just stashed them under their beds. We've matched them for DNA and fingerprints."

Margot took a long draw on her cigarette and for a while they smoked without talking. Was this meant to bring closure? The funeral the first step and now catching his killers the final full stop? She wasn't sure she would ever be able to think of it that way. It was hard to see how justice had been done. Twenty or so years in prison a fair exchange for the loss of her husband? She didn't think so. She'd often wondered what she would do if she ever came face to face with his killers. Some small part of her was even disappointed they'd been found; in her wilder moments she'd entertained ideas of tracking them down herself, hunting them through the backstreets of Paris, doing unto them what they'd done to Hugo. She had a wry smile to herself. Perhaps a career in the judiciary wouldn't have suited her after all.

Pierre had gone quiet and when Margot looked up she was surprised to find he'd got quite emotional. He was rubbing his forehead, head angled away, shielding his eyes.

"Pierre?" She leaned in, a hand on his forearm.

"I never should have left him. I was his partner and I let him get killed."

"Hush now. There's nothing you could have done."

"But if I'd stayed—"

"Then you would have got killed as well. And then there would be two grieving widows. Not to mention one little baby, missing her father."

"I know." He let out a small sob. The emotion quickly tumbled out of him and he took a handkerchief from his trouser pocket and noisily blew his nose. "I'm sorry. I'm tired, that's all."

"You mustn't blame yourself. Hugo knew the risks. There's no reason for you to feel guilty."

Margot wrapped her arms around him and pulled his face onto her shoulder. When he was feeling better, he took her hands in his own and gripped them tight. "He was one of a kind, Margot."

Margot blinked back tears. "The best."

———

They finished off the second bottle of champagne with dinner and then Margot opened the Muscat. Leaving the plates unwashed, they went back to the sitting room where the heat from the log-burner had turned the air into a thick smoky fug. Pierre was beginning to wilt in the heat so he moved the armchair closer to the front door where there was a draught. Margot kicked off her shoes and lay down on the settee, the Muscat having gone straight to her head. When she briefly closed her eyes, the room carried on turning.

"The washing up!" Pierre declared, rising abruptly to his feet.

"Leave it," Margot replied. "I'll do it in the morning."

He gave a silly little snicker and flopped back down in the chair. When Margot looked across, she could see he was pie-eyed. She smiled as she tossed him the packet of Gitanes.

"Here – a present from your bad influence."

"You really are the worst."

"Don't ever forget it."

She stared up at the ceiling, sad and content. It seemed such a long time since she'd last let her hair down like this; ages since she'd got so drunk. "Oh, I do miss this."

"Then we'll have to come down more often," Pierre said with enthusiasm. "I'll bring Camille and Noémie. We can go for walks along the beach. You can show us the galleries. It'll be fun."

"That would be nice," Margot said, though knew it would

never happen. Camille had never been part of their little gang. She would never countenance them sitting around drinking and smoking like this.

"So tell me, Margot – how are you getting on with your new life?"

"Truthfully?"

"Truthfully."

Margot propped her head with a cushion and reached for her cigarette where she'd left it smouldering in a groove on the ashtray. She filled her lungs with smoky, overheated air and sighed melancholically.

"Oh, Pierre. Sometimes I'm so bored I think I'm going out of my mind."

"Then come back."

Was it really that easy? With all the memories she'd dumped there? Probably not. And, if she was being honest with herself, did she really miss it that much? Trade deep blue skies and sparkling Mediterranean sunshine for drizzle and pollution? She couldn't survive without heat. It had always been a mystery to her why ancient people had chosen to live in colder climes when places like southern Europe existed. But equally, she couldn't just stay here and wither away. "I need to do something useful with my life."

"So go back to being a lawyer?"

"Too dull."

"Then re-train."

"As what?"

He shrugged. "You've always liked fashion."

Margot regarded him from the tops of her eyes. "I'm fifty years old next year."

"So?"

"Women start to become invisible as that age."

He smirked. "Not to a sixty-year-old."

Margot threw a cushion at him. Her aim was poor and it hit the radiator instead.

"Trust me, Margot – you don't look fifty. You don't even look forty."

"Yes, I do. And I'm getting fat, look—" She lifted the hem of her top and pinched an inch of flab from her belly. "I drink too much, I eat too much ... I'm turning into a fat old widow who lives by the sea."

"Margot – you're not old and you're not fat. Stop feeling sorry for yourself."

Margot sighed theatrically. He didn't understand. Men of his age had no idea what it felt like to age as a woman. The irony was she used to love wearing a bikini, revelled in the sense of empowerment it gave her – a swing of her hips could reduce many a man to a salivating schoolboy.

Pierre had retrieved the cushion from the floor and tucked it behind his head. Eyes blissfully closed, he looked like he was about to doze off. Margot let the frustration fizzle out of her and then ground the stub of her cigarette into the ashtray. Booze always had this effect upon her; she really must cut down. No more than five bottles of wine a week, starting from tomorrow. Or maybe next week.

The LP came to the end of the track and the needle started to jump so she got up and turned off the record player. The heat was starting to irritate her now so she closed the vents on the log-burner and opened the door to the stairs. It was late, and Pierre had to go back tomorrow. She gazed fondly down at him, snoozing so peacefully.

"I'll make some coffee," she said softly.

His eyelids sleepily rose up. "No more Muscat?" he bemoaned.

Margot smiled as she took away his glass. Sweet child. "No more Muscat."

She kissed him on the forehead and then went to the kitchen to make a pot of coffee.

When she returned, Pierre had perked up a little and had gone back to perusing Hugo's record collection. Margot set the coffee tray down on the table and poured out two cups.

"It's not completely uneventful down here," she said. "Something horrible happened the other day."

Pierre cast a glance over his shoulder. "Oh. What was that?"

"Two bodies were found, one of them just outside the harbour."

"A boating accident?"

"Sort of. They were migrants, probably coming over from north Africa."

"Ah," Pierre said and took a cup from the tray. He went back to his armchair and settled into the cushions with a knowing nod of his head. "I see."

Margot disliked the assumption he appeared to be making and regarded him in consternation. She put down her cup. "That makes their deaths no less important."

"Of course not. I didn't—"

"One of them was only a boy, six or seven years old."

"That's tragic."

"Just imagine how his mother will feel, assuming she even finds out."

Pierre put down his own cup and shifted to the edge of his seat. "I'm sorry, Margot. I didn't mean to appear insensitive."

"I know. It's just that people can be so judgemental. To hear some of the locals talk you'd think they deserved to die. It's the people who put them on the boats we should be mad at."

"Of course," Pierre said, and leaned back again. "Unfortunately, there's not much we can do. They know the risks and they just keep coming. It's been going on for decades, centuries even."

"But people make money out of it. It makes me so angry."

"They broke up a smuggling ring only last month. They were charging eight thousand euros for a crossing."

"That's obscene."

"And many of them end up trapped in unpaid labour. But all it needs is someone with a boat. There's a never-ending supply of people willing to pay."

Margot had a sip of her coffee. She wasn't naïve. Everything that Pierre had said was obviously true, but it wasn't always right to look at the bigger picture. Every death was an individual, not a statistic. They each had a life of their own, hopes and ambitions, dreams and desires, no matter what their background. No doubt the little boy had dreamed of one day becoming a footballer, playing for his favourite team, just like most boys of that age.

"They're saying he drowned at sea and got washed up on the beach," Margot said, "but it doesn't add up to me."

"How so?"

"All he had on when they found him was a pair of football shorts. Then when I went for a swim on Saturday I found the matching shirt. It was hidden behind a rock in the cove."

"You're sure it was his?"

"It was too much of a coincidence not to be."

"Did you hand it in?"

"Yes, though the gendarme I spoke to wasn't very helpful."

"I'm sure they'll do their best."

"Hmm," Margot said, unconvinced. She set down her cup again. "What I don't understand is how the shirt got to be in the cove when his body was found a kilometre away."

"Presumably it came off when he was in the water."

"How?"

"He could have fallen out of the boat, someone grabbed him, the shirt got pulled off ... Any number of things."

"But the cove is north of the harbour. And surely the boat would have been coming up from the south."

Pierre nodded thoughtfully, unable to come up with an answer.

"Besides, the place where I found it was too high for it to have been washed up. The tide wouldn't go in that far."

"So what do you think happened?"

"I think that at some point he was on the beach. Alive. And he wouldn't have taken the shirt off and just left it there – you can imagine how much a football shirt would mean to a boy of that age."

Pierre nodded, seeming to agree.

"There's more to it than what the gendarmerie would like to believe. If they'd simply drowned and got washed up there would have been cuts on their bodies from the rocks."

"And were there?"

"Not from what I could see. A post-mortem would reveal it, of course."

"Have they ordered one?"

"I doubt it."

Pierre breathed in deeply through his nose. "If they think the cause of death was obvious they probably won't bother. What's also unusual is for smugglers to operate this far up the coast, I will say that. Normally they choose somewhere remote, down on the coast of Spain or the Balearics."

Margot nodded and looked into his eyes, then shuffled forward so she could reach his forearm. "Do you think you could look into it for me? Keep an eye on what's happening."

Pierre pulled a face. "It's not really my—"

"Please, Pierre. I really don't want to speak to that gendarme again. He's such an oaf."

Pierre gave it some thought and then finally conceded a small nod. "All right. I'll see what I can do."

Margot smiled.

He drained his coffee cup and then got to his feet. "But right now I have to go to bed. Otherwise I may just fall asleep in your chair." He leaned down and kissed her on the cheek. "Goodnight, Margot."

"Goodnight, Pierre."

Margot stayed up a little while longer. Whatever happened she wasn't going to let it rest. Everyone deserved justice.

5

Pierre was late getting up and when he did finally appear at the bottom of the stairs he was grey-faced and hunched-up, complaining of a headache. Margot brewed a fresh pot of coffee and laid out some cheese and apricots for breakfast, but the sight of it turned his stomach and she had to eat alone in the courtyard. She couldn't help feeling guilty: she rarely got hangovers, no matter how much she drank. It was one of the things her friends hated about her.

She made him a packed lunch and then took him to the station in a taxi. They hugged goodbye on the platform. Margot made him promise to come back and visit in a few weeks and he said he would, though she knew it was a promise he was unlikely to keep. She walked back to town in a sullen mood.

By the time she got there the beach was busy. To make matters worse, it was a school holiday and the place was crowded with families. She skirted the beach via the concrete walkway and then took the steps down to the headland path. Happily, the cove was still deserted. She stripped down to her swimsuit and then launched herself into the water.

She swam with vigour, pushing on through the pain when

her calves started to burn. All she could think about was Hugo's killers – the three young men hacking him to death in that alley. He'd lost his life and she'd lost a husband simply because he'd strayed into a gang dispute. The futility of it made her blood boil.

Lost in thought, she failed to keep track of time. When she did pause to look up, she found she'd swum out much further than she normally would. Not only could she see the lighthouse on the tip of Cap Béar, but a good stretch of the coastline beyond. Looking back to shore, the rocky beach seemed very far away. She trod water, feeling a creep of anxiety, realising she'd strayed a little too far out of her comfort zone. The current out here was strong, and a keen breeze had brought on a swell, making her rise and fall uncomfortably. She began to feel nauseous, and had to work hard with her arms to keep her face above water.

And although there were no clouds in the sky Margot's world suddenly went dark. Confused, she turned her head just in time to see the bright white lines of a sailboat loom up out of nowhere. Her brain seized. The boat was heading straight for her; she was caught like a rabbit in the headlights. The smooth clean hull rose up on the crest of a wave, its sail snapping in the wind, looking certain to come crashing down on top of her. Margot snatched a breath and dived as quickly as she could.

Adrenaline brought new life to her limbs and she swam hard, but the boat was moving at considerable speed and the undertow pulled her with it. Flipped onto her back, Margot was horrified to see the underside of the boat passing just metres over her head. The eddying water sucked her back up and she was tossed like a ragdoll into the foaming maelstrom of its wake. Stunned and confused, Margot kicked away. As soon as she was out of danger she glared at the stern of the rapidly receding vessel.

"You idiot!" she yelled, and tried to wave a fist.

At the helm, the man at the wheel showed no sign of having heard. His back to her, he leaned with the boat as it rolled on through the water, oblivious to the tragedy he'd nearly just caused. The last thing that registered in Margot's brain before she headed back to shore was the name on the backboard: *Carpe Diem*.

———

Margot hauled herself up onto the rocks, exhausted and confused. Plonking herself down on the small strip of shingle, she tore off her bathing cap and coughed seawater from her lungs. Unbelievable! Those overgrown boys with their ridiculous playthings. Her mind reeled as she glared back at the sea – the yacht was now just a blurry shape, disappearing into shimmering haze. She hissed through her teeth. The lunatic could have killed her!

Margot retrieved her swimming bag and hurriedly towelled herself down. She started to put on her clothes, half a mind to go and report him to the harbourmaster, but then told herself to slow down. She took a deep breath. She wasn't going to let it spoil her day. People like that weren't worth it.

She gulped some water from her drinking bottle and then finished getting dressed. After tying up her swimming bag, she climbed up onto the rocks. Her eyes roved the scene before her, searching for the place where she'd found the football shirt. She probably should have taken a photo, compiled a proper record, if not for the police then at least for her own peace of mind. She identified what she thought was the spot and estimated it to be a good ten metres in from the shingle. Its height was at least a metre above the level of the sea. There was never much of a tide here; the marks on the rocks confirmed that the water never went in that far, just as she'd suspected. Freak weather events aside, there was no way the shirt could have washed up there.

She jumped across the rocks until she reached the southern edge of the cove and then climbed to the highest point, hands on hips. She tried to imagine what it would be like out here at night, stumbling around in the pitch black, tired and hungry, hundreds of miles from home. It would have been a long sea crossing. Even a fast boat would have taken ten hours to get here from the coast of north Africa. Pierre was right – if this was the location they'd chosen to haul out it was a strange one to pick. There were plenty of more isolated stretches further down the coast so either whoever had smuggled them was inexperienced or something had gone wrong. Perhaps there had been an accident, they'd ended up here by mistake, in the confusion the boy had got separated and somehow fallen into the water. But then, how had the other man ended up down by the fort?

Someone needed to carry out a proper search. There could be other clues here, and if the police couldn't be bothered then why didn't she search it herself? She'd spent enough time in the company of police officers to know what to do.

A wide visual search revealed nothing of significance so Margot hunkered down and worked methodically, moving slowly from one side of the cove to the other. Where the rocks gave way to shingle, she got down on her hands and knees and worked her way forward centimetre by centimetre. She wasn't quite sure what she was expecting to find – maybe some blood on a rock, a piece of damaged boat. If nothing else there was plenty of litter – after just ten minutes she'd recovered more stray plastic than she could carry. She left it in small mounds ready to collect with a bin bag.

But then something more interesting caught her eye: lodged in a space between two large boulders was what looked like a bag. Margot lay down on her side and carefully fed her arm into the slot. When her hand emerged, she found herself holding a child's backpack, and her heart started to beat more quickly when she realised it was the same colours as the football strip – garnet and blue.

Instinct made her look round. Was someone watching? The beach was still empty, however, and silent apart from the fizz of water washing up through the shingle. For several long moments she sat on her haunches, trying to understand the significance of what she'd found. She took some photos of where it had been lodged and then moved to a smooth wide rock where she sat with the backpack on her lap. The bottom was wet on her thighs. Unclicking the buckles, she found it fully packed and neatly layered. On top was a waterproof coat, then a jumper, then a pair of boy's shoes. A zipped pocket on the inside contained a plastic wallet stuffed with papers, and although she didn't pull it all the way out, Margot was excited to see a mobile phone safely hidden inside. The lower half of the bag was soaked through, but the contents of the plastic wallet had escaped undamaged, it seemed.

She spent a few moments thinking, but then came to her senses and put everything back. She stuffed the backpack into her swimming bag and then went on her way.

———

She took her time going back around the headland. The bag was evidence and she would have to hand it in to the police, but given Captain Bouchard's attitude last time she was in no hurry to return to the gendarmerie. Maybe she should look through it first. She was the one who'd found it, after all.

The beach was still busy so Margot kept to the concrete walkway and carried on round towards the harbour. At the turning to Rue Voltaire she paused. A short walk up the hill would take her to the gendarmerie, but she was still in two minds. Her eyes drifted across to the marina where a yacht was mooring up. Something about it struck her as familiar. Spotting the name on the backboard Margot was hit by a surge of adrenaline. *Carpe Diem*. Blood rose to her forehead. Teeth gritted, she marched straight over.

The skipper was too busy tying up his mooring rope to notice Margot bearing down upon him. He was older than she'd expected, salt and pepper hair, a thick, greying moustache covering his top lip. Sunglasses were perched on the crown of his head and he was scruffily dressed in an unbuttoned Hawaiian shirt and shorts that had long ceased to be fashionable.

"Hey, you!"

The man looked round, as did a couple of nearby fishermen.

Margot halted on the jetty directly above him, hands planted firmly on hips. "You idiot! Why don't you look where you're going?"

The man slowly straightened, his forehead creasing into a frown. He looked around again, as if unsure he was the one being addressed. With his bushy eyebrows and bronzed face Margot thought he might be Spanish and guessed he hadn't understood, but just as she was searching her mind for a suitably pithy comment in Spanish, he said, in French:

"Are you talking to me, Madame?"

"Of course I'm talking to you!"

"Do I know you?"

"You could have killed me."

"When?"

"Just now! When I was swimming in the cove."

He looked around once more as if the cove might be hiding somewhere over his shoulder. "But I was sailing at least a kilometre offshore."

"Yes! That was where I was swimming."

"Really? So far out?"

There was scepticism in his tone and it angered Margot all the more. How dare he doubt her? She jutted out her chin.

"I've a good mind to report you."

"What for? I didn't see any buoys."

"You need your eyes testing."

"If you were swimming so far out shouldn't you have been using a tow float? I really don't see how I did anything wrong."

Margot bared her teeth. Only a man could say that. "You drove your stupid boat straight at me, you old fool!"

In her anger, she swung her foot, intending to kick the mooring rope, but she'd forgotten she was wearing her ballet flats and the shoe flew clean off. It hit the rope dead centre before dropping through the narrow gap between hull and jetty, hitting the water with a comical *plop*. Margot's eyes widened. In the silence that followed the man seemed reluctant to meet her eye, and when he did look up he was clearly having difficulty containing a smirk. And it infuriated Margot all the more.

"Just watch where you're going in future!" she snapped, and retreated inelegantly down the boardwalk, feeling the eyes of the fisherman pursuing her every step of the way.

6

Margot forgot all about the gendarmerie and went straight home. She took off her one remaining shoe and threw it in the bin, and then sat in her courtyard, arms tightly folded, simmering. How dare he laugh at her? The temerity of the man. She lit a cigarette and blew angry jets of smoke into the air.

It was several minutes before she'd calmed down. She was still tempted to report him, but there would probably be no point. There were far more important things to think about than some stupid yachtsman.

She took off her swimsuit and tossed it into the washing machine and then put on a loose white dress. After pouring herself a small cognac, she retrieved the backpack from her swimming bag and took it out to the table in the courtyard, though for a while sat with it unopened on the seat beside her, mindful of what an intrusion this was. If some misadventure should befall her one day would she want a stranger going through her things? This bag might have been the boy's prized possession: his schoolbag, a favourite gift, something he'd bought with saved-up pocket money. It wasn't right, but if it offered some clue as to what had happened to him then she had to look. Margot took a deep breath, and then unclicked the buckles.

The waterproof coat was a cheap one, nothing in its pockets, no labels inside, something that could have been bought anywhere. The jumper was neatly folded. The black leather shoes looked new and unworn. Margot imagined his mother packing it for him on the eve of his big trip. How proud she must have been.

She put the clothes to one side and then took out the plastic folder. The first thing that struck her were two maps: Michelin Map no. 734, '*National Map of Spain*', and Michelin Map no. 725, '*National Map of Southern France*'. Both of them were new, and when she unfolded and carefully examined them they didn't appear to have been marked in any way, no 'X marks the spot' or highlighted roads. Tucked into a fold on the map of France was an envelope containing two €20 notes. The mobile phone was an old-model Nokia with a cracked screen. The other items were a collection of loose papers and a diary which promptly drew Margot's attention. It was written in French, in a child's hand, and every page had been filled up to April 14, the day before the bodies had been found. The final entry read:

We met M. Etienne in the woods. Papa gave him a hug. M. Etienne said we would go to Spain tomorrow. Papa gave him our money and M. Etienne rubbed my hair. His hand smelled of petrol. He gave Papa a picture of his boat and a map. We slept in woods and I was cold.

Margot flicked back to the front of the diary. On the title page:

This diary belongs to Aswan. Aged 7. 987Q+R4, Tiaret

So there it was: the little brown shape on the rock now had a name – Aswan. The boy in the Barcelona shorts whose favourite player had been Dembélé. A thin slice of her heart melted.

Margot photographed the page with her phone and also noted down the address in her own diary. At some point she would write to them and let whoever was there know what had happened. She turned to another page:

We were in the lorry a long time. My legs hurt from walking but Papa said the driver would not stop. Then the lorry got broke and we stood on the road. It was very dark. Some men came and fix it. Then they were angry and shouted. They made me scared. Papa said M. Etienne would come soon and make us safe. He said when we got to Spain he will get work and we will go to Barcelona. Papa said we will go to the Nou Camp every Saturday.

Margot paused. Could the body that had been found by the fort be the boy's father? It seemed plausible. If Aswan had got into danger his father would surely have stayed with him, though how the backpack, the shirt and the two bodies had ended up so far apart was still a mystery.

She photographed the rest of the pages and then put the diary to one side. The bundle of loose papers came next. Many of them were notes scribbled on scraps of paper in handwriting so bad she couldn't decipher. There were a number of receipts, one dated April 12 from a shop in Algiers. Scribbled in large letters on another piece of paper was an address in France: 27 Rue Baudin. Margot took a picture of that, too.

It seemed unlikely the Nokia would still work but after a few seconds of holding down the power button the screen came to life. The battery was down to one bar so Margot wasted no time clicking through. Just one number was stored in the contacts. Seven incoming calls were listed in the call log: the first on April

9, the last on the 12th. All seven were listed as 'Number unknown.' No outward calls had been made.

A single received text message: '7 4 3 1'.

She pressed through the menus to find the phone's own number but the battery promptly died. Not that it mattered; it had all the hallmarks of a burner phone.

Margot left the phone for now and went back to the address. 27 Rue Baudin. She typed it into the maps app on her phone and got back four results, one of which, she was surprised to see, was close by. Rue Baudin was in the commercial port, just a few kilometres up the coast. An internet search came up with a vehicle repair shop – Garage de Paolo – which, according to its website, carried out repairs on all makes and models. Margot stared at the screen, perplexed. Why would Aswan's father have written down the address of a vehicle repair shop?

She put the papers back in the folder and returned everything to the bag just how she'd found it. She had all the information she needed for now; it was safe to hand it over to the police.

––––––––

The next morning the story made the newspapers. When Margot called in at the tabac, a half-page photo of the body on the rocks was emblazoned on the cover of the local daily. She snatched it from the rack. *Invasion de Migrants* claimed the headline. The photo had clearly been taken by someone who'd been in the crowd that day because it was just as Margot remembered – the little brown shaped morphed into the rock. Heat flushed through her as she speedread the article. They'd interviewed one of the fishermen who'd gone out on the RIB: '*Everyone in the town is devastated by the discovery,*' he was quoted as saying. Was that so? Margot buried the paper in a bin on her way out.

She marched on up the hill to the gendarmerie. A younger

man was on duty this time and he greeted her through the screen with a cheery bonjour. Margot was more succinct.

"Captain Bouchard, please."

"Can I ask what it's regarding?"

"It's about the bodies that were washed up. The *Invasion de Migrants*," she added with emphasis, though her bitter tone seemed lost on the young man.

"And your name?"

"Margot Renard."

The gendarme started to turn, but froze midway. He sent a glance back in her direction before tilting his head to the half-open door of the inner office. Despite the fact that someone was clearly in there the gendarme received no audible response. He manufactured a small cough, and then stepped back to the counter. "I believe Captain Bouchard is busy right now." His voice had suddenly climbed a semitone. "Can I help?"

Margot angled her head to try and see through the same door. She couldn't properly see in, but a strong smell of charcuteric was coming from close by. A piece of cutlery scraped on a plate, and now both Margot and the young officer looked at the door in silent anticipation. Whoever was in there seemed to pick up on it because the cutlery went quiet. As the silence became strained, Margot returned her eyes to the young gendarme. "You're sure he's not there?"

The gendarme pulled a face. "It is lunchtime, Madame."

The clock on the wall showed 12:30. Margot had never got used to the long French lunchbreaks. A good breakfast and a full evening meal were usually enough to sustain her. Whenever she'd been down here with Hugo he would always lunch alone in the kitchen and afterwards sleep for an hour in the garden leaving Margot to kick her heels, bored, for two hours.

The tension continued to build but Margot wasn't giving in.

"I have something the captain needs to see," she said.

"Well, if you leave it with me I'll be sure to pass it on," the gendarme replied.

"Yes, I could do that ...' Margot trailed away and then raised her voice in the hope it would carry: "or I could take it to the newspapers instead. I'm sure they would be interested to hear what I have to say."

An ugly scrape of a chair leg broke the stalemate. A moment later, Captain Bouchard appeared in the doorway, having to stoop to get under the frame. He sneered at the young gendarme who knocked over a pile of papers in his eagerness to get out of the way. When he came to the screen, the big man leaned over the counter with his palms planted wide as if he were about to deal with an unruly child. Margot straightened her spine, up for the challenge.

"Yes, Madame."

Even through the Perspex she could smell wine on his breath.

"I was asking about your investigation."

"What of it?"

"Have you made any progress?"

"The investigation is over."

Margot flinched. "Already?"

"Yes."

"And what did you conclude?"

"It's fairly obvious what happened: a boat was seen out that night, it was overloaded with migrants, some of them fell overboard, two of the bodies washed up. It's not the first time it's happened."

"Have the deaths been certified?"

"The certificates were signed this morning."

"And what was the cause?"

"Accidental drowning."

Margot scoffed. "How can you say it was accidental when you haven't even carried out a post-mortem?"

"A post-mortem is only ordered where death was not accidental or caused by natural causes."

Margot narrowed her eyes. "I know the law, Captain. I trained as a barrister."

"In which case you should know that the matter is out of our hands. I've passed my report to the Procureur."

Margot simmered. "And what about the people who put them on the boat? Are you just going to let them get away with it?"

Captain Bouchard heaved a tired sigh. If his eyes had rolled any further back into his skull he might just have lost them. "Is there anything else?"

Margot glared at him. She was tempted not to give him the backpack, much use it would do, but finally she pulled it from her swimming bag. "I found this in the cove."

The captain studied it through the Perspex. "You seem to have developed a knack for finding things."

"That's because I look."

The captain narrowed his eyes.

"It was hidden behind a rock, near to where I found the shirt."

The captain relaxed his shoulders, looking a little less combative. He grudgingly opened the hatch so she could pass it through.

"If you look inside you'll find a diary," Margot went on. "There's no doubt it belongs to the boy. And it's possible the man you found down by the fort was his father. Which could be confirmed with a DNA test, of course. Assuming you'll see fit to reopen your case."

Captain Bouchard didn't contradict her but the look on his face suggested it was a prospect he would not look forward to.

7

As the day passed Margot's frustration grew. She called Pierre at work to see if he could find out what the gendarmerie were doing, but he was snowed under and hadn't had a chance to look into it. The garage was the best lead they had and someone needed to follow up on it – she had half a mind to go there herself. The only other clue was the name 'Etienne' which she'd found mentioned several more times in Aswan's diary. The impression she'd got was that he was a friend of the family, and although it was Etienne who had accepted the money from Aswan's father it was unlikely he was the ringleader. Whoever else might be involved was being given plenty of time to cover their tracks.

She spent the day anxious and unsettled and when night fell went up to the bedroom in the attic. With the lights turned out she trained her binoculars on the sea. The Mediterranean was one dark featureless mass. How many other boats might there be out there right now, making that same dangerous crossing?

Margot swung the binoculars closer to shore and focussed on the harbour. The fishing boats were amassed on one side, the yachts and pleasure boats lined up on the other. She scanned the jumble of tall masts to see if *Carpe Diem* was amongst them, and spotted what she thought was it tucked in at the end. A light was on inside, but the blinds were down and she couldn't see in.

She lowered the binoculars, her mind settled. If she didn't hear anything from Pierre by noon tomorrow she would go to the garage herself.

———

After her swim, Margot went home and changed into a V-neck top and a pair of skinny jeans from Comptoir des Cottonniers. She took Rue Voltaire into town and turned right at the war memorial to take the alley into Place Saint-Marc. The square was lined with a range of shops selling knickknacks and souvenirs, and although it was a well-known tourist trap Margot habitually called in – tucked away in one corner was her favourite café, Le Paname. It was busy inside so she waited by the door. Raymond, the young waiter, spotted her immediately and greeted her with a friendly wave, and when Margot took a table under the canopy he appeared beside her before she'd barely had time to light her cigarette. He eagerly stood waiting with pencil and notepad.

"Good morning, Margot. How are you today?"

Margot shook the life out her match and dropped it in the ashtray. "I've had better days."

"Oh, I'm sure things will improve. What can I get you?"

Margot watched his eyes travel from his notepad to her legs. He'd had a schoolboy crush on her for years now and she couldn't resist teasing him. A few summers ago, she and Hugo had spent the whole of August down here and Margot had become friends with Raymond's mother. Raymond had been falling behind with his studies and Margot had agreed to give him some home tutoring, but Raymond, sixteen at the time and with teenage hormones coursing through his veins, had spent more time looking at her legs than listening to what she'd had to say. They'd taken to spending their sessions discussing Shakespeare in the garden, and Margot had the horrible suspicion she was the one who'd started him smoking, even though Raymond had insisted he'd had the habit already. He'd just been trying to impress her.

"I'll have a café crème, please."

"Coming right up."

He went back inside with a happy little smile.

When he re-emerged, Margot waited for him to finish arranging the coffee things and then reeled him in with a smile.

"Raymond."

He almost stood to attention. "Yes, Margot?"

"I wonder if you might help me."

His eyes bulged. "Yes. Of course."

Margot leaned back and admonished herself. It was nice to know she could still stir up such desires in a young man but she really oughtn't encourage him.

"A friend of mine has a problem with her car. Is there a garage nearby you could recommend?"

"Well, there's the Citroën dealer on the industrial estate. You know, the big one."

Margot nodded. "I know it. But someone mentioned Garage de Paolo ... near the port."

Raymond pulled a face. "I'm not sure I would send your friend there."

"Oh. Why not?"

He sent a glance over his shoulder before moving a little closer. "Just between you and me, the owner is a bad sort."

Margot's interest suddenly picked up. She flicked the ash from her cigarette as she leaned in. "What kind of bad sort?"

"They say he likes young ladies."

"And?"

"He has strange tastes."

"How do you mean?"

"I heard there's a room above the garage where he likes to take pictures. He ties them up in chains and does all kinds of weird stuff."

"With their consent?"

Raymond shrugged.

"Do the police know about this?"

Raymond appeared to want to smile, perhaps at her naivety. "I'm sure they do, but given who his brother is they're not going to do anything."

"Why – who is his brother?"

"Enzo Bellucci."

He said it with an ominous tone as if it were obvious who that was, but Margot had no clue.

Another customer was signalling for his attention and Raymond dithered. "I'm sorry. I have to go."

"Just a second." She caught his arm. "Tell me more about Enzo."

"All I can say is, they're not the kind of people you want to get involved with. Tell your friend to go to the Citroën garage."

Margot nodded and let him go.

————

As she was heading back down the hill Margot was distracted by a shout, and the *thump-thump-thump* of heavy, running footsteps.

"Madame!"

The town was busy with shoppers and several heads turned to see who was causing the commotion. Margot's eyes widened when she spotted a man hurtling down the street towards her, a red object raised above his head.

"Your shoe! I rescued it."

He came to a halt directly in front of her, juddering the last few metres so sharply that Margot had to take a step back. He seemed very pleased with himself, but he was so out of breath from the exertion that all he could do for the first few moments was pant noisily and grin stupidly. It was the skipper from *Carpe Diem*, Margot realised, though he was dressed a little more smartly than before. He had on a pair of sharp white slacks, and his pink linen shirt was a vast improvement on the Hawaiian monstrosity she'd seen him in yesterday. He'd also slicked back his hair and had a shave – the smell of cologne coming off him was actually quite appealing.

"I fished it out with the boat hook," he went on. "I gave it a good clean. I don't think there's any damage."

He attempted to hand it over, but Margot kept her hands to herself. She cast a disdainful look at the shoe. It was her ballet flat, all right, but she had no intention of accepting it. "You really think I'm going to wear that again?"

"But—"

"You found it, you keep it."

He returned a baffled look; then a smile of understanding crept across his lips. He nodded slowly, and lowered the shoe. "Of course. How thoughtless of me. I'll have to buy you a new pair."

"Don't be ridiculous." Margot turned on her heel and made to walk on, but he called out,

"I didn't get the chance to apologise. Not just about the shoe; for nearly running into you, as well. I honestly didn't see you out there."

She turned back. "Then you obviously weren't paying enough attention."

"Of course. You're absolutely right. I cannot admonish myself enough. And I assure you, Madame, it will never happen again." He gave a little bow of his head.

"I trust not."

Margot waited. If this was an attempt to chat her up he clearly wasn't very good at it. He already seemed stuck for his next line and stood there, looking abashed. She knew she wasn't making it easy for him – fixing him with a cool stare and an unyielding face, a stance she'd perfected over the years.

"I've been wandering around for over an hour," he said, "hoping I might find you."

"And here I am."

"And here you are."

She gave him another chance, waiting to see what he might come up with. When he didn't say anything, however, she turned again, prompting a last-ditch attempt:

"Perhaps I could take you to lunch some time."

"I don't think so."

"Then dinner?"

Margot came to another sharp halt. Against her better judgement, she turned and faced him for a second time. He wore a look of hopeful expectation, and something about it weakened her. She let her eyes slip to his chest. He was quite handsome, in a provincial kind of way. Beneath the shirt she could pick out some definition in his chest, and for a man who must have been fifty he had no discernible paunch. Margot's eyes returned to his. There was a mellowness there that spoke of a gentle soul. Maybe he wasn't quite the rich layabout she'd initially taken him for. Nevertheless.

"I'm sorry. I'm far too busy."

He quickly offered his hand. "My name is Raul."

Margot looked down at it, tanned and weather-beaten, but

didn't shake it. She did, however, surrender a small smile. "That's nice to know."

She turned for a third time.

"If you change your mind you know where to find me. I'll be in the harbour all week."

"I won't change my mind, Monsieur," Margot called back, and this time she carried on walking.

————

When she got home, Margot poured herself a large cognac and phoned Pierre. There was no answer from his office phone so she tried his mobile.

"Pierre – is everything all right?"

A cacophony of street noise made it difficult to understand his response. He was a little out of breath and somewhat distracted when he said, "Sorry, Margot. I'm out on a job."

A siren screamed by in the background. Someone shouted as if in pain. A tight knot formed in Margot's stomach as her mind flashed back to an image of him and Hugo chasing the hit men through the streets of Petites Écuries. A glimpse into a world she thought she'd turned her back on. She regretted calling him now but held on.

"Does the name Enzo Bellucci mean anything to you?"

"Who?"

"Enzo Bellucci."

More muffled sounds. She really ought to have hung up.

"It doesn't ring a bell. What's it about?'

Margot pinched shut her eyes. "It doesn't matter. I'll call you later."

"Are you sure?"

"Yes. I'll let you get on."

"Okay."

"And Pierre ..."

"Yes?"

"Please take care."

When the line went dead she slid her phone across the table and glared at it. Would she ever be free of that torment?

That night, Margot sat at the bureau in the corner of her sitting room and wrote a letter to the address she'd found in the front of Aswan's diary.

To whom it may concern,

It sounded rather formal but she had no names, or even any idea who might end up reading it.

I'm writing in connection with a boy named Aswan, aged 7. It was in his diary that I came across this address.

I don't know if this is where Aswan lived, or if there's any family connection at all, but if it does and you are related in some way I'm sorry to say that I write with bad news. It appears that Aswan may have died in an accident at sea. The body of a boy of his age was found on a beach in France in a town called Argents-sur-Mer, and although the body has not yet been formally identified, the discovery of this diary leads me to suspect that the victim may be poor Aswan. An older man was also found further along the coast and I fear this may be his father.

It may be that the authorities in Argents have already tried to contact you (I've passed on your address), but if not, I would urge any relatives to get in touch with the gendarmerie here. In particular, if you are aware of any connection with a man named Etienne you may be able to help find out why Aswan lost his life in such tragic circumstances.

If you are a relative, all I can say is I feel your loss deeply.

She hesitated, but then wrote:

I can only imagine what it must be like losing a child.

Not in the least bit true but it seemed the right thing to say.

Margot read it through and immediately felt sunk with disappointment. Words were so inadequate. She couldn't help thinking she was wasting her time. She signed it anyway and sealed it into an envelope.

She took the bottle of cognac up to the attic and sat at the window. The lights were on in the harbour, but she resisted the temptation to get out her binoculars. Laughter came from below; moving her face closer to the windowpane revealed an elderly couple walking by, dressed up to the nines. They were holding hands like a pair of young lovers, exactly how she'd imagined herself and Hugo at that age.

She switched on the lamp; flinched at the sight of her own reflection. What was she becoming instead – someone who stared out of windows and got her kicks from teasing young men? She swiftly reached out and closed the shutters.

No, that was not who she was. Standing there, at the top of the empty house, Margot stiffened her resolve. She was the one who'd found the backpack and she had every right to act upon what she'd uncovered. She couldn't keep asking Pierre for help, and if the gendarmes were dragging their feet because of who might be involved her blood was going to boil. Either Captain Bouchard acted soon or she would take matters into her own hands. She wasn't scared of anyone, despite Raymond's warning.

She poured half the glass of cognac into her mouth; the rest she emptied into a plant pot.

8

The lobster seemed lodged in his gullet. Enzo threw down his napkin and dug his fist into his chest, battling with indigestion. The waiter, hovering nearby, looked on anxiously.

Beside him, Marielle sighed. "Sweetheart, why don't you take one of your pills?"

Enzo brushed away his wife's interfering hand. He hated taking pills, or anyone fussing over his health.

"I've got some ginger capsules down in the car," Crystal put in, seated on his other side. "Shall I send Mutt down to fetch them?"

Across the table Marielle's *tut* was scathingly audible. She muttered something about shoving the capsules where the sun don't shine, and the air in the restaurant turned a few degrees chillier. Enzo groaned inwardly. The last thing he was in the mood for was a catfight between his wife and his mistress. They were both capable of going the full twelve rounds. "I'm fine," he said, but Marielle wasn't letting up.

"If Bunny wants to fill you full of New Age crap then let her."

Crystal ignored the comment. "You eat too quickly, that's the problem."

Marielle said to no one in particular: "He does everything too quickly, that's *my* problem."

Crystal took the bait and fired back: "Not in my experience," and Marielle shot a dagger across the table with her eyes.

Enzo rubbed his face, wishing he was elsewhere.

"Don't you have *filing* to do?" Marielle sneered.

"Don't you have *pans* to wash?" Crystal sneered back.

"Just give me the goddamn pills!" Enzo snatched the bottle from his wife's hand and chugged a couple down with the remainder of his glass of Bollinger. Anything for a quiet life.

It was an uncomfortable feeling to acknowledge but sometimes he regretted instigating this particular *ménage à trois*. Crystal, his PA, was a lively one, the feistiest mistress he'd had in years, and ever since that weekend in Paris when he'd taken her away on business and Marielle had walked in on them, she'd revelled in her role. Crystal had quickly cottoned on to the fact his wife would never leave him (she loved the trinkets too much) and never passed up an opportunity to provoke her, leaving Enzo caught up in the middle. And *not* in a good way.

Mutt appeared by his side. "Boss."

"What is it?"

The big man leaned down to his ear. "We've picked up a kid. The one who was bothering us last week."

Enzo looked up. "Who is he?"

Mutt pulled a face. "Some weird shit. He's down in the car. Do you want me to deal with him?"

Enzo turned back to the two women. Despite all the table finery the scene before him looked more like a battlefield. If looks were daggers the air between them would be a bloodied mess right now. Glad of the distraction, Enzo slid back his chair. He nodded to Mutt: "No. I'll do it." Snapped his fingers at the waiter: "Another bottle over here." And then tipped his head to his two companions: "Excuse me, ladies. Business calls." He manufactured a smile as he got to his feet.

On their way down in the elevator Mutt handed him a business card. Black and gold stars decorated one side; "*Need something to get you thru?*" printed on the other. At the bottom, a mobile number.

"He was handing them out on Felix Pyat," Mutt said. "One of our boys called it in."

"What's so weird about him?"

Mutt smirked as much as his overstuffed face would allow. "You'll see."

The Mercedes was parked in the two-storey garage at the rear of the restaurant. Mule got out of the driver's seat and opened the back door, then buttoned his jacket over his bulging torso while he stood on guard. When Enzo climbed in, he found a pasty-face rockabilly slumped in the seat beside him, dolled up like a full-on greaser: sharkskin suit, skinny tie, Dickies denims. His hair was styled in the most ridiculous pompadour you could ever have the misfortune to see; the odour of his pomade more fragrant than a hipster's posing pouch, though the petrified look on his face detracted from the coolness of his image somewhat. His wrists were bound with a cable tie.

Enzo shared a private chuckle with Mutt, and then elbowed the kid full in the face, so hard blood spurted from his nose. He nodded to Mutt who passed back a handkerchief.

"Bleed on my upholstery and I'll kill you."

The rockabilly clamped the handkerchief to his face. He wore the stunned look of a kid who'd never been hit before.

Enzo flicked his lighter and torched the end of a cigar, puffing on it until the air filled with thick grey smoke. How he loved that smell. He tossed the business card into the boy's lap. "This yours?"

The kid's eyes were like roving saucers, rapidly assessing,

trying to decide the best way out of the scene he'd landed himself in. He did the right thing and nodded.

"What's in the bag?" Enzo indicated the messenger bag in the footwell between them. The kid seemed to have gone mute so Enzo signalled to Mutt who promptly snatched it up and went through. At the side was a false lining concealing his stash: two bags of pills, three grams of hash, a small bundle of cash, two mobile phones. Mutt held it up to show Enzo who shot the kid a derisory look.

"Is this it?"

The kid nodded.

"You working for anyone?"

The kid shook his head.

"Good. Because if one of my boys went out with a stash as crap as this I'd kick his arse all the way from here to Lyon." With a weary sigh, he tossed the bag and the drugs into the kid's lap. It wasn't like the old days. Now it was all Snapchat and text-a-drug, kids could set themselves up from anywhere. They had no respect for boundaries. "You do know the third is my district?"

"Is it?"

"You were seen there three times last week."

The kid moved his shoulders, more of a twitch than a shrug. "I'm sorry," he said, and Enzo had to chuckle.

"You're *sorry*?" He turned his face to the window while he laughed himself out. Lights shone in his eyes as a vehicle swung out of the car park. Enzo took a long draw on his cigar, and then turned to blow smoke in the kid's face. There was nothing here for him to worry about here. The kid was a user-dealer, small fry. But still, lessons had to be taught.

"What's your name?"

"Sacha."

"Sacha. Well, let me tell you something about myself, Sacha. I'm old school. I like boundaries. I don't stray into anyone else's patch and I don't expect them to stray into mine. That's a perfectly reasonable point of view, don't you think?"

The kid seemed eager to agree.

"You can see where I'm coming from, can't you?'

He nodded again. They were both on the same wavelength, apparently.

"Good. Because now you might see value in the lesson I'm about to teach you."

The kid blanched, went so white he looked like he might just throw up.

"Are you good with your hands?"

"W—what?"

"I said, are you good with your hands? Do you enjoy combing through that stupid pompadour you've got going on there, putting on your poncey makeup, that kind of thing?"

Sacha nodded.

"Are you left- or right-handed?"

The boy's eyes switched frantically between the two men. He had the look of a caged animal, knowing that something bad was coming his way and desperate to figure a way out of it. His words tumbled out: "Hey look – I'm sorry. I won't do it again. I promise."

Enzo tapped Mutt's shoulder. The beefcake took a hammer out of the glovebox and held it up between the front-seat headrests.

"Now, my colleague here, he's very good with his hands. He can do all sorts of things with a tool like this. He can put up some shelves, make a really nice fence. Or, he can mincemeat out of a man's face."

There was a small clenched sob as the kid dropped his head. Enzo leaned down; he could hardly believe it but the kid was actually crying. He shook his head in dismay.

"Oh, Sacha, you disappoint me. If you want to play in the big boys' league you need to toughen up. Taking a beating is an occupational hazard."

The kid started sobbing now, pleading to be let go, and it was not a pretty sight. Enzo pinched the bridge of his nose, suddenly fatigued. He really did not want to be sitting here with this snivelling little greaser, and neither did he want to go back up to the restaurant. Why did other people have to make his life so complicated? He heaved a sigh.

"All right, Sacha, let me tell you how this is going to be. I can see you're young, naïve. I'm willing to believe you didn't realise whose territory you were straying in to. So I'll have my boys go easy on you. When I get out of this car they'll take you for a little drive. They'll park up somewhere nice and quiet. And then they'll break three of your fingers – two on your left hand for pissing on my patch and one on your right for being such a baby. Do you understand?"

The kid squealed and started bouncing on the seat. He doubled up and tried to pull the door handle with his teeth, but Mutt reached back and pinned him in place with one fat fist. And then the atmosphere in the car changed. Enzo ruffled his nose; sniffing the air he picked up the stench of urine. He looked down at the kid's trousers where a dark patch was spreading across one leg, and screwed up his face.

"Oh Jesus Christ – don't tell me you've wet yourself?"

The two men had a groaning contest.

Enzo reached over and pulled the door handle. "Get the hell out of my car."

The kid couldn't believe his ears. "You mean I can go?"

Enzo blasted: "I said, *get the hell out of my car, you snivelling piece of shit*," and the kid moved so fast he tripped, feet pedalling air as he face-planted the tarmac. When he finally got up, his pompadour had collapsed into a greased-up atrocity.

Enzo shook his head. Kids these days.

9

A TV news crew was setting up in the harbour when Margot came back from her swim. A female presenter was rehearsing her lines to camera, gesturing over her shoulder at the beach of rocks where Aswan's body had been found. A small group of onlookers had gathered, a ghoulish reminder of the day the bodies had been discovered.

As soon as she got home, Margot dug out the number of the local car rental shop. Her plan was simple – she would hire a car and take it to Garage de Paolo on the pretence that something was wrong with it. Play the damsel in distress and have a snoop around while they fixed it. According to an internet search, Paolo Bellucci was the garage's sole proprietor. A quick search on Enzo Bellucci revealed little other than the fact he was named as a director of a shipping company in Marseilles. The lack of information was hardly surprising – she didn't imagine they were the kind of people who left an on-line trail.

She downed her third coffee of the morning and stared at the clock: 10:06. She'd been prevaricating for over an hour now, sitting at the kitchen table, smoking cigarette after cigarette, wondering if she should talk herself out of it. Another ten minutes rolled by. Perhaps she should try and contact Pierre again, or go back to Le Paname and see if she could get something more out of Raymond, though she quickly dismissed that second idea. She wouldn't want to put him in danger.

Finally, at 10:45, Margot summoned her courage. She phoned the rental shop and then ordered a taxi.

———

The satnav directed her onto the main road and then up along the narrow strip of land that separated the sea from the saltwater lagoon. A left turn at a miniature roundabout brought her back inland and she drove across a wide flat plain, home to a caravan park that had seen better days. The directions ended on a concrete apron next an inlet lined with large brick warehouses. Margot drew up alongside an elderly gent walking his dog and lowered her window to ask for directions to Rue Baudin. The streets he told her to go down had a tatty, run-down feel.

Garage de Paolo was tucked away amongst an assortment of old brick buildings. After a slow drive-by, Margot turned right to go under a railway arch and then looped back around the block. Despite the emptiness of the streets she couldn't escape the feeling she was being watched. She passed the garage for a second time and then did a U-turn further up the street. She pulled in at the end of a line of parked cars. When she turned off the ignition the only sound was the drumming of her pulse in her ears. Had Hugo ever got nervous when he'd been out on surveillance?

She had a good view of the garage from where she'd parked. The big roller door was up, but a tow truck parked on the forecourt blocked any view of the interior. In the half hour she sat there no one went in or came out. Margot gave it another five minutes while she finished her cigarette, then popped the bonnet and got out of the car. After checking that no one was looking, she loosened the fuse on the starter motor relay.

A personnel door lay to the left of the roller door but Margot squeezed past the tow truck and went directly into the work-shop. Despite the huge open door, the interior was gloomy. A car was up on a ramp, but the only mechanic in evidence was lying on his back under a Hilux, the lower halves of his legs sticking out from underneath. A small office was situated on one side, and through the half-open door Margot could hear a man speaking on the phone. The personnel door she'd seen from outside led straight into an open-plan waiting area, but no one was in there. Tinny radio music came from close by. There were no other doors that she could see, and crucially, no staircase. Raymond had spoken of a room above the garage, but there was no obvious means of accessing one from here.

A dog barked, making Margot jerk her head. A small terrier looked up from its basket, but settled back down when she offered it a smile.

The mechanic didn't appear to have noticed so Margot stepped closer.

"Hello," she said, peering under.

A grumbled curse came from beneath the truck. Margot stepped back as the man rolled out on a creeper and stood up. His expression changed from irritation to pleasure as he took her in. He gave her an up-and-down look before settling his eyes on her chest.

"I'm looking for Paolo."

The man got to his feet. He indicated the office with a tilt of his head, but the person inside was still on the phone so Margot remained where she was. She hoped the mechanic might go back to work, but he lingered, licking his lips as his eyes roved over her. Margot inwardly cringed. Pathetic creature.

"What can we do for you?"

"My car's broken down."

"You work around here?"

"I was just passing."

He moved a step closer. Margot cringed again, though more at her own stupidity this time. She should have come up with a better story – this was hardly the kind of place you would stumble upon by chance. But she held her nerve. "I'll pay extra if you're busy."

The mechanic continued to stare, doing his best to look menacing, but Margot was not going to be intimidated. One step closer and she would be reaching for her pepper spray. Fortunately, the man in the office came off the phone at that point and the mechanic's face dropped. Margot enjoyed a small smile as she crossed to the office, looking back over her shoulder as she went. The mechanic returned to his creeper.

"Can I help?"

Margot jumped at the sound of the voice. She turned to find Paolo standing right in front of her. He must have been five centimetres shorter than she was, though his demeanour suggested he was not someone to be trifled with. He had a lumpy face, olive-skinned and heavily pock-marked. Margot let out her breath.

"You startled me."

"Are you booked in?"

"I was just speaking to your colleague."

"What's the problem?"

"I take it you're Paolo?"

"You are?"

She'd been intending to give a false name but in the heat of the moment completely forgot which one she'd chosen. He was radiating unfriendliness but she forced a small smile. "Is there any chance you could have a look at my car? I just tried to start it and it was completely dead."

He hadn't once lowered his eyes. For a man who liked to take pictures he seemed strangely uninterested. Maybe she was too old for him, or perhaps he was making an effort not to look. He was certainly difficult to read. A silence developed and she began to fear he'd seen right through her, but finally his mood lightened.

"Where is it?"

"Just down the street." She held up the keys. "The white Clio."

Paolo took the keys and whistled to the mechanic who took his time coming over. When he was halfway there, Paolo tossed him the keys.

"We'll see what we can do."

"Thank you. Shall I wait over here?" Margot indicated the seats in the corner.

Paolo nodded and went back to his office, this time closing the door behind him.

———

Margot picked the cleanest of the four chairs and moved it so she could sit facing the workshop. A range of magazines covered the table – she glanced at some back issues of *PHOTO* before settling upon a copy of *Art et Décoration*. She kept the magazine open in front of her while her eyes roved over the top, imagining herself as a spy in an old-fashioned movie.

The mechanic had gone back to working on the Hilux and seemed to have forgotten she was there. Margot lowered the magazine. The walls of the office were made from stud and plasterboard, and although the door was glazed the glass was obscure and all she could see through it were vague shapes. From the street it had been obvious that the garage was part of a jumble of buildings and there had to be more to it than what she could see from here, a back way in at least. There must have been something other than this waiting for Aswan and his papa.

The mechanic finally put down his tools and sauntered out through the big roller door. Margot closed the magazine and laid it gently on the table. She glanced around the corner of the office to check the door was still closed and then quietly got to her feet. The dog's eyes tracked her as she moved back to the ramp but it chose not to bark this time. Now she could see there was a door on the far side. Checking again that she wasn't being watched, Margot turned the handle and tentatively peered in. A lobby led to a toilet and a storeroom, beside it a grubby kitchenette. The smell coming out of there was pretty foul so she quickly pulled it shut.

A squeal of tyres drew her eyes to the forecourt. The tow truck was still blocking the entrance but through a gap she could see that a vehicle had pulled in – a white pickup with a green and white logo. The driver barely had time to get out when the office door flew open and Paolo emerged. Margot froze, but he marched straight out without even noticing her.

She moved closer and concealed herself behind one of the steel stanchions. Outside, Paolo had gone around the back of the pickup and was arguing with a dark-skinned man in blue overalls. Both men were quite animated and the argument kept them swaying back and forth, making it difficult to keep them in sight. Despite the animosity between them, they were speaking in voices too low to be overheard. Some sort of agreement was reached and the two of them set off down the street on foot.

Margot's pulse quickened. Alone in the garage, her eyes snapped to the office where the door had been left wide open. The mechanic had been gone for at least five minutes. She would have to be quick. After snatching another glance onto the street, she hurried into the office.

She went to the far side of the desk and perched on the

edge of the armchair, pulling all the drawers. They were all crammed with papers and junk apart from one which was locked. The computer was still switched on, but without knowing what she was looking for there was no point wasting time clicking through. Next, she ran a fingertip along the shelf of lever arch files, checking labels, but nothing caught her eye. He was hardly likely to keep anything incriminating in plain view. She scanned around, desperate to find something, and spotted a door on the far side of the filing cabinet. It wasn't locked. After turning the handle, she found herself peering into an inner lobby. And there was the staircase, leading up into darkness.

Margot's heart was beating so rapidly she feared it might burst but she had to take a look. A quick glance back to the empty workshop and then she went in. The floor was covered in a hideous orange carpet and a strong smell of petrol was coming from close by. A short corridor led to a door marked PRIVATE, but Margot ignored it and headed straight for the stairs. Her feet moved lightly on the hard metal treads. Eyes turned upwards, she found another short corridor and paused at the top, peering into darkness. The walls of the corridor were painted black, as was the ceiling and the floor. There were no doors – just a red velvet curtain five metres down at the end.

Voices drifted up from downstairs. Margot hesitated. She was desperate to go on, but it was far too risky. She turned on her heel and quickly went back.

Paolo and the mechanic were on their way in. She'd cleared the door by perhaps a metre when they spotted her at which point they abruptly went quiet, suspicion writ large their faces. Margot tried to look innocent as they halted in front of her, but her mind raced, convinced she'd been rumbled, tempted to make a run for it. She hadn't left a name, they wouldn't be able to trace her. Paolo looked like a man who was weighing up his options. Perhaps the police had already been round and put him on his guard. Somehow, Margot held her composure.

"I was just coming to find you. I thought you'd deserted me."

Paolo cleared his throat. "You had a loose fuse."

"Did I? I wonder how that could have happened."

He rocked his head. "A number of ways."

"You managed to fix it, then?"

He nodded.

"Thank you." She reached for her purse. "What do I owe you?"

Paolo continued to hold her eye, saying nothing. Margot still couldn't read him. He tipped his head towards the mechanic who strolled back to the Hilux, and for a moment Margot thought he was going to call her bluff. But he twitched a small smile instead.

"No charge." He held up the car keys.

Wrongfooted, Margot stared blankly back. She was off the hook, but part of her wasn't ready to go just yet. She still had no idea why Aswan had had this address and she was tempted to come straight out and ask him, present him with her evidence and tell him she'd already been to the police. But her courage finally abandoned her.

"That's very kind," she said, and accepted the keys.

Back in the car, Margot gripped the steering wheel with unsteady hands. Her mind was already running ahead. She had no idea what they were up to in there but something suspicious was definitely going on. She would come back after dark and find out what lay beyond that red velvet curtain.

10

On the other side of the hot tub Crystal's friend was giving him the come-and-get-me eyes. When she swished through the bubbling white water to take her share of the two lines of coke that Enzo had carved out for them, her sparkling blue eyes never left his. Her soft inner thigh nestled against his as she lowered her nose to the tile. Enzo held her hair while she vacuumed it up, and then kissed Crystal on the lips as she came over to join them: a threesome treat he'd been promised as a reward for not siding with his wife at the restaurant last night.

Crystal's friend had been awestruck when she'd seen the new house. Enzo rarely invited people into his home, but with his wife away and this treat on offer he'd given in to temptation. Watching them swim naked in the pool earlier he'd been undecided which of them he was going to enjoy the most. Crystal was the eldest and knew how to please him, but her friend had the better body, curves a porn star would kill for. Maybe he could come up with a challenge of some kind. Get them to see who could keep him going the longest. Crystal's friend suddenly raised her head.

"Where's yours?"

She seemed surprised he'd only carved out two lines.

"Enzo never touches the stuff, do you lover boy?" Crystal said, reaching across for the tile.

"How come?"

"It kills his libido."

The coke quickly kicked in and soon they were both all giggles and jiggles.

True, Enzo never touched the stuff, but no, it did not affect his libido. It was a fool's game, he knew that better than most. If you were dumb enough to get suckered in you only had yourself to blame.

They settled down on his either side and Enzo lay back, ready to enjoy. But despite the fantastic prospects on offer he found himself strangely unmoved. He couldn't stop thinking about his wife. A few hours ago she'd jetted off to the Alps to go skiing with a girlfriend. Her family owned a big old chalet up there – seven bedrooms, views of Mont Blanc. They'd had a huge late snowfall; Marielle had sent him pictures of happy smiling faces, glistening in white sunshine, and it had got him reminiscing. As kids, he and Paolo had used to love playing in the snow.

The frivolity in the hot tub quickly grew tiresome so he prized himself free. Two faces looked up in pretend disappointment as he swished to the side.

"Enzo no want to play?" Crystal said, putting on a baby voice.

Enzo looked back at them with mild annoyance. Sometimes he got the feeling they only came for the free coke. He clambered up onto the hot tiles and pulled the champagne bottle from the ice bucket. "Bolly's got warm," he said, and collected his robe on the way out.

In the changing room, Mutt was welded to the sofa, staring at a giant TV.

"Hey, lard-ass – you think this is what I pay you for?"

Mutt pulled a face and levered himself up. "Sorry, boss."

Enzo pushed the warm champagne bottle into his chest. "Go fetch."

He took Mutt's place on the sofa and lit a cigar. He reached for the remote and flicked away from the sports channels, feeling suddenly grumpy. He must be getting old. Passing up the chance of an amazing threesome to watch the news instead – was this what life would be like from now on? Maybe it was time to start taking the little blue pills. A man in his position needed to keep up appearances.

He almost flicked past it – a bulletin on the local news about some dead migrants that had been washed up – but held off when they said where it had happened. He jabbed the button to turn up the sound:

"The two bodies, believed to be father and son, were found within a kilometre of each other on a popular stretch of coastline near Argents-sur-Mer, close to Perpignan. Police are working to identify them, but so far few leads have been uncovered. An eyewitness reports seeing a boat out that night – an Oceanus RIB – and the gendarmerie are keen to trace the boat's owner."

Mutt came back with a fresh bottle of champagne and held it out, but Enzo stared blankly back at him. He turned off the TV, his mind elsewhere.

"You okay, boss?"

Enzo went on staring, and then finally nodded. An Oceanus RIB – that sounded familiar.

He got to his feet and slapped Mutt on the arm. "You take it in," he said. "They're all yours."

Mutt could hardly believe his ears. "Boss?"

"Family calls. I need to go and speak to my brother."

―――――

Enzo got dressed and took the elevator up to the living room level. He went into his office where he retrieved an encrypted phone from the safe. It could have been a coincidence but the more he thought about it the more likely it seemed. A while back Paolo had got into a little migrant importation. Every few months he and his friend Etienne would make a trip down to North Africa, pick up a boat-load of losers. And Etienne's boat was an Oceanus RIB.

"Paolo – it's me."

Silence from the other end of the line. Enzo expected little else. When Dad died fifteen years ago his kid brother had wanted nothing more to do with the business and had been determined to go his own way. Even now, after years of life going nowhere, Paolo barely tolerated him.

"I've just watched the news. You been up to your old tricks?"

"None of your business."

"If there's something going on I really need to know."

Paolo didn't answer. He'd never been the most talkative of people but some silences meant more than others. Enzo sat down in his chair.

"You need some help?"

"Haven't you got better things to do?"

Enzo clenched his jaw. He had a good mind to describe to him exactly what he'd passed up on to make this call but the kid would only get jealous. "I'm coming up to see you."

"Stay out of it."

"I wish it were that simple but trouble affects you then trouble affects me. I really don't want any attention right now."

Another silence.

"Will you be at the garage later?"

"Maybe."

Enzo squeezed the phone. "For God's sake, Paolo. Just grow up, will you?" He checked the time. "It's eight o'clock now; I'll meet you at the garage at eleven. You got that?"

There was another short silence before his brother hung up. Enzo punched the red button and tossed the phone onto his desk. Maybe one of these days he might not bother bailing him out, let him go to the wall, for all the thanks it got him. But even as he thought that Enzo knew it wouldn't happen. Not this time. Not next time. Not ever. Paolo was the only family he had now.

11

At six o'clock Margot switched her phone to silent. Pierre hadn't got back to her and in some small way she was relieved. As soon as he found out what she'd been up to he would only get worried and insist she leave it to the police. She was too keyed up to eat a full meal and only picked at a salad. She put on a set of dark clothes, slipped into a pair of soft-soled shoes, tucked her hair into a black wool beret. She chain-smoked three cigarettes while she waited for her phone to finish charging. The garage closed at seven, but she didn't set out until nine. Walking back to the street where she'd parked the car she was surprised to find a spring in her step. It had been months since she'd last felt such a tingle of excitement.

It was a moonless night and the roads were dark. When she got to the port, she parked on the other side of the railway arch and sat at the wheel, eyes on the garage. The place was all closed up – the tow truck gone, the shutters down. No light shone in the waiting room window, and the street was quiet apart from the thrum of muted music coming from a bar at the end of the street. She gave it another half-hour and then, at 9:53, went for a closer look.

A large rat scurried away from her as she walked through the railway arch. She went a little way down the street before crossing over, and then slowed as she approached the garage. A security light blinked on, scalding her retinas. Margot briefly paused while she pinched shut her eyes, then turned left at the next corner.

A jumble of two- and three-storey additions were tacked onto the rear of the garage and it was impossible to discern any boundaries. A high brick wall meant she couldn't even see in. The first opening she came to led to an access road at the rear of the properties, little wider than an alley. Margot hesitated before going in, eyes probing the darkness. No one appeared to be down there, but the air itself was menacing.

High walls ran along both sides. She felt her way forward with her palms on the brickwork. A parked car materialised, beyond it was another wall, meaning she was walking into a dead end. If anyone challenged her now she would be trapped. Soon she came to a pair of tall timber doors with a personnel door tucked into an alcove. Margot halted as another security light came on, revealing her surroundings in harsh white light. If she was imaging the layout of the building correctly she was still in line with the rear of the garage. She waited for the light to go out, and then switched on her torch.

She stepped into the alcove, careful not to trigger the lights again. Her heart sank when she spotted the illuminated keypad – the door was secured with an electronic lock. Hugo had once told her about the tricks lock-breakers used, but without specialist equipment there was no way of getting past a lock like this. She was about to start looking for another way in when inspiration struck: '7 4 3 1'. The text message on Aswan's phone. Could whoever have given him this address also have texted him the door code?

She punched in the numbers, flinched when a small green

light came on. Margot's pulse quickened when she heard the *click*. She turned the handle, pushed the door, and after peering through to make sure no alarms were going off, quietly stepped inside.

It was pitch dark but the acoustics suggested she'd entered a cavernous space, a storage unit or a small warehouse. With the aid of her torch she soon located a bank of light switches, but she didn't risk putting any of them on. The space was so congested its full extent was impossible to judge; the floor so jampacked she had to shuffle from spot to spot. Margot's roving torch-beam revealed several cars crammed into the space to her left, three vintage 2CVs amongst them. On the opposite side was a collection of motorcycles in various stages of restoration. A custom chopper was raised up on a bike lift; beside it an over-the-top scrambler with a pink leather seat. Scattered between the various vehicles were tools and spare parts and racks of shelving; every step of the way she had to be careful not to knock over a box or bump into something solid and heavy. There was no sign of the staircase she'd seen earlier, or the door with the red velvet curtain.

As she neared the edge of the space, the ceiling lowered and it became apparent she was walking beneath a mezzanine level. In the corner, her eyes picked out a dog-leg staircase and Margot ascended cautiously, her footsteps silent on the chequer-plate treads. It opened onto another storage area, just as cluttered as the space below, and her eyes went straight to the only door. It opened easily, but when she went to take a step forward she almost jumped out of her skin – five metres below, a solid concrete floor would have been the next thing to greet her.

There was no barrier. Margot took a quick step back and held onto the doorframe. She stood on the verge of a much larger space, an abandoned factory of some kind. High-level windows let in a little ambient light, and her torch-beam moved over a shadowy shop-floor that had long been stripped of its machinery. Pieces of heavy equipment lay abandoned, their chunky iron components relics of an earlier age. Heavy-duty chains hung from girders, and small, swept-up piles of broken glass littered the floor like puddles of precious stones. And, weirdly, in the centre of it all was another custom motorcycle, this one a purple Harley sporting a set of ludicrously high ape-hangers. Unable to make sense of it all, Margot closed the door.

She checked the time – it had gone ten-thirty and she'd still found no clue as to why Aswan and his father might have come here. Growing impatient, she quickly descended the stairs.

And from this angle she spotted a door that had previously been hidden to her. A flash with her torch revealed a sign saying PRIVATE. When Margot opened it she was relieved to find herself at the end of the corridor she'd discovered earlier – the hideous orange carpet the obvious giveaway. She strode the ten metres to the back door of Paolo's office and this time found it locked. Not that it mattered: her focus switched immediately to the stairs. She paused with her hand on the handrail, one foot on the bottom tread. If someone found her here right now the consequences were unthinkable and she briefly considered turning back. She could be out the back door in ten seconds flat. But curiosity was a hard thing to resist.

She paused again at the top of the stairs, skin prickling with nerves. A car raced by, the raucous bark of its uncapped exhaust making the walls vibrate. She approached the curtain and drew it aside, holding it back with the gold rope tie. Directly behind it was a solid black door, a shrunken skull for a handle, a keyhole below. Margot was certain her luck would run out and she would find it locked, but the door opened easily when she turned the handle. A squeak came from the hinges, making her suck her teeth. She reached for the light switch and tentatively flicked it on. A series of fluorescent tubes blinked on revealing a large room dominated by a table, at least five metres in length. An assortment of boxes and papers and prints and books covered the table, and more were piled up on the floor. Margot worked her way around the edges of the room first, her eyes drawn to the large, high-end printers that lined one wall. A small photographic studio was set up in the corner with lights on tripods and backdrops strung from a pole. A camp-bed was tucked into the next corner, looking like it had recently been slept in, and a dozen or so rolled-up sleeping bags lay nearby. A side table was laden with tins of food, a gas stove, half a loaf of bread. Several pairs of shoes were lined up beneath the bed and there was a free-standing rail with clothes. An inner door opened onto a toilet – Margot peered in and noted the single toothbrush in a glass on the shelf. Next to the toilet, a black curtain screened a darkroom.

Margot turned back to the table. It was so cluttered it was hard to know where to begin, but her eyes quickly settled upon a pile of EU passports. Thirty or forty of them were arranged in small piles, and when she examined them they looked brand new and genuine, or at least very good forgeries. Her eyes quickly returned to the printers. Is that what they were doing up here – manufacturing fake documents and supplying them as part of the package? Passage to Europe and a shiny new passport?

There were hundreds of photographs spread across the desk, some in boxes, many in albums. Margot took her time looking through, captivated by what she found. They were clearly the source of the rumours Raymond had passed on – many of them were in black and white and the subjects were young women, tied to chairs or bound in chains in a location very much like the abandoned factory she'd seen next door. The subjects were all naked, or near naked, and some of them were quite explicit, but they weren't pornographic. They were artfully staged and interestingly lit and wouldn't have looked out of place in a Paris gallery. Whoever had taken them undoubtedly had talent.

Margot was so engrossed she barely registered the sound of voices and when she did tune in, her head snapped up in disbelief. A light was shining up the stairs. Through the open door she could hear men's voices, moving closer. She raced to the door and switched off the light, then listened with her back to the wall. The men were coming up the stairs, hard-soled shoes clanging on the metal treads.

She searched the greyness for a way out. There was a window but it was too high up. The footsteps reached the landing, giving her only seconds to hide. She ran to the black curtain and hid in the darkroom, snatching a breath when the lights clicked back on.

They didn't seem surprised to find the door wide open. When Margot eased back the curtain to create a slit, she saw two men standing on the far side of the table, one of whom was Paolo.

"You ever think about tidying up?" the other man said.

Paolo didn't seem impressed. "Just say what you've come to say and then get out."

The second man moved slowly around the table and sat down in an armchair, his back to the darkroom. There was a *clink* of a heavy metal lighter, followed by silence as he lit a cigar. As the smoke started to billow, he leaned back in his seat and made himself comfortable. Whoever it was clearly had no intention of leaving soon.

12

Enzo stretched to pick up one of the passports. They were immaculate, barely distinguishable from the real thing. "How much do you charge for one of these – five, six hundred?"

Paolo took the passport out of his hand and tossed it into a bag. "Everything's not about money."

Enzo put his feet up on the table and blew a column of cigar smoke into the air. He watched without comment as Paolo continued tidying his stuff, and then glanced around the room with a feeling of dismay: the camp-bed, the tinned food, the rolls of toilet paper. Why did his brother choose to live like this when he could have so much? All he had to do was swallow some of his pride and come and work for him. Enzo had made the offer plenty of times.

And all these photos – piles of them, spread across the table. Enzo shuffled through ... silhouetted nudes, a pair of legs, some tattooed freak with her ass to the camera. Why couldn't he just take a straightforward god-damn snap? The kid was stuck inside his own head, that was his problem. Growing up he'd wanted to be an artist. At eighteen, he'd applied to an art school in Florence, bragged about the fancy life he was going to have. He did well in his exams, got offered a place, was all set to move away from the family home, but Dad had refused to pay the fees and there was no way Paolo could rustle up the money himself. He'd got a job as a grease monkey instead. Stupid kid was wasting his time, anyway; he was never going to fit in with that arty crowd. But he wouldn't listen, and he'd gone on taking his pictures, setting himself up in this crappy garage and turning this room into his studio. Sure, Enzo could see the allure of the naked ladies and had one time tried to persuade him to turn his hand to pornos, at least make some money out of it. But Paolo had refused, deluding himself into thinking it was all about 'the art'.

"You've been getting up to your old tricks with the Algerian, I take it?"

A pair of moody eyes turned to look at him. "His name's Etienne."

Etienne, yeah. Good old-fashioned French name that. Enzo had never liked him. His family had come over as illegals twenty-five years ago and for some reason the authorities had allowed them to stay. He and Paolo had been in the same class at school, and in their early twenties had decided to bring over a few migrants themselves: Etienne had the boat, Paolo the talent for forging documents. His brother had a naïve notion he was doing good, helping them find a better life in Europe, and would charge the bare minimum, throw in a few fake documents, even let them bed down for a few nights if they needed to. There was good money to be made from that game, but the kids were clueless.

"So what happened?"

Paolo went on bagging up his things. Enzo gave him a few moments and then took his feet off the table. "Come on, Paolo – talk to me. Whatever happened I can sort it out."

"You reckon?"

"They fall off the boat and drown, or what?"

"Just stay out of it." Paolo turned his back while he unlocked one of his cupboards. He shuffled some things around to make space for the passports.

"It's not your fault if they did. They know the risks. If they can't hack it they should go back to where they came from."

Paolo's head jerked round this time and Enzo tried hard not to grin. It was nice to know he could still find the right buttons to press.

"Is that what happened?"

No response.

"If you're in any kind of trouble I really do need to know. Look at it from where I'm sat: my only brother gets mixed up with some dead migrants and the first I hear about it is on the TV. How do you think that makes me feel?"

Enzo would never show it but he was genuinely hurt. His mind went back to those two kids playing in the snow. That year they'd had a massive downfall and school was shut for days. Kids from every street had come out to play. Maybe the last time he'd ever been truly happy. He snapped back.

"Has Etienne got rid of the boat?"

"He came round this morning."

"And?"

"He said he would take care of it."

"Was there any other evidence?"

Paolo was taking his time locking up the cupboard so Enzo got up and went over.

"Any documents, phones, clothes? Whatever you used that night needs to be got rid of."

"I'm not stupid." Paolo sneered at him and went back to the table. Enzo followed, one last trick up his sleeve.

"Look. I've got something big going on. There's a shipment coming in soon and I don't want any attention coming my way.

So if it's money you need—" He reached into his jacket and pulled out a roll of cash. He tossed it onto the table where it bounced towards the edge. "You know I'm here for you."

Paolo's eyes went after it like a hungry dog. Standing at his shoulder, Enzo could sense the desire coming off him. The kid would take it, he always did. And Enzo would go on bailing him out, no matter how many stupid capers he got himself involved in.

Enzo retrieved the cash from the edge of the table and pressed it into his brother's chest. "Take it. It's yours."

Paolo's hand twitched as he reached up for it. "I'll pay it back."

Enzo nodded. "Let's go down to the office. You can write me a receipt."

———

Margot listened for the closing of the door and then cautiously came out from behind the curtain. They'd turned off the lights, so she switched on her torch and carefully made her way back to the door. When she tried the handle, however, she found it locked. Damn. She quickly scanned for another way out. The only possibility was the window, though it looked as if it hadn't been opened in a while. Eyes searching the table, she found the passports gone. Foolishly she'd neglected to take any photos.

She moved a chair over to the window and at full stretch was just about able to raise the catch. Hooking her hands onto the thin metal frame she hauled herself up, kicking her legs to feed herself through. Luckily there was a flat roof below which she dropped onto with the gracefulness of a cat burglar. Reaching back up, she managed to close the window without making a sound.

Rooftops surrounded her. It was close to midnight and no

lights shone from any of the buildings. Unsure of her next move, Margot paused. It was obvious from the conversation that Paolo was involved in smuggling the migrants, but it wasn't exactly hard evidence. She could only hope that together with the contents of the backpack it would be enough to persuade the police to carry out a search.

She moved to the edge of the flat roof and peered down into the lane at the rear of the garage. It was a drop of at least five metres, but fortunately there was a sturdy drainpipe which she managed to shimmy down. She hurried round to the front of the building, and then paused at the corner. The bar at the end of the street was buzzing with life and some revellers had spilled onto the pavement. A black Mercedes was parked on the garage forecourt, and when Margot leaned out she could see light escaping from the waiting room window. It was a short hop across the street to the railway arch, another fifty metres to where she'd parked the car, but there was no way of getting there without passing the front of the garage. She had to risk it.

The security light caught her unawares. When it came on, Margot couldn't help turning her head. As bad luck would have it, the front door opened just at that moment and two men emerged. Suddenly, it was like she'd been caught red-handed: the two men stood staring while she froze in the middle of the road. When Paolo locked eyes on her she knew she'd been recognised. But she quickly turned her head and carried on walking.

Margot felt their eyes following her every step of the way, though neither of them came after her. As soon as she was through the railway arch she increased her speed, and then broke into a run when she reached the line of parked cars. Tucking herself in behind the wheel, she closed the car door as softly as she could, and wasted no time manoeuvring out of the parking space. It was only when she was back on the main road, speeding towards home, that she realised she'd neglected to switch on her headlights.

———

Enzo stared into his brother's surprised eyes and asked the question both of them appeared to be thinking:

"Who the hell was that?"

Paolo stepped into the street, confused. A hundred metres away a white Clio was heading away from them at speed, headlights out. When Paolo turned back, a look of realisation was dawning on his face.

"Goddammit."

"What?"

"I know that car."

Enzo stepped closer. "Who was it?"

"Some woman. She came into the garage earlier."

"To do what?"

Enzo followed like a shadow as his brother marched back inside. "Paolo, who was she?"

Paolo halted in the middle of the workshop, rubbing the back of his neck. "She reckoned her engine wouldn't start but it was just a pulled fuse."

Enzo frowned. "You mean she faked it?"

Paolo shrugged irritably.

"What the ..." The pressure in Enzo's temples started to build. His head throbbed as he paced the workshop, desperately trying to make sense of what had just happened. He had a sixth sense for trouble. You needed to in his line of work. Halting, he pushed a flattened palm up into the air. "And where the hell did she come from just now?"

"Hell knows."

"For god's sake ..."

"She was probably just some reporter, snooping around."

"But how did she get your address?"

Paolo had no answer.

"Jesus, Paolo!"

Enzo strode into the office. For several long moments he kept his back turned, afraid of what he might say if he let loose. Sometimes his brother's incompetence astounded him.

There was silence for a while. Then Paolo said, "I didn't get her name, but I took her registration."

Enzo's jaw slackened. He turned slowly to face his brother, still out in the workshop. "All right. Give it to me. I'll deal with it."

13

It was well after midnight when Margot got back to Argents. She drove into the main car park in the centre of town and reversed the Clio into a dark corner, hidden from view of the surrounding buildings. Streetlamps lit the way as she walked home, but she kept her wits about her even though no one was around. Only when she'd made it safely back to her house and had closed the door behind her did she even think about relaxing.

She poured herself a large cognac. Perched on the edge of the settee with just the table lamp on, her hands shook ever so slightly. It was late, but she was keen to get her thoughts in order, jot down a record of what she'd seen and heard, remember as many details as she could. She would go to the police first thing in the morning, though the thought of seeing Captain Bouchard again turned her stomach. Better to call Pierre first, see what he could do. She drank the cognac in three gulps, and finally went to bed in the early hours, tossing and turning and waking again at four.

At nine o'clock she called Pierre's office in Paris, but he was busy on a case so she had to leave a message. For thirty minutes she sat and stared at her phone, waiting in vain for him to call back. Needing to clear her head, Margot put on her Speedo and went to the cove.

The poor night's sleep had left her with a headache and she'd barely swum out five hundred metres when her energy started to decline. Her arms and legs were as loose as jelly, her joints achy. To make matters worse, it started to rain, and not just lightly – hard heavy raindrops shot down from the sky in a way that reminded her of Paris. She swam straight back in and climbed up onto the rocks, shivering under the onslaught.

"There you are!"

Margot spun at the sound of a man's voice. She was stunned to see Raul working his way towards her along the headland path, an open umbrella over his head. Annoyed at having her space so rudely invaded, Margot began gathering her things.

"So this is where you come to swim." He reached the end of the path and stepped up onto the rock next to hers. "Awful weather, isn't it?" He offered her the cover of his umbrella, but Margot shied away. "Don't you have a coat?"

"I'm wet already."

"But you're shivering."

Margot looked at him in consternation. "I'm fine," she insisted, and snatched up her bag. She pulled out her clothes and started putting them on, despite the fact she was still soaking wet. She felt clumsy with him watching and struggled to get her trousers on, almost toppling as she hopped on one leg.

"Here – let me help."

"No!" She turned away from his proffered hand.

Despite her protests, Raul kept moving the umbrella around to try and keep her covered. The fact he was still watching made

Margot increasingly uncomfortable and she came close to losing her cool. Why wouldn't he just go away?

"I saw you come in just now. You're a very strong swimmer."

"I've had plenty of practice."

"Isn't it rather dangerous, though? Going out so far."

"Only when people drive their boats at you."

He laughed. "You're never going to let me forget that, are you?"

Not likely. Margot pulled off her bathing cap and shook out her hair. It sprayed the front of his trousers and made him step back, but she didn't care. She gave him a look as if to ask why he was still there, though he didn't seem to get it. "You're not out playing with your *toy* today?" she sneered.

"No. I'm waiting for a telephone call. My daughter's just gone into hospital. I may have to go to Madrid."

Margot immediately stopped what she was doing. "You mean you're leaving Argents?"

Raul seemed surprised by the question and didn't answer right away. Margot lowered her eyes, realising her mistake. That probably wasn't the first thing she should have said. The sound of the rain pattering his umbrella abruptly got louder.

"Hopefully it won't be for long," he said.

She finished getting dressed, a little less hurriedly now. Some shingle had found its way into her sandal so she shook it out before sliding it onto her foot. "Is she all right, your daughter?"

"They said it was just a precaution. She's been having a difficult pregnancy. I'm sure she'll be fine."

Margot fastened her bag, knotting the drawstring a little more tightly than was necessary. The rain was running down her face now despite Raul's attempts to shelter her.

"Are you going back into town?" he asked.

She nodded.

"In that case why don't we find a nice warm café? I can buy you a coffee."

"I'm sorry, I need to get back."

He came a little closer, ostensibly so they could both be under the umbrella. Margot had no choice but to look closely at his face. Her gaze travelled tentatively across his soft pink lips, up to his pearly blue eyes, just like Hugo's. There was something comforting about the way he was looking at her and it made her heart feel a little bit softer.

"Are you sure you're all right?" he said. "You seem a little troubled."

"I've got a lot on my mind, that's all."

"If there's anything I can do to help ..."

Margot shook her head. "You're very kind, but I have to go."

He accompanied her back around the headland, but as soon as they reached the harbour they went their separate ways.

———

Margot went home and changed into dry clothes. She sat at the kitchen table and stared at her phone, but the screen didn't change: no missed calls. Before she knew it, half the morning had gone. When she called Pierre's office she was told he was still busy. No, she didn't want to leave a message. Running out of options, it seemed she would have to go and see Captain Bouchard, though perhaps not just yet. Despite the bad weather, she walked to the car park where she'd left the Clio and then drove it back to the rental shop.

The man at the desk must have remembered her because he greeted her by name.

"Was everything satisfactory?"

"Yes."

"You had no problems with the car?"

He was looking at her rather oddly: glancing up from the tops of his eyes while his hands got on with the paperwork. Margot frowned at him. What was he implying? Did he know she'd taken it to the garage? Did they automatically do that when a hire car came in for repair? Margot cursed herself, feeling an amateur. She should have come up with a better plan.

"Everything was fine," she said and determinedly held the man's eye when he looked up. She scribbled her signature on the bottom of the form.

She took a taxi back to town. Paolo would have taken her registration, that was to be expected, and he could have used it to find out where she'd hired the car from, though she couldn't believe the rental place would have given out any of her details. Surely they wouldn't have passed on her address. Unless they'd been got at in some way – who knew how far Paolo's and Enzo's influence extended. Margot had the taxi driver take her straight to the gendarmerie.

The same young man was on duty. His face lit up as soon as he saw her come in and he seemed pleased to see her this time.

"Ah, Madame Renard. Back again so soon?"

"I need to speak to Captain Bouchard. It's urgent."

The gendarme pulled a face. "I'm afraid the captain is not here today." And it was obvious from his tone that this time he was telling the truth. "He's away on a course."

"Is there anyone else I can see?"

"I'm afraid we're a little short-staffed at the moment. One of our investigating officers is off sick and the other is out on a job."

Margot let out a sigh. Why did it seem like everything was conspiring against her?

"Can I take a message?"

Margot shook her head. "No. I'll try again tomorrow."

The rain had stopped when she came back out. Shafts of warm sunlight were poking through the clouds, and the tourists were emerging from the shelter of the shops and cafés as she headed back down Rue Voltaire. Unable to escape the feeling that people were looking at her, Margot detoured into Place Saint-Marc where she was relieved to see Raymond serving tables outside Le Paname. She dragged a chair over to the corner and sat with her back to the square.

"A café crème?" Raymond prompted when she was slow to order.

"Please." Elbows on the table, shoulders slumped, Margot radiated gloom.

"Bad day?"

"You could say that."

"Did your friend manage to sort out her car?"

"Friend?" She queried him with a frown, but then quickly cottoned on. "Oh yes. My friend. The one with the car." She leaned back in her seat while Raymond wiped the table. She struck a match and lit a cigarette, her mood mellowing as she pulled in that satisfying first lungful. "No," she said, and blew a small cloud of smoke into the air. "I'm afraid my friend may have done something rather foolish instead."

"Oh?" Raymond was all ears.

"She didn't go to the Citroën garage."

"Oh," Raymond said again, though this time in a much lower tone.

Margot defused his curiosity with a smile. It would have been nice to confide in him but it was far too dangerous. He was such a sweetie.

"Sometimes I think my friend doesn't have a clue what she's doing," she muttered, and all Raymond could do was walk away looking a little bit perplexed.

As she turned the corner to go into her lane Margot was halted by the sight of a man outside her house. A tall, thickset man with a number 1 buzz cut was standing by the fence, looking up at her windows. Margot came to her senses and started walking towards him, but the moment she opened her mouth to speak the man turned and walked away. She had half a mind to go after him, but went in through her front door instead.

She dropped her keys into the bowl. As she moved through the living room and into the kitchen something felt different. Was that magazine on the bureau exactly as she'd left it? Had that black mark on the flagstones been there before? She checked the windows, but they were all still shut. She spent a few more moments listening to the silence, certain that someone had been inside her house, but then pushed the thought away, convinced she was being paranoid. Nevertheless, she went back to the front door and slid home the bolts.

———

Margot was in the courtyard, smoking in the dark, when Pierre finally called back. It was eight o'clock and she'd been sitting there, staring into the air, for well over an hour.

"I'm sorry, Margot. It's been one of those days." He sounded tired.

"Are you still in the office?"

"Yes. It's this case ..."

She pictured Camille at home with the baby, wondering what time he would be back. So many long nights she'd lain awake waiting for Hugo to finish work.

"What did you want to talk to me about?"

Margot hesitated. Now she was on the spot she wasn't sure what to say. "I think I may have done something rash."

She was expecting him to make a joke at her expense but he was clearly not in the mood. Margot imagined him sitting back in his seat, rubbing his eyes, forcing himself to take an interest in the conversation.

"What have you done now?"

"You remember those two dead migrants?"

"Yes."

Margot told him about the backpack and how she'd come across the address of Garage de Paolo. "I wanted to find out why the boy had that address so I went there last night."

"And did what?"

Margot drew in a breath. "I didn't break in. I just wanted to have a look round."

"And?"

"I overhead them talking, Paolo and his brother. It was Paolo who was involved in the smuggling, he virtually admitted it. And they've been faking passports, I saw the evidence with my own eyes. We have to get the place searched as quickly as possible."

"Margot, slow down. Who are you talking about?"

"Paolo Bellucci. His brother's Enzo Bellucci."

"*Enzo* Bellucci?"

"Yes."

"Isn't that who you asked me about the other day?"

"Yes! but you were busy."

Pierre went silent. Margot heard him tapping away at a keyboard; she got the feeling he was only now looking him up. After a few moments he gave a sharp intake of breath.

"Pierre, what is it?"

"So you broke into the garage and listened in on a conversation between Enzo Bellucci and his brother?"

"I didn't break in. I had the door code, it was on Aswan's phone. That's evidence in itself."

A series of exasperated noises came from the other end of the line. "Have you any idea how dangerous that was?"

"Don't patronise me, Pierre."

"Did anyone see you?"

"I don't think so ... I mean, perhaps."

"What does that mean?"

Margot drew in another long breath. "They were just coming out the front door as I was heading back to the car. I think they probably did see me."

"But did they know you'd been snooping around?"

"Possibly. I'm not sure."

"Oh, Margot!"

"That's all the more reason to get to the place searched," Margot responded quickly. "They're getting rid of evidence, Pierre. They'll have covered their tracks by the time the local gendarmes do anything. There must be something you can do."

Pierre sighed lengthily. Margot didn't like putting him in this position but he was the only one she could turn to.

"All right," he said at last. "I'll make some calls."

"Thank you."

"But you have to promise me you won't do anything else foolish."

"I'll try. But what do you know about him?"

"You know I can't tell you, but it's nothing good. Are you at home?"

"Yes."

"Then stay indoors. Don't do anything until you hear back from me. Okay?"

If anything, his serious tone did the opposite of reassure her but Margot wasn't going to argue. She assured him she would not go out and then hung up.

———

After a nightcap, Margot went up to the room in the attic. She turned off all the lights and opened the window, leaning out to look both ways along the lane. No one was there.

She took her binoculars from the shelf and trained them on the harbour. A bank of mist had come in from the sea, reducing the streetlamps to fuzzy yellow blurs. She scanned the jumble of tall white masts to see if *Carpe Diem* was amongst them, but it was hard to tell. She lowered the binoculars and sighed. Perhaps his daughter had phoned and he'd gone off to Madrid. Or perhaps she'd been too abrupt with him. In spite of everything she did rather like having him around.

At 00:03 she called it a night. She went downstairs to make sure the doors were all bolted and then retired to her bed.

―――――

It felt like dream and reality had decided to combine. Fuelled by her escapade at the garage, Margot had been chasing villains in an open-top sports car, pursuing them up a winding mountain pass with her hair blowing in the wind. Tyres squealed on hairpin bends and gunshots rang out as the villains fired back at her. Then the gunshots became a series of *thuds* inside the house and Margot woke with a start. That noise had come from downstairs.

Her face was damp with sweat.

Her eyes were wide and searching.

The digital clock showed 03:13.

She listened, but the house went quiet again.

Perhaps it had been a dream; she contented herself to wish it away and sank back into the pillows.

But then came the tinkle of breaking glass and this time Margot sat up with conviction. That sound had definitely come from inside.

Snatching back the covers, she swung her legs out of the bed. Perched on the edge of the mattress she strained to hear, her pulse beating loudly in her ears. She went to the window and pulled the blind just in time to see a figure hurrying away. And despite the poor light, Margot was certain it was the man she'd seen earlier.

She quickly put on her dressing gown. She thrust open her door and went onto the landing, but was instantly halted by a terrifying sound: a drawing of air, a hiss and a crackle. Margot's eyes widened in disbelief. No. It couldn't be what it sounded like, surely not. But then a wisp of smoke crept out from under the sitting room door.

Panic seized her.

She ran down the stairs and reached for the door handle. She paused to cover her mouth with a corner of her robe. Part of her was afraid to go in, certain in the knowledge of what she would find, but adrenaline made her thrust open the door.

A wall of heat stopped her dead in her tracks.

Now there could be no mistaking dream from reality. Margot's sitting room was on fire.

14

Margot dashed through the kitchen and out into the courtyard. The logical part of her brain was telling her to call the fire brigade, but she couldn't just stand by and watch her house burn. The hosepipe was already connected so all she had to do was turn on the tap and run back in. Standing on the threshold of her living room, squirting water into her house, she could barely believe what she was doing. The fiercest flames were in front of the window, but small fires were popping up everywhere, filling the room with thick black smoke. Margot couldn't bear to leave it. She could only hope the neighbours had heard and would call for help. Her heart fluttered as black smoke billowed out from her bookcases, horrified by the damage it would be doing. She tried to get closer, but the heat was too intense.

Time warped and it seemed she'd only been there a few minutes when the room started to flash with red and blue light. Shouts came in off the street; someone started banging on the front door. Still Margot delayed, unable to tear herself away. She had to stay and fight, however useless her efforts might be. But then the door burst open and a jet of water shot in, making the decision for her. Margot dropped the hosepipe and ran.

A fire officer was charging down the passageway and they almost collided. He grabbed her by the forearm and pulled her into the lane, and then ushered her into the safety of the waiting fire truck. The next thing she knew someone was stretching an oxygen mask over her face and telling her to stay calm, but that was the last thing Margot could do. With stinging eyes, she leaned forward to look through the big windscreen, desperate to see what was happening. The sight of her lovely blue shutters going up in flame was almost too much to bear.

———

It didn't take long to put out the fire. Once the flames had been extinguished and the worst of the smoke had died down, two of the officers went in to carry out checks. They emerged a short time later and gave the all-clear. The water was turned off and the crew stood down. Tall columns of grey-black smoke funnelled out through the remains of her front window as they packed away their equipment.

"You were very brave, Madame," the fire chief said when he came to check on her. "It didn't spread much beyond the sitting room. Your little hosepipe kept it at bay."

Margot was too numb to respond with anything intelligible.

An ambulance drew up and a paramedic gave her a once-over. Her eyes were still stinging and she felt sick from inhaling the smoke, but she refused to go to the hospital. Monsieur and Madame Barbier took charge of her, and when the emergency crews left they insisted she go in with them. They poured her a glass of something strong and sat with her for the few hours that remained of the night. Everyone agreed what a horrible experience it had been.

At first light, Margot and Madame Barbier went back to assess the damage. Margot ducked under the tape that had been fixed across her front door and hesitantly stepped into the blackened mess that used to be her sitting room. Just a small fire, the fire chief had said, but the amount of destruction was shocking. Her bookcases were gone – Hugo's record collection reduced to a puddle of melted plastic; her books turned to ashes. The tin that had housed her photographs lay on the floor, its lid to one side. Those photos that hadn't been destroyed by the fire were ruined by water. The only crumb of comfort was that Hugo's medal had survived unscathed. The flames may not have spread beyond the sitting room, but everything else in the house – the carpets, the walls, the curtains – were covered in soot and stank of smoke.

"How on earth did it happen?" Madame Barbier asked, trailing at a respectful distance. "Could it have been an electrical fault?"

Margot shook her head. She pulled out a stool from beneath the kitchen table and sat down, numb to her core. She couldn't explain how the fire had started but the fleeing figure in the lane surely had something to do with it. For now, she chose not to think about who might have sent him.

———

Madame Barbier had to go to work at eight but she promised to return later to help clear up the mess. Ten minutes after she'd gone, another figure darkened her doorway – Margot was surprised to find Captain Bouchard standing on her threshold. He greeted her with a small nod of his head before stepping inside, uninvited, his eyes travelling around the room with an increasing level of surprise. Margot stood on the spot, observing him coldly, sickened by the sight of his thick leather boots clomping through the remains of her sitting room.

"What a horrible mess."

"Thank you."

His eyes snapped to hers, not quite getting the sarcasm. "I understand you were at home when it happened."

Margot nodded. "Upstairs. In bed."

"You had a lucky escape."

"I don't feel very lucky."

The captain had the kind of demeanour that was unsuited to showing compassion, even if he might be feeling it. After a failed attempt at a smile, he went back to picking his way around the room. It seemed no square centimetre of the floor or wall space was going to escape his attention.

"Do you have any idea how it started?"

Despite everything that had happened Margot was still reluctant to come clean with him. The chances of receiving a sympathetic ear seemed slim.

"I heard a noise downstairs, glass being smashed." It was all still a bit hazy, even though it had only been a few hours. "I went to my bedroom window and saw a man running away."

Captain Bouchard paused, turning to frown at her. "Running away from your house?"

"Yes."

"You're suggesting this wasn't an accident?"

"You're the policeman."

He straightened his back. "Arson is a serious crime, Madame."

"You think I don't know that?"

Margot quickly admonished herself. This wasn't the time for point scoring.

"Could you describe him?"

"I couldn't see very well. It was dark. He was tall and well-built. When I came home this afternoon I'm sure he was standing outside, looking up at my windows. I didn't think much of it at the time."

Captain Bouchard spent a few moments mulling that over. He nodded to himself a couple of times and then moved towards the broken front window. His eyes scanned the debris on the floor until he spotted something of interest, at which point he crouched next to the pile of broken glass. With a pencil he took from the top pocket of his tunic, he moved around some of the shards until he'd isolated a small piece. He picked it up and held it under his nose. Margot stepped closer.

"What is it?"

The captain stood. "Most of these pieces of glass are from the broken window. You can tell from the way it has shattered. But this one—" He extended his arm and held the shard in the air between them "—is from a bottle."

Margot peered at it.

"What's more, it smells of petrol."

"You mean—"

"The burn pattern on the rug also suggests an accelerant was used. You see the 'V' shape?"

Now that he pointed it out Margot could see it clearly.

"It has all the hallmarks of a petrol bomb," the captain declared. He lowered his arm and faced her squarely, a deep frown creasing his forehead. "It's hardly a common crime in Argents-sur-Mer. So tell me, Madame, why would someone want to throw a petrol bomb through your window?"

Margot looked away. It was time to do some explaining.

———

The captain escorted her into the gendarmerie via a back door and led her down a corridor that turned through several corners. He opened a door to a small, windowless room and indicated one of the two chairs on the far side of a table. Margot pulled one a little way out before sitting down, shuffling to get comfortable on the hard wood seat. It had been a five-minute walk from her house to the gendarmerie but for the entire three hundred seconds neither of them had uttered a word.

The captain closed the door behind him. He seated himself on the nearside of the table and took off his cap, placing it squarely in one corner. He leaned forward with his fingers laced, elbows on the table, a posture that intensified his stare. "Am I to take it you know who was responsible for the fire?"

Margot folded her arms. "I have my suspicions."

"Would you care to share them?"

The logical side of her brain told her to open up to him, that they were both on the same side, that she'd got herself in far too deeply and needed help, but she still had to drag the words out of herself. She sighed wearily, and then described her visit to the garage, who she'd seen there, what she'd overheard. "From what I understood, it was Paolo who was behind the migrant smuggling. I think the boat was owned by a man named Etienne."

"And the man who was talking to Paolo?"

"I assumed it was his brother – Enzo Bellucci."

The captain appeared unmoved. A silence formed as he took a pen from his pocket and wrote something down on a notepad. When he was done, he leaned back in his chair and allowed his eyes to roam, almost as if he'd forgotten Margot was still there. He nodded to himself a number of times before bringing his attention back to the table.

"Where did you hire the car?"

She told him. "You'll speak to the owner, I presume?"

"Naturally."

"If he was the one who gave them my address I want him prosecuted."

The captain raised an eyebrow but otherwise didn't respond.

He made another small note on his pad. Margot went on, "I'm guessing they found out where I lived and threw the bomb through my window as a warning."

"More than that, Madame. If they knew you were at home at the time their motive could have been far more serious."

Margot raised her chin. "I won't be intimidated, whatever their motive." A little bit of ice set into her veins. She didn't like being threatened, and she would not be bullied by anyone. An animal was at its most dangerous when it was being backed into a corner.

Captain Bouchard didn't speak for a while and the silence lengthened. Margot cleared her throat. "Well," she said. "What are you going to do about it?"

He looked away, seeming unsure. "We need to check for fingerprints. I'll have a crime-scene squad sent to your house as soon as possible."

"What about the garage? And the fake passports?"

"That's a separate matter. I'll have to consult with a different department."

Margot tutted in frustration. "By the time you've finished 'consulting' all the evidence will be gone."

"We have to follow procedure. I only have your say-so that the passports are there at all."

"I handed you the backpack. You had the same information as I did. Why didn't you go there and see for yourself?"

The captain went a little bit red in the face. "The matter was in hand."

"*Pah!*"

He leaned forward, spreading his hands. "You can't take the law into your own hands just because you feel like it."

"I wouldn't have needed to if you'd been doing your job properly."

"Enough!" The captain sprang from his seat and slammed

the table with the base of his right fist. "We follow procedure for a reason. We can't have people blundering into the affairs of criminals and then expecting the police to bail them out. This is not a game. We have enough crimes to deal with as it is."

Margot glared back at him. She was sorely tempted to accuse him of being too scared to go to the garage but she held her tongue, despite the anger raging inside.

"This is a police matter and you will stay out of it. Do I make myself clear?"

Margot had no intention of staying out of it and she would not be silenced. This man was an imbecile and needed taking down a peg or two, but she could not win this battle, not here. "Perfectly."

"Good."

The captain calmed down. He returned to his seat, smoothing down his hair with a flattened palm. He was clearly a man who did not like to be riled. Margot watched him with narrowed eyes. He may have won this battle but he would not be winning the war. The air cleared.

"Now. Is there someone you can call? A friend or a relative?"

She nodded. She would call Pierre.

"I would like you to ask them to come and collect you. And until they do I would strongly advise you remain here, in the gendarmerie."

Margot frowned at him. "But my friend lives in Paris. It'll take him hours to get here."

"It is for your own safety, Madame. These people have already made one attempt on your life. There's no guarantee they won't try again."

If she wasn't mistaken there was genuine concern in his voice. And that had a greater impact on her than anything he'd said so far.

15

It was like her parents had been called in by the head: Margot sat in the corridor outside Captain Bouchard's office while inside the pompous oaf lectured Pierre on her errant behaviour. How galling to have her fate decided by that jumped-up clown! When she'd called Pierre after being hauled in this morning, Captain Bouchard had taken over the phone and emphasised the seriousness of the situation. Pierre had come straight down, but for eight hours Margot had had to sit on a wooden chair in the waiting room, slowly going out of her mind with boredom. The longer it had gone on the more ridiculous the whole situation had seemed.

And even now, after all that time, the two of them had been in there for over twenty minutes, discussing it man to man, cop to cop. It was enough to make her head boil. Seething, she took a cigarette from her bag, and while the corridor was still empty, smoked a good quarter before crumpling the evidence into her ashtray.

Finally, the two men emerged. They parted company with a firm handshake and Pierre came over with a small nod. The matter of her irresponsible behaviour had been settled, it appeared, and she was free to go. Margot got to her feet with undisguised relief. Captain Bouchard paused to sniff the air as they turned to leave; Margot treated herself to a smile on their way out.

"You'll be pleased to know the *Procureur* has opened an *instruction*," Pierre said as they crossed the road to the mini-roundabout and took the pedestrian exit onto Rue Voltaire. "The examining magistrate has ordered a full post-mortem."

Progress at last. It seemed her actions had served a purpose after all.

"They've also tested the DNA," Pierre went on, stepping up behind her on the narrow footpath as a car went by. "The deceased were father and son, just as you suspected."

It was six o'clock and the bars and restaurants were starting to get busy. Margot couldn't face the prospect of going home just yet so she steered Pierre into Place Saint-Marc and under the canopy of Le Paname where the lights were on and soft music was playing. The smell of chips frying in duck fat wafted out from inside, making her stomach grumble. After being cooped up inside the gendarmerie for all that time Margot was glad of some fresh air so she remained outside while Pierre went in to get drinks.

She'd only been sat down a minute when her eyes alighted upon a familiar figure. Salt and pepper hair, pink linen shirt. Margot straightened her spine. On the opposite side of the square, the skipper from *Carpe Diem* was standing under the awning of the little chocolate shop, studying something in the window. Margot knew the shop well; the owner made a mouth-watering range of caramels and she could rarely resist the temptation to go in whenever she was passing. After disappearing inside for a few minutes, he emerged with a small white box tied up with ribbon. Who was he buying chocolates for? Margot smiled as she imagined him strolling her way, passing her table, a look of surprise taking over his face when he realised she'd been sitting there watching him the whole time. She stubbed out her cigarette and started to prepare a suitably pithy comment, but he took the other route out of the square instead and didn't even notice her.

Pierre came back with the drinks. Margot produced a smile. "Are you going to tell me now what you know about Enzo Bellucci?"

One by one, Pierre removed the coffee things from the tray and arranged them on the table between them. "We shouldn't even be having this conversation. I promised Captain Bouchard you would stay out of it."

"I trust you had your fingers crossed."

Pierre rolled his eyes. He picked up his espresso and snatched a sip. "Officially, he owns a shipping company in Marseilles; unofficially he runs an organised crime group."

"Is Paolo part of the business?"

"As far as we know he takes no active role. Their father died fifteen years ago and the two of them moved over from Italy. There was a rift of some kind."

"The impression I got was that Enzo knew nothing about the smuggling. He was offering to make it all go away."

"Given his connections I wouldn't put it past him."

"Who's he got in his pocket?"

"No one we know of, but money talks. You know how it is."

Margot lit a fresh cigarette. "What's his bag?"

"Drugs. Extortion. The shipping company's legitimate but who's going to notice the odd container going astray?"

"So why hasn't he been arrested?"

Pierre regarded her as if she were naïve. He took another sip of his coffee and put down his cup. "Come on, Margot, you know how these things work. Unless you've got cast iron evidence you can't go around arresting people like that. His lawyers would make idiots of us."

Margot wearily shook her head and looked up at the darkening sky. A dot of white light blinked away as a helicopter headed out to sea. Anyone would think the police were afraid of him. Sometimes it seemed like they were all still stuck in the playground, with the bullies and the gangs trying to run people's lives. But Margot wasn't giving in to them. The more she learned about these people the more determined she was to do something. She tapped the ash from her cigarette.

"Do any of the drugs end up in Paris?"

Pierre looked at her with soulful eyes before laying a hand upon hers. "There's no connection between Enzo's group and the people who killed Hugo."

Margot withdrew her hand and moved her eyes elsewhere. She took a long draw on her cigarette. Maybe there was no direct connection, but they were all links in a chain, each one as guilty as the next. She turned back.

"I heard him say he's got a shipment coming in."

Pierre's ears pricked up. "Did he say where or when?"

Margot shook her head. She played with her thoughts for a while and then shared a small smile with herself. No, he hadn't said where or when, but the idea of finding that out suddenly appealed to her.

———

The crime-scene officers were just packing up when Margot and Pierre got back to the house. No fingerprints had been found on any of the fragments of glass, and there was nothing amongst the debris that might shed light on the perpetrator's identity. Hardly surprising. Professionals rarely left traces.

Pierre was needed back in Paris but he seemed reluctant to

leave. Every time Margot tried to bid him farewell he made an excuse not to go.

"Have you got somewhere to stay tonight?"

She couldn't stay here, that was for sure. Everything was still soaking wet or reeked of smoke. "Madame Barbier offered me her spare room. And the insurance company said they would pay for a hotel."

"You must let Captain Bouchard know what you decide. But no one else."

Margot touched his arm reassuringly. It was seven p.m. and he really needed to be heading back. "Honestly, Pierre. I'll be fine. Thank you for coming down."

Still, he remained to help clear up. They bagged up everything that was beyond repair and then Pierre carried the bags down to the bin store at the end of the lane. It was all such a horrible mess. Shortly after he'd gone out for the second time another figure appeared at her front door. Margot's eyes widened when she turned to find Raul looking in from her doorstep.

"Oh my God! Madame – this is *your* house?" His eyes travelled around the room in amazement.

Margot paused, dustpan and brush in hand. "What remains of it, yes."

He stepped inside. "I heard the fire engine last night. Someone said the house belonged to the police inspector's widow ..." He seemed perplexed.

"That would be me."

"I had no idea."

"Really? I'm famous throughout the town."

"Was anyone hurt?"

"No. It's just me here and I'm fine."

Pierre came back just at that moment and halted on the threshold, giving Raul an up-and-down look. Margot could sense his policeman's brain ticking over and quickly explained: "Pierre, this is Raul. A new acquaintance of mine." And then to Raul: "Pierre's a policeman. He used to work with my husband."

Raul stepped forward and the two men shook hands. "I'm very pleased to meet you, monsieur."

Pierre tipped his head.

"And forgive me." Raul turned back to Margot. "I only came round to be nosey. But now I'm here you must let me help."

He took the dustpan and brush from her and quickly set to work. He was down on his hands and knees before Margot could utter a word of protest. Not that she minded; an extra pair of hands would certainly help. She fetched another roll of bin liners from the kitchen.

"What an awful thing to have happened," Raul said. "How on earth did it start?"

Margot was too tired to go through it all again. She squatted down next to him and tossed some more of her damaged books into a bin liner. "Oh, you know – a discarded cigarette, a fallen candle. It doesn't take much."

"And you were at home at the time?"

She nodded. "I managed to stop it spreading with my hosepipe."

"But your things ..." Raul abruptly stopped what he was doing and cast his eyes over the debris in front of them as if horrified by the way he'd been treating her possessions. He looked like he wanted to drop the dustpan in disgust.

"They're just things," Margot said. "They can all be replaced."

Though just at that moment she spotted a half-burnt photograph on the floor and recognised it immediately. It was one of their wedding photos, taken at the reception at the Pavillon Royal when Hugo had drunk too much Pernod and was sat slumped at the table, his cheek propped with a fist, while two of his nieces painted his face with comedy eyebrows. How they'd teased him.

With a heavy heart she stretched to pick it up. The rest of the set were just as badly damaged. Raul moved to her side. "Your husband?"

Margot nodded.

He lightly touched her shoulder. "Perhaps not all things can be replaced so easily," he said softly.

And maybe it was the thoughtful way in which he said it that caused her resolve to break, or it could have been the accumulation of emotion building up inside her. Whatever the reason, Margot's façade slipped and she let out a small, clenched sob.

Pierre moved to come over but Raul got there first. He slid an arm across her back and tenderly squeezed her shoulder. Together they retrieved the remaining photos with the greatest of care.

———

Pierre and Raul carried out the remains of the furniture and stacked it outside Monsieur Barbier's house – he'd kindly offered to take it to the dump in his truck. By the time they'd finished clearing the sky was growing dark. All that remained of Margot's sitting room was a foul-smelling blackened shell.

A neighbour brought round a bottle of cold red wine to lift their spirits so the three of them retired to the courtyard – the wrought-iron table and chairs were pretty much the only usable pieces of furniture Margot had left. The electricity company had advised her to keep the power switched off so they sat in the glow of a dozen tea-lights. As fatigue caught up on her, the reality of losing her home finally started to sink in and her mood took a dive. No comfy bed to retire to, no novel waiting on her bedside table. Houses were more than just bricks and mortar. At nine o'clock Pierre finally made the decision to go.

"You will be all right tonight, won't you?" he said, standing.

Margot picked herself up. "Of course." She stood and kissed him on both cheeks. Holding hands, she smiled fondly. "There's no need to worry."

"Will you be staying with Madame Barbier?"

"Actually, I thought I'd try a hotel. I'd better make some calls."

She picked up a tea-light and went to retrieve her phone. She tried Le Méridien but they were full. The only other hotel she liked was Le Place Bleu but all they had available was an apartment on the roadside elevation and she could imagine how noisy it got. She put on a brave on as she wandered back to the courtyard.

"Looks like I'll be staying at Madame Barbier's after all. Everywhere's full."

"You don't sound so keen," Pierre said.

"They're very nice but they haven't got much space." And they were a couple of old fusspots, she added to herself.

Raul got to his feet. "You're welcome to stay on my yacht," he said, and turned to Pierre as if to gain his approval. "It's plenty big enough for two."

Margot blinked in surprise. "That's very kind of you but I couldn't possibly."

"You would be doing me a favour. It would be nice to have company."

"But I hardly know you."

"Then you can get to know me."

Margot hesitated. Of the options available to her this was easily the most tempting. But she remained silent, leaving Raul to continue,

"You'll have your own cabin. *Carpe Diem* sleeps up to eight. And you can lock your door."

"In case you decide to murder me in my sleep, you mean?"

"Do I look like a psychopath?"

"Looks can be deceptive. Besides, how do you know you'll be safe from me?"

There was a pause while he gave that some thought, a smile not far from his lips. "It's a chance I'm willing to take."

"Then perhaps we should both lock our doors," Margot said, and was surprised when a spark passed between them.

Pierre noisily cleared his throat, making Margot look round. For a moment she'd almost forgotten he was there.

"Where is this yacht?" he asked.

"It's moored in the harbour," Margot said. "It's called *Carpe Diem*."

"I'll need to let Captain Bouchard know. Just to be safe."

Raul puffed out his chest. "She will be perfectly safe with me, Monsieur. I give you my word."

Margot and Pierre shared a longer look. Raul still had no idea about the true cause of the fire and she felt guilty about involving him whilst keeping him in the dark. But then, it was only for one night. She retrieved her glass from the table and downed what remained of her wine.

"Very well," she smiled. "Thank you, Raul. I would love to spend the night on board your yacht."

16

Carpe Diem was much bigger on the inside than Margot had imagined. Four wide ladder steps led down from the cockpit to a large salon where a semi-circular sofa curved around a polished oak table. The seats were thickly padded and upholstered in soft cream leather. On the port side, a large galley came equipped with twin sinks, two large freezers, a microwave oven, a stove on a gimbal, all of which would have looked at home in a professional kitchen. Raul led her through the galley to a short corridor at the end of which was the guest cabin – Margot was amazed when he opened the door to reveal a room with a full-size double bed, a wardrobe, lamps on side tables and an adjoining room complete with a toilet, sink and sparkling white shower cubicle.

"There are fresh towels in here." He indicated one of the many cupboards. "And extra pillows in the drawer under the bed."

It was as luxurious as a high-end hotel. Everything Margot touched was made from either polished wood or thick quality leather. She couldn't begin to imagine how much a boat like this had cost.

"Shall I leave you to unpack while I start on dinner?" Raul said, depositing her overnight bag on the chest at the end of the bed. "I'm making steak au poivre. I hope that's all right?"

He seemed keen that she agree. Margot nodded eagerly; the only thing she'd eaten all day was a cheese and ham sandwich at the gendarmerie and that had tasted like Captain Bouchard had made it himself.

"Is there somewhere I can put this?" She unzipped the side pocket of her bag and took out Hugo's medal. "I didn't like leaving it in an empty house."

Raul raised a hand to accept it and Margot placed it in his palm. He studied it, seemingly impressed. "Was this your husband's?"

She nodded.

"It's a police Honour medal."

"I know."

"He must have been a very brave policeman."

"He was killed while on duty."

"How tragic."

"At least they caught the bastards."

Raul lowered his eyes, unsure how to respond, the medal still resting on his hand between them. Margot sighed.

"I'm sorry. It's all still a bit raw."

"Of course. I'll put it in the safe underneath the navigator's chair. The combination is 1066."

"The year you were born?"

His eyes flicked upwards, not sure how to take that. Margot leaned in and laughed. "Only teasing."

Raul left her to freshen up while he went to start on dinner.

Ten minutes later she emerged to find him hard at work in the galley. Pans and ingredients were spread across every surface, and the smell coming off the steaks he was searing instantly made her stomach grumble.

"Is there anything I can do?"

"Everything is under control," he said, and just at that moment emptied a glass of alcohol into the frying pan and promptly ignited it which perhaps was not such a good idea in the confined space of a yacht since it immediately triggered the smoke alarm. He had to jab the button several times to get it to stop. "Perhaps you could choose a wine," he said, and indicated the cupboard in the corner.

He had a good selection, perhaps fifty bottles. Margot chose a five-year-old Fitou and took two glasses out of the wall cupboard.

"I thought we might eat up on deck," Raul said. "It's a lovely evening."

"Shall I lay the table?"

"It's already done."

She felt in the way standing there doing nothing so she went up on deck and sat at the table in the covered area of the cockpit.

"Turn on the switch at the end of the table," Raul called up from below.

Margot leaned down and found what she assumed was the right one; when she flicked it, ambient light strips came on along the edges of the bench seats and all around the canopy.

"Found it," she called back, and couldn't resist smiling. It was quite the cosy haven.

She rearranged the cushions so that she could sit sideways and look out over the harbour, and then poured herself a large glass of wine. She lit a cigarette and admired the view while she smoked it. From this angle the town looked dreamily quaint with all the boats lined up in the marina and the harbourside cafés buzzing with life. On the promenade, the blue and red festoon lighting snaked all the way down to the cliffs on the far edge of the town.

The food was delicious and Margot ate greedily. "I'm sorry I have no dessert," Raul said when she pushed forward her empty plate. "I wasn't expecting company."

"That's a shame. Pudding's my favourite."

His eyes sparkled with mischief. "However, I do have this."

He shifted the dirty crockery to one side and then raised one half of the table-top; it turned out to be the hinged lid of a freezer compartment. He reached in and pulled out a tub of Crème Brûlée ice cream. "Only the one tub, I'm afraid."

"You mean you're not having any?"

Ignoring her comment, he took two spoons out of a drawer and handed her one. "We share."

Later, when they'd finished the Fitou, Raul lifted the other half of the table-top to reveal a wine cooler; Margot had to fight her urge to grin when she looked in and saw that it was full of champagne. This really was her kind of boat. He pulled out a bottle of Pommery and held it over the side, twisting the bottle and shooting the cork high over the water. He poured out two glasses and raised his.

"To new friends."

"And the end of a very bad day."

They clinked glasses.

The champagne was the final straw and one glass was enough to send them into a postprandial lethargy. Raul laid himself flat on the bench seat, wriggling his back to make himself comfortable while Margot lit another cigarette and blew perfect smoke rings into the air. Live music drifted in from one of the bars as a female vocalist sang to the accompaniment of a Spanish guitar. After the day she'd had this was bliss.

"Who were the chocolates for?"

Raul sleepily opened his eyes. "Chocolates?"

"I saw you buying them in the square."

He pulled himself upright. He smiled across the table as he retrieved his glass. "You were spying on me?"

"Hardly."

"They were for my daughter."

"Is she all right?"

"She's fine. I didn't have to go in the end."

Margot tapped the ash from her cigarette onto an empty plate. She froze when she caught him pulling a face. "You don't mind me smoking, do you?"

He shook his head, though the look suggested otherwise. She had one last draw and then stubbed it out. "I know, it's a filthy habit. Hugo was always nagging me to quit."

"We all have bad habits."

She put the packet away in her bag. How ironic to have him concerned about her health when just a few days ago he'd almost run into her. She sat up to the table and refilled their glasses.

"So what brings you to Argents-sur-Mer?"

"I'm sailing solo around the world. It's been my ambition ever since I was a boy."

"How long have you been going?"

"Three months."

"And where did you start?"

"Cadiz."

"Cadiz?" Margot raised her eyebrows. "And in three months you've only got as far as Argents? At this rate it will take you twenty years to sail around the world." She hid her smirk inside her champagne glass. It was hard to resist teasing him.

He pulled himself up to sit properly at the table, seeming to relish the chance to respond. "It's not a race. Life's better at a slower pace."

"Is it?"

"Rush through and you'll miss all the scenery."

His eyes probed hers. There was a quality to his stare that she found quite beguiling, like he was determined to see right into her and discover her innermost secrets. But Margot hardened her heart. How many other women had he wined and dined like this on his way up from Cadiz, who'd sat in this very seat, enjoying his fancy champagne?

"And I suppose the life of an ocean nomad suits you, does it? A girl in every port?"

Raul threw back his head and laughed heartily. "You misjudge me, Madame."

"Do I?"

"Yes: I'm an aging lothario, sailing the world on one last jolly – is that what you think of me?"

Margot shrugged.

"Nothing could be further from the truth."

"So what is the truth?"

The twinkle returned to his eye. He emptied his champagne glass in one clean draught and then leaned in more closely. Holding up the fingers of one hand, he counted: "One, I am not a rich man. Six months ago I sold my house and my business. *Carpe Diem* is all I have now. Two, I'm nowhere near as old as I look. The stress of bringing up three daughters has aged me prematurely. Three—"

"How old do you think you look?"

"Thirty-two, thirty-three tops."

Margot spluttered. "Sixty-two more like."

He narrowed his eyes. "You really are too kind. Three—"

"And how old are you?"

"You should never ask a gentleman his age. Three—"

"Fifty-two?"

"You flatter me."

"Eighty?"

Now he returned a phlegmatic look. "I'm fifty-five. A man's golden years. Now, will you please let me continue?"

Margot bit her tongue.

"Three, sailing single-handed around the world is by no means a jolly. It's a challenging task, even on a yacht as magnificent as *Carpe Diem*. And four, as for lothario ..." He sat back and chuckled again, arms folded over his chest. "No, I do not have a girl in every port. One woman has always been as much as I can handle."

"Your wife?"

"Yes."

"So where is she now? Afraid she'd go crazy if she had to listen to you rant on for an entire lap of the world?"

"No. She died."

"Oh."

Silence fell like a weight. A lump formed in Margot's throat and it took her a moment to swallow. She put down her glass, eyes lowered. "I'm sorry."

She watched Raul's hand move across the table and reach for her forearm. When he squeezed it, Margot looked up and found him smiling.

"Don't be sorry. It's been five years now. Life goes on."

"How did she die?"

"Ovarian cancer. It was all very sudden. One day everything was perfectly normal, then the next day I found her sitting on the bathroom floor, groaning in agony. By then it had reached stage four. The doctors gave her six months to live; she was gone within three."

"That's so sad."

"But I try not to think about the sad times. We were married for twenty-six years and when she died it broke my heart, but I have so many happy memories to look back on. She blessed me with three beautiful daughters. I couldn't have wished for anything more."

He was smiling so warmly Margot couldn't help but smile back. She turned sideways on the bench again and shuffled so that she could pull her knees up to her chin. Would she ever feel that way about Hugo?

"What do you miss most about her?"

Raul leaned back. "Her smile, perhaps. Even when she was annoyed with me she wouldn't stay mad for long. She could see through my uncouth exterior to the fine fellow I am at heart."

"With Hugo it's the company I miss. We were like two sides of the same coin; I never imagined life without him. I thought we'd be together forever, be that old couple you see holding hands."

"That's very romantic."

"I came here to make a new start but the house feels so empty."

"It takes time."

A distant *whoosh* made them turn their heads. Somewhere in the hills a firework had been set off and a rocket was racing up into the night sky. There was a moment of silent anticipation before it exploded into a shower of red and white sparks. A cheer went up from one of the bars.

"It's been almost ten months but I can't imagine I'll ever stop missing him."

"Grief can be a stubborn old thing."

Margot heaved a long sad sigh. When another firework went up and it looked like a fiesta was about to begin, Raul rolled back the canopy and they watched the light-show with the last of the champagne.

―――――

The air turned chilly so they went below. It was after eleven and Margot felt sleepy, but Raul wanted to stay up. He got out a mixing glass and filled it with ice from one of the freezers while Margot retrieved a bottle of gin and a bottle of vermouth he had open in the fridge. They were going to make cocktails.

"What are your plans for tomorrow?" Raul said as he poured a good measure of gin and vermouth into the mixing glass. He stirred vigorously, and then garnished two Martini glasses with a pickled onion. The thought he might be trying to get her drunk crossed her mind but Margot had no fear on that score. She'd not yet met a man she couldn't drink under the table.

"I need to get some quotes for fixing up the house. Why?"

"Would you like to go sailing? The weather forecast is good."

She shook her head. "I get terribly seasick."

"I have some pills."

"They don't work on me."

"And yet you swim in the sea ..."

"Being *in* the water is different to being on it. Or maybe I'm just odd."

Raul made no comment.

In any case, her mind was on other things. She wanted to keep in touch with what happened when the police searched the garage. There would surely be other evidence hidden away in there. How she would love to be a fly on the wall when the police stormed in. It occurred to her that Raul was still in the dark about what she'd been up to and it didn't seem very fair, given he'd provided her with this safe haven for the night. She waited while he finished the cocktails, watching him pour the mixture into the glasses. Margot had sip and nodded her approval, but then slid her glass to one side.

"I've not been entirely honest with you."

Raul looked surprised. "Oh, about what?"

"The fire wasn't an accident. Someone threw a petrol bomb through my window."

He swallowed his mouthful and stared at her, eyes widening to the size of saucers. "A *petrol* bomb?"

"That's what the police think."

He seemed baffled. "But why on earth would someone do that?"

Margot locked eyes with him. She may have only known him for a few days but she was confident she could trust him. She told him the whole story, omitting no detail. Raul listened with increasing incredulity until by the time she'd finished he had a hard time closing his mouth.

"What on earth possessed you to get involved with people like that?"

"I wanted justice for Aswan. The police weren't interested, what else was I to do?"

"But why put yourself in so much danger?"

She exhaled in annoyance. "I've just told you. The only mistake I made was giving my details to the car hire company. I should have been more careful."

Raul tried to blink the surprise out of his eyes and abruptly sat back, pointedly shaking his head. "I can't decide whether you're brave or foolish."

"Maybe I'm both."

"Or completely reckless."

She tutted, tired of having to keep explaining herself. "If we all just sit back and do nothing people like that will keep getting away with it."

"Unfortunately, people like that are pretty scary."

"They don't scare me."

"Well, they ought to."

Margot stiffened her resolve. She leaned across the table. "No, Raul. They're just men. Overgrown boys. They're cowards and bullies and we shouldn't give in to them. People being afraid of them is what gives them their power. But someone has to stand up to them."

"And you're the one who's going to do that?"

"Yes! If I have to."

"And if you get yourself killed in the process?"

"Then I'll die knowing I tried to make a difference."

Raul got up from the table and walked to the far end of the galley, rubbing the back of his neck in frustration. Margot observed him with curiosity, surprised by how concerned he seemed to be.

Neither of them spoke for a while. She didn't want to argue with him but he had to understand. When he returned to the table, Margot tried to bring him round with a friendly smile.

"It's nice that you're concerned but I'm not naïve."

"I never said you were."

"I feel very strongly about this. My husband gave his life trying to do what he thought was right."

"But that was his job."

"Job or not, it's motivation that counts." She breathed in. " 'The only thing necessary for the triumph of evil is for good men to do nothing.' "

"Now you're quoting John Burke at me?"

"John Stuart Mill, actually. It's based on an earlier quote: 'Bad men need nothing more to compass their ends than that good men should look on and do nothing.' "

"Well lah-di-dah. Is that a fact?"

"Political Science was part of my law degree."

He narrowed his eyes. "That hardly seems fair."

She smiled again. Finally, Raul smiled back. "All I can say is I'm glad I'm on your side."

"You wouldn't want me as an enemy," she said immodestly and downed the remainder of her cocktail. Raul had nothing more to add.

A yawn crept up on her. Margot covered her mouth with a hand and then stretched her arms. "Anyway. It's been a long day. I'm off to bed."

He nodded. She left him to clear up the cocktail things.

In her cabin, Margot unpacked her overnight bag and set out her toiletries on the bathroom shelf. She spent a few moments studying her reflection in the mirror above the sink, dismayed by the black rings around her eyes. This time last night she'd been doing the very same thing in her bathroom at home. What an eventful twenty-four hours it had been.

She got ready for bed and then sat on the mattress, testing it for firmness. It was very comfortable, as were the pillows. When she laid down her head and closed her eyes, however, sleepiness abandoned her. She sighed, and tossed onto her other side. Her eyes switched focus to the door. Raul's cabin was at the opposite end of the boat and she probably wouldn't have heard if he'd gone to bed, but she had a feeling he was still up.

She lowered her feet to the carpet and crept to the door. There was no sound, apart from creaks from the hull as the boat rocked gently on the water. She eased open the door and went silently out. Raul was still seated at the table, exactly where she'd left him, staring sadly into the bottom of his Martini glass. Perhaps ten seconds passed before he noticed her.

"Is everything all right?"

"I just came out for a glass of water."

"There are some bottles in the fridge."

He made a move to get it for her but Margot told him to sit back down. She filled a tumbler and drank half of it while she was still at the counter. She turned to face him, and smiled.

"I'm sorry I called you an old fool the other day."

He shrugged. "I've been called worse."

She could imagine. "It wasn't your fault. I shouldn't have been swimming out so far."

"I would have been mortified had I actually run into you."

Margot had another sip of water. "The other day, when I thought your boat had gone, I assumed I'd frightened you off."

"You really think I scare that easily?"

"I can be quite intimidating when I want to be."

She waited, hoping he might come up with a sparring retort, but he seemed content to just look at her. Never mind. Margot poured the rest of the water away. "Goodnight, then."

"Would you have been disappointed?"

"About what?"

"If I had gone away."

"You flatter yourself."

"Yet here you are."

There was another pause. Margot's mind was fading fast but she couldn't let him have the last word. "It was either this or Madame Barbier's spare room and her husband snores terribly."

"Maybe I snore."

"You do and you'll be going over the side."

Raul laughed loudly. "What have I let myself in for?"

You'll see, Margot almost said, but ended with another cheery goodnight.

17

A series of gentle knocks woke Margot with a start. A square of shining blue light was hanging over her face and it took her a moment to realise it was the skylight. Which meant it was daytime, and well past the hour she would normally get up. It seemed liked only ten minutes had passed since she'd lain her head down on the pillow.

"Margot. Are you awake?"

Raul's voice sounded on the other side of the cabin door. Coming to her senses, Margot scrambled out of bed. "Just a minute."

"Would you like some breakfast?"

"I'll be right out."

She staggered across to the bathroom and opened the valve on the shower.

Twenty minutes later, she'd put on a white ruffled blouse and a pair of seersucker pants and was following Raul up on deck.

"Sleep well?"

"Like a log." She hated to admit it but she'd slept better than she had in months.

The table in the deck salon had been dressed in a clean white cloth and covered with an impressive array of breakfast things. Margot's eyes roved hungrily over the dozen or more dishes arranged before her: figs and apricots, honey and yoghurt, soft boiled eggs and a rack of toast. She'd no sooner sat down than he brought up a plate of ham and cheese and a pot of strong black coffee.

"You breakfast like this every morning?"

"Without fail." He rearranged the dishes to make room for the coffee and the extra plates. " 'Breakfast like a king, lunch like a prince, and dinner like a pauper,' said somebody once." He sat down, smiling privately, pleased with his little joke.

Margot contained her amusement. "Are we keeping score now?"

"No. I've already given in."

Wise man. She shook out her napkin and they greedily tucked in.

The weather was fine and she'd planned on going for a nice long swim, but by the time they'd finished eating her stomach was so full she feared she would sink to the seabed. Raul insisted on clearing up so Margot installed herself on one of the two pedestal seats while she checked her phone. One message from Pierre: *'Margot – are you all right? Please call me back as soon as you get this.'* She lit a cigarette and called his office.

"Don't worry, Raul's been doing an excellent job of looking after me," she said when her host came up to collect some more of the breakfast things. He blew her a friendly kiss.

"I've made a few calls," Pierre said. "Though I probably shouldn't be telling you this."

Margot turned away from some noise on the jetty, pressing the phone closer to her ear. "Go on."

"You're not to let anyone know this came from me."

"You know me, I'm the soul of discretion."

"A post-mortem has been carried out on the two dead migrants. The lab report showed that the adult male died from an injury to the head – a blow to the face with a blunt object."

"So he didn't drown?"

"No. There was no seawater in his lungs."

"And Aswan?"

"His lungs were full of water. The pathologist's conclusion was death by drowning. He could have washed up in the place where he was found, but since the rocks there are smooth they couldn't draw any conclusions from the fact there were no scratches on his body. The father did have injuries consistent with being dragged over rocks. Given he didn't drown, he could have been killed elsewhere and then his body moved to make it look like he'd been washed up."

Margot mulled that over. No obvious sequence of events came to mind: Aswan had drowned but his father had not. Then somehow they'd got separated?

"All right. Thank you, Pierre."

"You didn't hear it from me."

Raul was just finishing clearing up when she wandered back to the deck salon. He paused, eyes seeking hers, sensing something was wrong. "Everything okay?"

Margot nodded, and despite Pierre's warning would probably have told him about the post-mortem report had she not been distracted by the sight of a familiar gendarme down on the jetty. He was heading their way, pausing at the stern of every boat to check the name. When Margot moved back to the consoles, Captain Bouchard spotted her immediately and squared his shoulders. He promptly gave up his search and approached *Carpe Diem* with a purposeful stride.

"I was informed I would find you on board a yacht."

"Have you searched the garage?"

"We have."

"What did you find?"

The captain returned a pinched smile. "Would you come with me, please?"

Raul appeared by her side. "Is there a problem, officer?"

The captain spent a moment taking him in before turning his attention back to Margot. "Judge Deveraux would like to see you."

"Who's Judge Deveraux?"

"She's the *juge de instruction*."

Margot frowned. "Why does the *juge de instruction* want to see me?"

"If you come with me you'll find out." The captain extended an arm.

Margot hesitated, her heart beating a little more quickly. She didn't like the direction in which this was headed and was tempted to refuse, but it was probably wise not to escalate the situation.

"I trust you're not arresting me," she said breezily.

The captain didn't answer, but the look on his face suggested few things would have given him greater pleasure. After one final glance at Raul, Margot stepped down from the boat.

18

The *Palais de Justice* was a grand old building that occupied the northern flank of Place Jeanne d'Arc. Captain Bouchard led Margot up two flights of majestically curving marble stairs and then down a series of oak-panelled corridors to a vestibule nestled under smooth plaster arches. Facing a door marked 'Judge Deveraux', he fussed with his uniform, easing his neck out of his shirt collar and tugging his cuffs free of his tunic, seemingly oblivious to Margot's presence. When he was done, he gave two sharp raps on the door with his knuckles. A voice inside bade them to enter.

They swept into a stately room with high ceilings and elaborate plasterwork, their shoes sinking into thick woollen carpet. One wall boasted a row of tall sash windows that looked down on the park at the back of the museum while the other three were adorned with oil portraits – old men in gowns, the subjects as dusty as the frames that housed them. The place had an air of faded grandeur.

"Please, take a seat."

The voice brought Margot's attention back to the centre of the room where Judge Deveraux was seated behind a large mahogany desk, writing with a fountain pen. Captain Bouchard pulled out a chair for himself and, as an afterthought, nudged one aside for Margot. The judge seemed intent on finishing what she was doing and only briefly looked up. "Bear with me for a moment," she said, before going back to her writing. Margot returned her polite smile.

While they were waiting, she set her eyes loose on a longer tour of the room. On the other side of the windows, a line of tall pencil cypress swayed in the breeze, revealing glimpses of bright blue sea. The subjects of the paintings were a dull-looking crowd, though on closer inspection Margot realised they were not all men. Taking pride of place on the panelling behind the judge's chair was a portrait of a woman in robes, and not just any robes – if she wasn't mistaken they were the robes of a judge from the *Cour de cassation*, France's supreme court. Margot's focus switched back to the lady herself and she looked upon her with renewed interest. In the curve of her aquiline nose and the tilt of her ears there was a clear physical resemblance.

The silence was rudely shattered by a coughing fit. The judge turned her chair to one side and hacked into a handkerchief. Margot promptly got up.

"Are you all right, Madame?" She filled a tumbler with water from the carafe and passed it over. The judge nodded, and gratefully accepted.

"Thank you."

She took a sip and returned a warm smile. Margot went back to her seat, rebuking the captain's indifference with a testy glare.

Recovered, the judge screwed the top back onto her pen and began shuffling her papers. "Thank you both for your patience. And thank you, Madame Renard, for coming to see me."

Margot inclined her head.

"I heard about the fire at your house. That must have been a dreadful experience."

"People have been very kind."

The judge smiled again. She found the file she was looking for and opened it, sliding the top few sheets to one side.

"Now. The reason I asked you here was to talk about your visit to Garage de Paolo. I've read the transcript of your interview with Captain Bouchard. In it you stated that you saw a number of forged passports in the room above the garage."

"That's correct."

"Based upon your account, the Police National raided the garage early this morning, but unfortunately, no such documents were found."

"That's hardly a surprise," Margot said. "They had plenty of time to get rid of the evidence." She cast a sideways glance at the captain who straightened on his seat.

"Your impromptu visit obviously alerted them," he countered.

"If you'd searched the place sooner I wouldn't have had to visit them."

"We were waiting for information."

"You had all the information you needed. I gave you the backpack."

"If you hadn't blundered in and raised their suspicions the evidence might still have been there."

"If you—"

"The point being," the judge interrupted, "is that you were trespassing. And now questions are being asked as to what grounds we had for carrying out a search. Mr Bellucci's lawyer has filed a complaint."

Margot balked. Sometimes she despaired at the absurdity of their legal system. "I know what I saw and I heard them discussing it."

"You're missing the point, Madame Renard. I was the one who signed the search warrant. You've interfered in a police investigation and you've put both the captain and myself in a very difficult position."

Margot looked down at her hands. If they were hoping for an apology they were in for a long wait. She didn't regret doing what she'd done and she wasn't going to take any of the blame. "If the captain had taken me seriously from the start none of this would have happened."

"I did take it seriously."

Margot scoffed. "I really don't think so."

The judge stepped in again. "We can't take the law into our own hands, no matter how strongly we feel. Given your credentials, Madame Renard, I'm sure you're well aware of the importance of that."

Heat rose to Margot's cheeks. She'd had enough of people telling her what to do. She was sorely tempted to walk out, let them prosecute her for trespass if that's what they wanted. "Have you finished?"

The judge seemed bemused. "I didn't ask you here to scold you. My job as *juge de instruction* is to seek the truth."

"So how do you explain their injuries?"

"What injuries are you referring to?"

"I know about the mortuary report. The father was killed by a blow to the face. He didn't fall off a boat and drown."

Wrongfooted, the judge frowned. "How do you know about the mortuary report?"

"I'm a policeman's widow; I have my sources."

The judge took a few moments to digest that. In the lull that followed Margot suddenly felt two inches taller. Emboldened, she went on, "His death was no accident. Somebody killed him. And it's obvious Paolo Bellucci was involved."

"You have no evidence of that," the captain said.

"Have you interviewed him?"

"He was spoken to at the scene."

"And?"

"He denied any involvement."

Margot snapped shut her eyes in disbelief. "Of course he would deny it. But Aswan had his address. How do you explain that?"

From the sides of her eyes Margot saw the captain shrug. "A coincidence."

"And the door code? Was *that* a coincidence, too?"

"Door code?" the judge put in enquiringly.

"Yes," Margot said. "The only text message that had been sent to the phone I found in Aswan's backpack was a four-digit number that turned out to be the code to the lock on the back door of the garage. That was how I got in."

The judge seemed puzzled. She turned to the captain with renewed intensity. "I wasn't aware of this."

Captain Bouchard shifted uncomfortably. "The phone that sent that text message is unregistered. There's no way of proving who sent it."

"But how many people conceivably knew the code?" Margot said.

The captain tried to respond but Margot's heckles were up and she quickly went on, "Given they were forging passports in there it's hardly likely he would give out the code to just anyone. Paolo Bellucci has to be your chief suspect. What is it going to take for you to arrest this man? Anyone would think you were afraid of him. Or is it that you just don't care about a few dead migrants?"

The room fell silent. Captain Bouchard puffed out his chest with indignation and Margot lowered her eyes, knowing she'd overstepped the mark. Her only way out was to mumble an apology, but when she raised her head to speak she found the judge's attention still focussed on the man by her side. She was not letting him off the hook so easily, it seemed.

"Captain?"

Now both women were looking directly at him, waiting for his response. The captain wilted a little under the pressure, clearly unused to finding himself under such scrutiny.

"I am afraid of no one," he said, rather limply. "And I care about every member of this community. I think you'll find my record illustrates that very clearly."

Judge Deveraux didn't seem convinced. She paused to gather her thoughts, and then leaned back in her seat, inhaling deeply. After taking off her glasses she laced her fingers, ready to make a judgement. "In light of what Madame Renard has just told me I would like Paolo Bellucci brought in for a formal interview. See to it, please."

Captain Bouchard went a little bit red in the face, but he nodded. When Margot turned back to the judge they shared a small smile.

19

"So, they let you go?" Raul said when Margot sat down beside him on the bench at the end of the promenade. He'd texted to say he would be waiting there and presently was engaged in eating an ice cream, busily wrapping his tongue around a smooth ball of something dark and chocolatey.

"I got a slap on the wrist but I think I'm in the clear."

"Have they arrested the garage owner?"

"Not yet. The passports had gone by the time they'd searched the place. Surprise, surprise. But they are bringing him in for questioning."

Raul emitted a few short groans of pleasure as he carried on devouring the ice cream. Margot narrowed her eyes. "Are you enjoying that?"

"Yes, thank you. Would you like one?"

She looked away. "I'll pass."

"So, what now?"

A child squealed nearby. On the other side of the barrier, a small group of toddlers were playing on the swings and one of the boys had snatched a toy from a little girl's hand. She was most put out by it. A look of thunder darkened her face as she shook her mother's arm. Poor little mite. The mother, oblivious, continued to chat on her phone. Margot often came down here when she had time on her hands. She snapped back.

"They're never going to pin anything on Paolo. His lawyer will find some way of wheedling him out of it."

"One rule for the rich and all that."

Margot lit a cigarette. "We need to find the man he was working with. Someone called Etienne."

"You don't know his surname?"

"No. But Enzo called him the Algerian. I think he was the one who owned the boat. And Aswan mentioned him several times in his diary. When I was at the garage that day I'm pretty sure he was the one arguing with Paolo."

Raul finished eating his ice cream and dropped the remains of the cone in the bin. He wiped his fingers with a tissue and tossed that in, too. "Do you think he's local?"

"It's a fair assumption."

"Shall I ask around the harbour? See if any of the other boat owners have heard of him."

Margot looked him in the eye. She hadn't planned on enlisting his help and was surprised by the offer, given how he'd reacted last night. She would never forgive herself if anyone got hurt acting on her behalf, but it certainly would be useful having him on board.

"Are you sure you don't mind?"

"Of course I don't mind."

"Very well. Why don't you do that while I run some errands? Then I'll meet you back here in, say, a couple of hours?"

Raul straightened himself up and smiled broadly, seemingly excited by his new role.

———

Margot had arranged to meet a carpenter at the house at eleven, but when he arrived he spent ten minutes grumbling about how the front door was a non-standard size and that it would take three weeks, at the very least, to get bespoke joinery. The decorator who was supposed to arrive at eleven-thirty didn't even turn up. When Margot called him, he said he was snowed under and wouldn't be able to give her a quote after all. She called the hotel, but they were still fully booked so she packed a few more things into a bag.

Back on the promenade, the bench had been usurped by a trio of elderly ladies so Margot sat on the wall nearby and watched the people milling outside the frontline shops. In Paris, she would often sit on a bench in Square Jehan Rictus, opposite the Wall of Love, and watch the world go by. If ever someone interesting caught her eye she would observe them, sometimes even follow them, curious to see what story they might have to tell. Hugo had said there was a word for what she was doing and it was called stalking and as a policeman's wife she should know better, but it had only been an idle pastime. Mostly.

It took her a moment to realise it but someone was looking back at her. Outside one of the shops a heavyset man stood staring. He was partially hidden behind a rack of clothing meaning she couldn't see him so clearly, but Margot was certain she was the object of his attention. She stiffened, an uncomfortable feeling beginning to take hold. She was all set to go over and confront him, but then a presence at her side made her turn sharply. Raul sat down beside her on the wall.

"Are you all right? You look like you've seen a ghost."

Margot turned quickly back to the shops but the man had gone. Perhaps he'd just been staring out to sea. She hoped she wasn't becoming paranoid.

"Well, go on then," Raul said, looking very pleased with himself. "Ask me what I found out."

Margot recalibrated. "What did you find out?"

"The police said they were looking for an Oceanus RIB boat, correct?"

"Yes."

"Well, I asked around the fishermen and several names came up, but only one of them matched the description you gave me – Etienne Hamidi."

"Who is he?"

"He works as a motorboat mechanic. He's got a hut in the boatyard. But wait, there's more. One of the fishermen I spoke to was angry with him. He said he'd arranged for Etienne to transport some cargo, but when he got to the boatyard Etienne claimed his boat had gone missing."

"When was this?"

"The day after the migrants were found."

"Did he tell the police?"

"I didn't ask, but he sounds like your man, don't you think?"

Raul sat waiting for her response. Margot took a few moments to think it over. It was too much of a coincidence not to be him.

"All right," she said at last. "Let's go and find him."

————

They took a taxi to the boatyard. Margot had the driver drop them at the entrance and he pulled up next to a big metal arch set into a high chain-link fence. They went in on foot, moving through a landscape that was littered with cranes and industrial ironworks. A concrete footway took them around an L-shaped basin to an inlet that was lined with featureless buildings. Several boats were up on ramps, and the air was thick with the smell of diesel and seawater. Apart from the muted clang and smash of metal being worked, the place resembled a ghost town.

On the opposite side of the inlet lay a row of sheds and tatty metal huts. They were too far away to read the writing on the signs, but one of them stood out – the green and white logo Margot had seen on the pickup truck. They crossed the water via a metal footbridge and then halted outside the motorboat mechanic's hut. The door was locked with a chain and padlock.

"Our luck had to run out some time," Raul said, rattling the chain.

Margot turned around. Flashes of bright white light revealed some welding was going on, and looking more closely she spotted a small group of men gathered at the rear of one of the factories. She nodded to Raul and they re-crossed the footbridge, then kept their distance as they neared the factory, shielding their eyes from the intense white light. After a few moments, the welder turned off his torch and flicked up his visor, looking at them with unfriendly eyes.

"We're looking for Etienne, the motorboat mechanic," Raul said. "Has he been in today?"

"No idea."

"When was the last time you saw him?"

The man shrugged.

"Do you know where he lives?"

"Rue du Port. One of the tenements, I think."

"Do you know the number?"

The man shook his head.

They thanked him and went on their way.

Rue du Port was only a kilometre away so they went there on foot, following the directions on Margot's phone. It was a rundown neighbourhood with graffiti-strewn fences and a dog running loose. Some hard-faced kids sneered at them as they walked by on the footpath, prompting Raul to quicken his pace.

"Perhaps we should let the police handle it from here," he

said, but Margot pushed on. In Paris, she'd walked alone through far worse neighbourhoods.

A pair of three-storey tenements lay at the end of the street. A flight of concrete steps led up to a lobby, but the doors were shut. None of the names on the buzzers resembled 'Hamidi'. As they were crossing to the second block, however, Margot spotted a truck with the green and white logo parked across the street. She pointed it out to Raul and they hastened up the steps to building number 2.

The door to the lobby opened as they approached. An elderly man emerged, and Margot reached for the door before it had time to close behind him.

"Merci, Madame." He tipped his head.

She slid a foot into the gap.

"One moment, Monsieur." The man turned and Margot smiled politely. "Do you know if Etienne is at home?"

"Etienne Hamidi?"

"Yes."

"Have you come about the noise?"

"Noise?"

He screwed up his face. "Blasted woman never stops wailing."

Margot looked blank. "They're in nine, aren't they?"

"Twelve."

Margot palmed her forehead. "Of course. I'm an idiot. Thank you."

They waited for him to leave and then stepped inside.

Number twelve was on the second floor and the corridor leading to it would have looked more at home in a prison. Raul slowed as they approached, and halfway there he reached for Margot's arm.

"Are you sure this is a good idea? What will you say if he is in there?"

Margot shrugged. "I'll think of something." They'd come too far to back down now.

She paused when they reached number twelve. Cocking an ear, Margot got the impression several people were inside. Two seconds after she'd knocked a young woman in a hijab came to the door.

"Mrs Hamidi?"

A look of alarm appeared in her eyes. She started to close the door but Margot gently held it back.

"We just want to speak to Etienne. We're not here to cause trouble."

Margot moved her head to try and see past. There were several people inside, and the sense of alarm appeared to be spreading. A door slammed shut, a man cried out. An elderly woman in an armchair began wailing. When a baby started crying, the young woman pushed the door more forcefully. The cacophony set Margot's nerves on edge but she pushed back, knowing the sound of grieving when she heard it. She would have gone in, but a man suddenly appeared in the gap, brusquely pushed past her, and ran off down the corridor. In the confusion that followed, the door shut in their faces.

"Margot!"

She'd already set off in pursuit. The man had taken the stairs and he was quick – by the time they got to the lobby he'd already crossed the street and was climbing into his truck. Raul held her back as the vehicle sped away.

"Come on, Margot," he said, still clutching her arm. "It's time we called the police."

20

Enzo was on his way out of the office when his phone buzzed in his pocket. He left Mutt to go fetch the car while he stepped onto the quay.

"Paolo, what's up?"

"The police called."

"And?"

A forklift was going by so if there was a response Enzo didn't hear it. He turned his back on the noise.

"What was that?"

"They want me to go in."

"When?"

"Tomorrow."

His mind ran ahead. From the tone of his brother's voice he could tell he'd already been drinking. "Listen. Stay where you are. I'll be over as soon as I can."

Mutt had brought the Mercedes round to the front and was stood waiting, but Enzo went to the driver's side and took the keys from him.

"I'll be back in a couple of hours. Don't wait up."

It was seven-thirty p.m. and the light was fading when Enzo

swung the car up onto the forecourt of garage de Paolo. He parked next to the tow truck and went in through the open roller door. The mechanic was on his way out of the wash room, drying his hands on a filthy towel, and it took no words to establish what was going on: they both looked over to the office where Paolo sat with his feet up on the desk. Enzo could smell the whisky from ten metres. He peeled off a fifty and cocked his chin at the mechanic.

"Close the door on your way out."

Paolo's eyes lazily took him in as Enzo stepped into the office, but he uttered no words and kept his feet up on the desk. It was wise to tread carefully when he was in a mood like this, when the darkness had him. From past experience Enzo knew it could go either way. He lit a cigar while he waited for the roller door to finish lowering, and when the clatter gave way to silence he pulled out a chair and sat down. When the workshop lights went out, all that remained was the glow of the desk lamp. He looked into the shadows of his brother's face and tried to catch his eye.

"You okay?"

Paolo drained his whisky glass. "Never been better."

"If they had anything on you we'd know by now."

It looked like the words had gone straight through him but Paolo nodded.

"Has Etienne got rid of the boat?"

"As far as I know."

"In that case you've got nothing to worry about."

Paolo snorted and stared into the bottom of his empty tumbler. Enzo hated dealing with him when he was like this but it had to be done. He shuffled his chair as far forward as he could.

"Listen to me, Paolo. I'll take care of this. They had no right to carry out a search. My lawyer's already got them tied up in knots. By the time he's finished they'll be wishing they'd never set foot in this place."

Paolo reached for the whisky bottle but Enzo got to it first. "Just tell me what happened and I'll make this all go away."

Finally, his brother looked him in the eye, a connection made. He let out a long sad sigh and then tossed the empty glass onto the table. "You want to know what happened?"

"Talk to me."

Paolo held his gaze for a very long time. There was no anger there, just resignation. Like he'd given in to the fact this was all too much. Enzo remembered that time years ago when Dad told him he couldn't go to art school and he'd raged for weeks. But there was nothing he could do about it and over the years it had eaten away at him. It wasn't how Enzo wanted things to be but *c'est la vie.* He nudged the chair. "Come on. Tell me how they died, that kid and his old man."

Paolo blinked. He pulled his feet off the desk and leaned forward, face in his hands.

"How many were on the boat?" Enzo prompted.

"Fifteen."

"Who were they?"

"The guy was Etienne's cousin."

"And the kid?"

"A nephew. His family wanted to bring them over."

Enzo nodded, pleased with the progress. Just keep him talking, that was the key. "So what happened?"

He spoke with lots of pauses. Enzo listened patiently, careful not to push too quickly. "When we got to Algiers Etienne met up with some friends. They all got hammered on the beach. Then on the way back the GPS died. We'd meant to haul out in one of the old dropping zones but we came up too far. It was getting light so we told everyone to get back in the boat, but they wouldn't listen. They started heading off into town."

"And the kid?"

"He'd got seasick. His dad was all in my face, saying they weren't getting back on the boat."

"And?"

"I lost my temper."

"You hit him?"

Paolo nodded.

"What with?"

"There was a wrench, in Etienne's toolbox."

"Did anyone see?"

Paolo rubbed his forehead. "Etienne, the kid ... maybe a couple of the others."

"What did the kid do then?"

"He got scared and ran off. Etienne tried to grab him but he got away. The last we saw he was running towards the water."

"So it was an accident."

Paolo met his eye. "It was still my fault."

"You were defending yourself from his dad. How were you to know the kid would run off?"

Paolo shook his head. Enzo went on,

"Then what?"

"We put the body on the boat and then dumped it by the fort. We searched for the kid but couldn't find him."

Enzo leaned back and mulled it over. It was worse than he'd expected but there was a way out. A draught was coming in from the dark open space of the workshop so he got up out of his chair and closed the door. He went back to the desk and perched on the edge, facing his brother squarely.

"Where's the wrench now?"

"Hidden in a drain out back."

"I'll take it. See it ends up somewhere more useful."

Paolo gave him a closer look. "Like where?"

"In Etienne's hut."

Now his brother came to life. "You're such a bastard."

"It's dog eat dog, brother, you know that. And I'm not having my own flesh and blood go down for this, especially as it wasn't your fault."

"What if Etienne tells them the truth?"

"He's got family here, hasn't he? He won't take much persuading."

Paolo screwed up his face. "You really are a piece of something."

He got up out of his seat and made a move for the door, but Enzo blocked him. Eyeball to eyeball, Enzo was determined to finish this now.

"Look, I know he's your friend but he screwed up. He was the one driving the boat. It was his fault you ended up in the wrong cove. None of this would have happened if he hadn't got stoned."

The light in Paolo's eyes dimmed a fraction. He was nearly there now. Just one more push.

"It's time to forget about Etienne and think of the future. When all this is over things will be different, I promise you. I want you to come down to the new house. Spend some time with me and Marielle. She'd love to see you again. And you'd like that, too, wouldn't you? And hey—" He grinned, and dug his brother in the ribs. "I've got this new PA. Crystal. Tits out here, you're going to love her."

Paolo said nothing but the acknowledgement was there in his eyes. Enzo gave him a few more moments, just to be sure, then opened his arms for a hug. Enzo slapped his back with pride.

———

To Margot's surprise, Captain Bouchard phoned her straight back. He'd spoken to the judge to arrange for a warrant to be issued and expected to search Etienne's hut first thing in the morning. They returned to the yacht in buoyant mood.

At nine a.m. the following day Margot and Raul were waiting at the boatyard's entrance. Five minutes passed before two police cars raced towards them along the street and then pulled up sharply beside the arch. Captain Bouchard emerged from the rear of one, quickly followed by three others.

"Where?"

Margot pointed; the captain directed his men.

The arrival of the police brought people out of the nooks and crannies and the boatyard swiftly came to life. Suspicious eyes tracked them every step of the way as Margot, Raul and two of the police officers worked their way along the concrete walkway. They marched across the footbridge in single file and then regrouped in front of the motorboat mechanic's hut

"Stand back."

Margot did as he said, though when she looked at the chain was surprised to see that the padlock had changed. This one was one silver, whereas yesterday it had been brass. Before she had time to voice her concern, however, one of the policemen snapped the chain with a pair of bolt croppers. A cat sneaked out as they opened the door, and sensing unfriendliness scampered away. The men filed in and quickly set to work.

It would have been nice to find a boat hidden away inside but the shed was largely empty. Workbenches lined three of the walls, and the floor was an oily dark expanse. Margot wandered in, her eyes travelling curiously around the space before the captain instructed them to wait by the door.

To their credit, the gendarmes conducted a thorough search. They went through all the tool cabinets, searched every cupboard, meticulously inspected the floor. And within half an hour their efforts had paid off.

"Captain."

The voice came from the back of the shed where Margot could see a gendarme gingerly holding up an object. The captain strode into the gloom and carefully took it from him. When they came back into the light it became clear he was holding a monkey wrench, the jaws of which were smeared with what appeared to be blood.

————

All six pairs of eyes were still focused on the wrench when a shout rang out nearby. Heads turned, the policemen moved out into the light. A fellow officer was sprinting along the road on the other side of the perimeter fence, heading towards a stationary pickup truck. It was some distance away, but Margot could see the green and white logo. As the officer closed in, the truck promptly reversed at speed.

A moment later hurrying figures were moving in all directions. Raul stayed close to Margot's side and they watched the action unfold from a distance. Barely had the truck sped out of sight than there was a loud bang, a crunch of metal on metal. A fleeing figure appeared, the policeman in hot pursuit.

"Is that him?" Raul asked.

They were fifty metres away but Margot had no doubt. "That's Etienne."

He was a fast sprinter but he was hopelessly outnumbered. Captain Bouchard himself had run through the main gate with an alacrity that belied his size and he made it to the street just in time to block that particular route of escape.

Etienne skidded to a halt. He spun to face his rearward pursuers, and then, realising he was trapped, launched himself at the fence. He made it up three hand-lifts; struggled on one more even as hands grabbed at him from below. But with two of them on him he didn't stand a chance. The three men collapsed into an ugly heap on the concrete.

Under Captain Bouchard's supervision, they frogmarched him back to the hut where everyone regrouped. There was a pause while they all stood regaining their breaths. When he was ready, the captain grasped Etienne's arm and marched him inside.

"This tool chest," he said, still breathing heavily from the run. "Does it belong to you?"

Etienne nodded.

"And this?" The captain held up the wrench.

Margot had to move closer to watch the Algerian's reaction. He made no attempt to deny it, but the look on his face was one of surprise rather than alarm.

21

The *chug-chug-chug* of a diesel-powered fishing boat roused Margot from her sleep. She eased herself up in the bed and peered out of the window: on the other side of the harbour, a small group of men were awaiting the arrival of the morning's catch. It was only six o'clock but she put on a clean Speedo and packed her swimming bag. Raul was still asleep so she eased open the hatch with care and set off for the cove.

She paused as she rounded the headland, watching the dawn break. The sun was a huge glowing orb, fanning rays across the sea and filling the cove with warm orange light. Pierre had called yesterday afternoon to say that officers from the crime-scene squad had searched the area and found traces of blood on the rocks close to where the backpack had been left. It hadn't yet been confirmed as belonging to Aswan's father but it seemed highly likely, and there was every reason to believe the blood on the wrench would also be a match. The case against Etienne seemed strong.

The fact it had happened here, in her favourite cove, would take some getting used to. The exact sequence of events might never become known to them but at some point during that night a scared little boy had been out on these rocks. In all probability he'd seen his father get hit in the face with a wrench. And then somehow he'd ended up in the water, struggling before he drowned. Just a few hours later, Margot had come down for her morning swim, oblivious to all that had gone on.

She only swam out a short way and was back on board *Carpe Diem* within the hour. All was still quiet below deck so she sat up top and smoked a cigarette while the town came to life. When Raul did get up, she went below and brewed a fresh pot of coffee.

"You've been for a swim?"

She nodded, and stared at the empty table between them. "Sorry. I should have brought something back for breakfast."

He dismissed her apology with a wave of his hand and went to the galley to prepare something. He came back with a plateful of ham and cheese, some toasted white bread and a jar of jam, and looked happier with some food in front of him.

"Penny for them."

"Pardon?" Margot frowned.

There was a pause while he swallowed his food. "You seem distracted. I thought you would be pleased now they've arrested the motorboat mechanic."

Margot placed a slice of toast on her plate and spread it with a thick layer of jam. "Only if they've got the right man."

"You have your doubts?"

"I don't doubt he was involved. I'm not sure he was the killer."

"But the wrench?"

"It could easily have been planted. Didn't you notice the padlocks had been changed?"

"No."

She finished chewing her mouthful and then swallowed. "Someone must have gone back there before the police arrived."

"Maybe Etienne did."

"But why would he lock it with a different padlock?"

Raul shrugged.

Margot shook her head. Something wasn't right. In all the excitement she'd not had chance to pass on her concerns but she would definitely be paying Captain Bouchard another visit. "That's not the only thing that doesn't add up."

"Go on."

Margot wiped a residue of sticky jam from her fingertips. "Why would Etienne leave the murder weapon in his own toolbox?"

Raul nodded. "That does seem rather foolish."

No one could be that careless. Something more was going on here and she would not be so easily taken in.

After breakfast, she walked up the hill to the gendarmerie. Both Captain Bouchard and the young gendarme were in the office behind the screen, hunched over some papers. They both noticed her, and the young man appeared to want to come over, but the captain kept her waiting, taking his time to finish discussing whatever it was that was occupying them. Finally, he straightened his tunic and came to the screen. "Yes, Madame?"

"I didn't get time yesterday to tell you about the padlocks."

He rolled his eyes and planted his palms on the counter, looking very bored. "Padlocks?"

"On Etienne's hut. The first time we went there the chain had been secured with a brass one, but when you arrived it was silver."

"There was only one padlock at the hut."

"Yes, but—"

"We have our perpetrator, Madame."

"You're just going to assume he's guilty?"

"He's confessed."

Margot flinched. "When?"

"This morning. He admitted to smuggling the migrants and to killing the boy's father."

"And he did it all on his own?"

"We have no reason to suspect otherwise."

"But Paolo—"

"Paolo Bellucci has been released without charge."

"What?"

"Was that all?"

Margot could hardly believe what she was hearing. It was all too neat, all too cleanly sewn up. While she was still reeling, the captain went on,

"May I suggest you now leave this matter alone?" And then, in a lower tone: "I really wouldn't want to see you get hurt."

———

Rue Garenne linked the gendarmerie to Place Jeanne d'Arc and with little conscious intervention Margot found her feet moving that way. She halted outside the *Palais de Justice* and looked up at the windows, in two minds whether to go in. She couldn't just stand by and let this travesty of justice continue, but would the judge be any more sympathetic? It seemed unlikely, but Margot wasn't giving in.

Without an appointment the receptionist said there was no possibility of seeing the judge, but Margot persisted and managed to persuade her to at least ring up. She was told she could have five minutes.

In contrast to the frosty reception downstairs, Judge Deveraux greeted her warmly. She came out from behind her desk at a sprightly pace and indicated two armchairs by one of the windows.

"Can I get you some coffee?"

Margot nodded; the judge briefly returned to her desk and

called through to her secretary. She moved with a gracefulness that belied her age, and Margot couldn't help noticing how toned her calves were, how straight her spine. Perhaps she'd been a dancer in her youth, or an artist's model. When she returned to her seat she sat with her legs crossed, knees angled towards Margot.

"Thank you for seeing me at such short notice," Margot said.

"The pleasure's all mine. What can I do for you?"

The secretary came in with a tray of coffee. Margot waited while he set it down on the table between them. When he left, she said,

"I understand Etienne Hamidi has confessed."

The judge lowered her eyes while she poured the coffee. "Yes. And I heard you were instrumental in leading us to him. You certainly have been very determined to get to the bottom of this case." She handed over a cup and leaned in, conspiratorially. "I probably shouldn't say this but I admire your persistence."

"May I be direct?"

The judge seemed surprised. She left her cup untouched on the tray and then leaned back in her seat. "Feel free to say anything you like to me."

"I really don't think Etienne is guilty."

There was a pause while the judge gathered her thoughts. She seemed disappointed that this was the subject Margot had brought up. "The evidence is all there. The victim's blood was found on the wrench. An eyewitness saw him taking his boat out the day before the bodies were discovered. We've now recovered the boat and found additional DNA evidence. Add to that his confession and the case against him is strong."

"Where did he confess?"

The judge seemed puzzled. "Where?"

"Was it at the gendarmerie?"

"I presume so."

"Did he see anyone beforehand?"

"I have no idea. Why would that be relevant?"

Margot allowed a pause to develop. She felt the need to choose her words carefully.

"Etienne seemed surprised that the wrench was found in his toolbox. I was there. I saw his reaction."

"What are you implying?"

"I think someone planted it. They broke into his hut and replaced the padlock with a different one, probably thinking no one would notice. But it had definitely been changed."

"And who do you believe did that?"

"Either Paolo Bellucci or his brother, Enzo. When I heard them talking at the garage it was clear that Etienne was just an accomplice. And now Enzo is trying to use his influence to get him off."

The judge's body language changed. Her eyes briefly glazed over and Margot shifted on her seat, fearing she'd overstepped the mark. Before she could backtrack, however, the judge continued,

"Madame Renard—"

"Call me Margot."

She smiled maternally. "Margot. Please believe me when I say this to you, I find few things more repellent than people with influence using their position to try and interfere in the judicial process. No one is above the law, no matter how rich or well-connected they may be. Throughout my career I've made it my goal to prosecute anyone and everyone I believe to be guilty, regardless of what feathers it might ruffle. But we have to have evidence. And there simply is nothing we can use against either of the Bellucci brothers."

"It wasn't Etienne who tried to burn down my house."

"We have no evidence to suggest who was responsible."

"It was someone who wanted to shut me up."

"All I can say is I'm glad they failed." Judge Deveraux offered one last smile before her tone turned serious again. "As far as this case is concerned, however, the evidence is clear. Etienne Hamidi has been charged with murder and that is the end of the matter."

Margot walked sullenly back to the harbour and when she got to *Carpe Diem* found Raul cleaning the deck with a hosepipe and brush. He turned off the water and gave her a cheerful look, but all she could offer back was a sad little face.

"Did you find what you were looking for?"

She frowned. "Sorry?"

"At the shops."

She got his meaning and shook her head. Raul followed as she went below and sat down in the salon.

"I didn't go to the shops. I went to see Judge Deveraux."

"Oh. I see."

"They've charged Etienne."

"And Paolo?"

Margot tightened her jaw. "Paolo's getting away with murder."

22

___

Seated on the harbour wall, Margot took off her pumps and handed them to Raul. She swung her legs over the side and searched the rocks below for a suitable place to jump down. The flat top of a large boulder provided a convenient landing spot. She reached back up to take the bunch of flowers that Raul was still holding onto.

"Do be careful."

"I will."

Margot remembered the day Aswan's body had been found and how she'd watched the teenage boys leap effortlessly down the beach of rocks. Now that she was here doing it herself, however, it wasn't as easy as it had looked. The gaps between the boulders were large, and she had to pause between each jump, concentrating hard. She couldn't help worrying how slippery the rocks might be, how much it would hurt if her foot got stuck. Twenty years ago she would have done it without thinking.

She made it to the water's edge without mishap and looked down at the smooth brown rocks on either side. Close up, they all looked the same and there was nothing to distinguish the spot that had proved to be Aswan's final resting place. A wave came in, forcing her to step back. She chose a rock at the edge of the waterline and wedged the flower stalks into a slit.

"Rest in peace, little boy." She transferred a kiss with her fingertips.

Raul held onto her forearms to help her climb back up. Some passers-by looked on in surprise when Margot clambered inelegantly over the concrete barrier. She dusted off her hands and sat still, recovering her breath.

"That was a nice gesture," Raul said.

"His mother's not here to do it."

"I'm proud of you." He leaned in and kissed her on the cheek. "If it wasn't for you no one would even know his name."

True, but Margot felt little satisfaction. In every other respect he was still anonymous. A statistic. A ghastly photo on the front of a newspaper. And if Raul was thinking that this meant closure he was sorely mistaken. Justice was a long way from being done.

———

They called in at her house to check on progress. The carpenter still hadn't started work and, if anything, being boarded up for a few days had only made the place smell worse. Margot lingered in the sitting room where the lumpy black marks of Hugo's record collection still scared the floor.

"Looks like I'll be homeless for longer than I thought," she muttered and turned as Raul approached. "I'd better move into that hotel."

But Raul firmly shook his head. "You'll do nothing of the sort. You'll stay on board *Carpe Diem* with me. It's the safest place."

Margot smiled. Having him as an ally was about the only good thing to come of this.

She went upstairs and sorted through the remainder of her

clothes. Most still stank of smoke but a few things had escaped unscathed. She packed what was salvageable and binned the remainder. While Raul was taking her bags back to the yacht, Margot called Pierre.

"I want you to tell me everything you know about Enzo Bellucci."

"You know I can't do that."

"Why?"

"You really need me to explain?"

Margot exhaled in frustration, making no attempt to cover the phone. "Come on, Pierre. I was the one who told you he'd got a shipment coming in. Quid pro quo and all that."

"It's being dealt with by the drugs brigade. I'm only a lowly lieutenant."

"But you still have contacts."

Pierre's exasperation came back down the line. "Margot."

"Yes?"

"You really must leave this to the professionals now. Please, I really don't want you getting involved."

After a few more words they hung up. It had been a longshot expecting him to give out any information but she'd been itching to take her frustration out on someone. And it didn't really matter. There were other ways of finding out.

———

Margot wasn't keen on using her phone to do an internet search on gangsters in the local area and so, after lunch, she went to the internet café in the library. The East Wing was a modern addition with a fancy first-floor restaurant and panoramic windows that looked out over the sea, but Margot ignored the view and installed herself in a booth in the corner. She typed "Enzo Bellucci" into a search engine. The first thing that came up was a link to his shipping company: EDB Transports Maritimes. According to its website, it was a large outfit with shipping routes all over the world. Enzo was listed as chief executive, but there was no biographical info and no photos. She switched to the images tab. As Paolo's older brother Enzo must have been at least in his mid-forties and several of the images that came up fitted that profile, but since she hadn't got a good look at him at the garage there was no way she could be sure.

There were no newspaper articles, nothing on social media, though that was not surprising – gangsters were hardly likely to be big on Insta.

She looked up the business information on Paolo's garage and found Paolo listed as sole director. Running out of ideas, she drummed her fingers on the desktop. Maybe if she phoned the office she could get Enzo's home address, pretend she had a parcel to deliver or something. It was a pretty lame idea but she jotted down the number just in case.

Some noisy new arrivals broke her concentration. Looking up at the clock she saw that it was 15:05. She'd told Raul she would only be gone an hour. She quickly deleted her search history, gathered her things, and headed for the exit.

She paused on the concrete steps to light up. While she was exhaling her first lungful, her eyes alighted upon a man standing on the opposite side of the street, and it could have been déjà-vu: the heavyset man with the buzz cut was staring straight back at her. Margot's blood instantly turned cold. This time he was slower to react and their eyes stayed locked for a good few seconds. But then she came to her senses, stubbed out her cigarette and hurried down the steps. The man turned quickly on his heels and slipped away.

He headed down Rue de la Libération, walking fast but not quite running. Meandering tourists kept getting in Margot's way, reducing her view to glimpses between bodies, and she had to brusquely push through. For a man of considerable size he was moving with speed and she had to jog to keep him in sight. He turned left into Rue Blanqui, hurried down the steep narrow laneway that led to the quay. By the time she next caught sight of him he'd gone all the way down to the bottom where the lane joined the plaza and the old ship's canon pointed out to sea. When Margot reached the same spot, she glanced swiftly around. The promenade was thronged with pedestrians and the man was nowhere to be seen. She halted, stamping her foot in frustration.

————

Margot took a roundabout route back to the harbour, checking over her shoulder to make sure no one was following. All was quiet on the deck of *Carpe Diem* so she went below where she found Raul dozing on the sofa, a cushion over his face. Cheese crumbs littered the table, and an empty wine bottle was rolling around on the floor. She tutted as she picked up the bottle, and set it down harder than necessary on the table-top. Raul woke up with a series of surprised unhappy grunts.

"I thought you might have been worried about me," Margot said as he cranked himself into a seated position. "I would have stayed in the library if I'd known you were sleeping."

He rubbed his crumpled face. "I was resting my eyes, that's all."

"Hmm," Margot said, unimpressed. She fetched them a bottle of water each from the fridge.

It was a few minutes before Raul was completely with it. Watching him tidy himself up, Margot recalled the scruffily-dressed man she'd accosted on the jetty that day and wondered how many other times he'd spent like this on his way up from

Cadiz. Maybe the death of his wife had affected him more than he was willing to admit.

"Is there any particular reason I should have been worried?" he asked once he'd come back to life.

Margot folded her arms. "Promise you won't be cross."

Raul sucked thirstily from the bottle of water, the wafer-thin plastic crackling in his hand. "You told me you were going to the library. Why would I be cross?"

"I've been doing some research on Enzo Bellucci."

His sank his cheek onto his fist and sighed wearily. "Go on."

"I looked up the address of the shipping company he owns. I was thinking I could use it to find out where he lives."

"Why – so you can go round there and firebomb *his* house?"

Margot's face darkened. "That's not funny."

He sat back. "I'm sorry. That was insensitive. But really, Margot, when is this going to end?"

"They need to be brought to justice."

"You can't fight them."

"Why not?"

"Because they're too powerful."

"That man tried to kill me."

"Exactly!"

"So you think I should just let him get away with it? Hide away like a frightened little kitten?"

"I never said—"

"I'm not going to sit here and do nothing, Raul. You should know me well enough by now to realise that."

Raul sighed again. He got up to clear away the mess he'd made and fetched a cloth from the galley. Margot took a deep breath and calmed down. It was nice that he cared but she wasn't giving up.

"Pierre told me he uses the company as a front for importing drugs. We know he's got a shipment coming in; all we have to do is find out where and when."

"Perhaps you could phone him up and ask."

"Be serious."

"I am being serious. I can't understand why you want to go anywhere near these people."

"I won't do anything rash. I'll bide my time, wait for the right opportunity." She smiled to lighten the mood. "Something will come up, you'll see."

Raul tilted his head upwards like he was hoping for divine inspiration. "The cosmic forces will align, yin will meet yang, karma will prevail – is that what you believe?"

"I believe in natural justice, yes. People should get their just deserts."

Raul took a long time thinking about it but finally he nodded, placated. He came back to the table and sat down, laying his hands on top of hers. "Yes. Okay. Very well. And perhaps with me on your side you might just stand a chance."

She wasn't sure whether he was being serious or not but Margot held her smirk, just in case.

———

They needed to stock up on wine so at five o'clock Raul set off to cave Saint Joan with two empty carrier bags. Alone on the yacht for the first time, Margot couldn't resist having a sneaky look round.

It was even more spacious than she'd previously thought. A door opposite her cabin led to another large space where two bunk beds were folded neatly into the side of the hull. Beside them, a large locker housed wetsuits and diving equipment. A little further along, another door opened onto a small engine room complete with banks of switches and dials. As she made her way back to the salon, Margot ran her fingertips along the smooth wooden panels, marvelled at the discovery of another small toilet tucked away in what she'd initially assumed to be a cupboard. It was all so cleverly designed, like a carriage on the Orient Express. She briefly poked her head up through the companionway to make sure Raul wasn't on his way back and then had a quick look in his cabin. It was much tidier than she'd expected – the bed neatly made, some family photos on the walls, a guitar on a stand in the corner. The door to his shower room was open revealing a shelfful of Dolce and Gabbana.

She went back to the salon and sat down in the navigator's seat. When she switched on the console, a chart came up showing their current position. One push of a button brought up a topographical map of the western Mediterranean. She zoomed out until it showed half the globe; all she had to do was pick a spot and let it plot a course. Where would she go if she owned a boat like this: the Greek Islands, the Adriatic? She could winter in west Africa; explore the Norwegian Fjords in summer. At some point she would cross the Atlantic and go through the Panama Canal, spend years exploring the remote islands and tiny atolls of the South Pacific. Sailing around the world was still the ultimate adventure. But to do it all on her own? Margot sat back in the seat and folded her arms. It would be a hard thing combatting loneliness.

She snapped out of the daydream and fetched her laptop from her cabin. She was meant to be doing research.

She typed Enzo's name into a lesser-known search engine and got back some different results. A page from an architectural journal came up that was full of pictures of an ultra-modern house. It was an incredible piece of engineering – a glass and steel structure seemingly built into the side of a cliff. The plans showed five bedrooms, a cinema room, an underground leisure suite. A separate wing would house a car collection. The infinity pool would be a state-of-the-art construction, projecting directly out of the rock with half of it appearing to hang in mid-air. The article said it was being built on the Mediterranean coast, though it didn't specify where. The client was Enzo Bellucci, head of EDB Transports Maritimes.

Margot lit a cigarette. It may have been a very big world but some things were the same all over – the rich and powerful exploiting the weak and vulnerable. Sometimes it seemed there was no yin to the yang at all.

Realising she was smoking below deck, she quickly stubbed out her cigarette and fanned the air with a towel. The clock on the wall showed six-thirty. Raul had been gone for over an hour yet Cave St Joan was only a ten-minute walk away. She went up on deck to look out for him, and five minutes later heard the *clink-clink-clink* of bottles being carried in a bag. Raul's familiar outline appeared on the jetty.

"You were gone a long time."

"Did you miss me?"

He came up the steps at the stern and presented her with a bunch of flowers. "The florist was shut. I had to walk all the way up to the supermarket at the top of Rue Voltaire."

Margot frowned at the flowers, white freesias and lavender. They were lovely, but she didn't take them.

"I never did say how sorry I was for almost running into you," Raul explained.

Margot felt a glow on her insides but still didn't take them. "There's really no need."

"Please." He raised them a little higher, a sprig of lavender almost touching her nose. "If only to make me feel better."

She conceded a small nod. "All right. Thank you."

They went below and Margot sorted out a vase.

He unpacked the food he'd bought for dinner while Margot put away the wine. He'd bought a 2015 Pinot Gris, three bottles of a local Sauvignon, a bottle of Louis Roederer. Flowers and a bottle of champagne – it had been a long time since she'd last felt so pampered. She took the Sauvignon over to the table and half-filled two glasses.

"I take it you've been doing some more 'research'," Raul said, gesturing at the laptop with a packet of chicken thighs.

"Don't worry, I didn't get very far." Margot sat down and clicked back to the article from the architectural magazine. "This came up." He left the shopping and came to sit beside her. Margot turned the computer so he could see. "This is what drug money can buy you. It says the build cost was over two million euros, never mind the price of the land."

Raul pulled the laptop a little closer and stared at the screen, his brow crumpling up. He scrolled down the page, taking rather more interest than Margot had expected. Intrigued, she watched him closely. As the silence lengthened she felt like giving him a nudge. "What is it?"

"I know this place."

"You do? How?"

"I passed it on the way up. It's a little bit further down the Côte Vermeille."

Margot turned her eyes back to the screen, her mind starting to race. She had a short sip of wine. The Côte Vermeille wasn't very far away, just a few kilometres down the coast, close to the border with Spain. "Are you sure it's the same one?"

"Yes. I remember these terraces, and these big metal rings – look."

There were some photos of the garden in progress, one of them showing a line of large bronze ring sculptures.

"Did it look like it was lived in?"

"I didn't pay that much attention. But it certainly looked finished."

Margot checked the date of the article – it had been

published eleven months ago, the house was surely complete by now. Her heart started to beat a little more quickly as she looked into Raul's eyes.

"How long would it take us to get there?"

"In *Carpe Diem*?"

She nodded.

He narrowed his eyes with suspicion. "Why would you want to go there?"

"Curiosity."

"I thought you got seasick."

"You said you had some pills."

"The pills that don't work on you, you mean?"

Margot sucked in her cheeks and pouted, but Raul was having none of it. He pushed the laptop away. "You seriously expect me to sail you down the coast to spy on the house of a gangland boss? Now I know you're out of your mind."

He got back up and went to finish his unpacking, but just then there was a thud from outside. Margot cocked her head, and their eyes locked again. "Did you hear that?"

They both listened. The wind had picked up and things on the boat had started to creak. Margot leaned over the back of the sofa and raised the blind on the nearest window. Outside was one dark sheet of water.

"It'll be nothing," Raul said. "But stay here." He opened the hatch doors and went up.

Margot waited anxiously. It would surely be nothing. No one knew she was here apart from Pierre and Captain Bouchard, and she'd been careful not to be seen every time she'd come back. For the longest time the hatch stayed empty and all she could see was a rectangle of dark black sky. She briefly had a vision of something terrible happening out there, but then Raul came back down the steps, closing the hatch doors behind him.

"What was it?"

"Just a buoy come loose."

"Are you sure?"

He came over and rubbed her shoulder reassuringly. "There's no one out there, Margot."

For now, they said nothing more about a trip down the coast.

23

Enzo stepped out through his front door and beamed at his Mercedes while it was still winding its way down the drive. He strode across the gravel and signalled to Mutt to pull up. When Paolo emerged from the back seat, scowling at the midday sun, Enzo opened his arms for a hug.

"Hey, Paolo!"

The brothers hugged, though it was heavily one-sided.

"You okay?"

Paolo nodded.

"Mutt, take my brother's things up to the guest suite." He patted Paolo's chest. "Come on in. I'll show you around. You won't believe what they've done with the place."

It was the first time Paolo had seen the house, the first time in years he'd agreed to see Enzo at home. Enzo took him in through the hall and straight over to the glazed wall that ran the full length of the house's top floor. On the other side of the glass, a fifty-mile panorama of sparkling blue sea opened up to them. Enzo watched his brother's face, hoping for at least a spark of appreciation.

"What a view, huh?" he prompted. "They used a hundred square metres of glazing in this place. Can you believe that? They had to bring the bigger sections in by helicopter."

Enzo waited, but Paolo's face stayed blank. He shuffled his feet. Perhaps he was expecting too much. A reconciliation like this would take time. Baby steps, that's what were needed. He forced the smile back onto his face. "Come on, let's go down and see Marielle."

It was an upside-down house. From the entrance on the top level, four more floors stepped down the face of the cliff to the basement level which was still sixty metres above the sea. They took the elevator to the lowest level where the main living room, kitchen and dining room combined into one giant space. Another glass wall separated it from the terrace and they went out through an opening into a blaze of sunshine, the infinity pool jutting out before them like something from an Escher illusion. Enzo walked him right out to the edge where they gazed down the cliff-face to the beach tucked away at the bottom. There was no more impressive location on this whole stretch of coast but Paolo remained stony-faced. Enzo balled his fists in his pockets. What the hell was wrong with this kid?

"Hi, Paolo."

They turned to see Marielle waving from a sun lounger at the far end of the terrace. "Long time no see."

She put on a beach sarong and came over. The chiffon was so flimsy it only served to emphasise her curves but at least it made Paolo crack a smile.

"Hi, Marielle."

"Good to see you."

"You too."

They smiled into each other's eyes.

Enzo cleared his throat, feeling like a third wheel. She and

Paolo had always got on. Years ago, she'd posed for him: they'd broken into an abandoned aerodrome and shot some pictures on a plane carcass, Paolo's usual weird stuff. She probably still had the pictures tucked away in a drawer somewhere. But Enzo wasn't jealous. If Marielle could loosen him up that was all well and good.

He left them chatting while he went to fetch the champagne and found them still head-to-head when he got back. Finally, there was something a little more human on Paolo's face as Enzo handed out the glasses. He waited for his wife to take a sip and then cocked his head. "Is that dinner I can smell cooking?"

Marielle gave him the evil eye. He would pay for it later but being a third wheel didn't suit him.

"Sorry, Paolo. Duty calls." She scowled as she handed him back the glass

Enzo slapped his brother on the back. "Come on. Let's talk."

He led Paolo across the terrace and into the garden on the far side of the seating area. They climbed a short set of steps and then took the path to the summer house perched high on the promontory. Enzo stood right on the edge as he sipped his champagne, nothing but cliffs and blue sky surrounding them. Beside him, Paolo at last seemed to be enjoying the view. It would be nice to think there would come a day when they could stand together like this and talk about something other than business, but maybe not just yet. Enzo stepped back into the summer house and sat down in the shade.

"I take it everything got sorted?"

Paolo nodded as he joined him. Enzo lit a cigar.

"You need to lay low for a while. Stay here for a few days. Then we'll sell the garage, get you somewhere smart to live."

"And we all live happily ever after?"

Enzo looked him in the eye. "You might not think it right now but some good will come of this."

"It didn't turn out so good for Etienne."

"He shouldn't have screwed up."

Paolo narrowed his eyes. "What did you say to him?"

"It doesn't matter what I said to him. It worked, didn't it? Anyway, he's an idiot. The dumb ass didn't even get rid of the boat. Did you hear about that?"

"It cost him a lot of money. He didn't want part with it."

"And look at the price he's had to pay for it now?"

Paolo couldn't argue with that. Enzo sat up in his seat.

"Look. Forget about Etienne. All that matters now is you and me. And I need your help."

"*You*, need my help?"

"Let's not play games. My shipment's coming in soon. I need eyes and ears on the ground. You come in with me now and you'll have more money than you know what to do with. But once you're in, you're in. You understand what I'm saying?"

It took a while but Paolo finally conceded a small nod. Enzo extended his arm, and they shook hands.

"We'll go over the finer points later. Why don't you go upstairs and wash up? I'll call you when dinner's ready."

In the kitchen, Enzo helped make dinner. He squeezed lemons for the dessert while Marielle stood at the counter with her nose in a recipe book, but he was crushing rather than squeezing them and Marielle took the juicer off him when she saw what a mess he was making. Enzo came away from the counter, drying his hands on a towel.

"Why won't he talk to me? He'll spend all day yakking to you yet he'll barely say two words to me."

"You're trying too hard."

"It's important. He looks at me like I'm something he picked up on his shoe."

Enzo watched from the other side of the island as Marielle did something with a chicken.

"What do you expect?"

"A little gratitude."

Marielle shook her head, that pitying look on her face.

"The only thing your brother has ever asked you for is to stay out of his life. What makes you think anything's changed now?"

"I just saved his ass, didn't I? If it wasn't for me he'd be looking at twenty years inside right now."

"He hates you and everything you represent. I thought you would have got that into your head by now."

Enzo curled his lip, and turned away. His wife had this annoying habit of telling him uncomfortable truths at times. Maybe he should return the favour someday. But she didn't know everything. They'd been close once, as kids. He would find a way.

"Here comes Bunny," Marielle muttered.

Across the living room, the office door had opened and Crystal was heading their way.

"Do you think she'd look so cute if I boiled her head in the microwave?" Marielle said, but Enzo ignored her and went out.

He intercepted Crystal in the living room, having had an idea. If money didn't work there was something else that would.

"Hey." He tipped his head and steered her clear of his wife's line of sight. "My brother's just got here. He'll be having dinner with us later. But when we're finished, I want you to come and join us."

"Is *she* going to be there?" A poison dart shot in the direction of the kitchen.

Enzo sighed. Jesus, what was it with these women? "She'll be out. It's her book group tonight. But look, I need you to cheer him up."

"Why does he need cheering up?"

"It's a long story, but listen. When Marielle goes out I want you to put on your bikini and come join us out by the pool."

Crystal rolled her eyes. "I'm not your whore, you know."

"Don't worry," Enzo winked. "He likes to look, not touch." He reached around and cupped her left buttock. "Unlike me."

24

The skylight in Margot's cabin was directly over her head and during the night she had a bad dream. In the dream she'd woken up to find a man's face staring down at her. After several long minutes he'd tried to break in and she'd reached up to the skylight and pulled it shut, but the man was too strong and tore it from its fixings. She woke up for real, hot and panting.

It was five a.m. and the harbour was quiet. The dim light from a passing fishing boat crossed her window and when Margot peered out she saw that it was misty. For the first time in a long time she had little desire to go swimming, but she packed her bag and put on a swimsuit. There was something she wanted to speak to Raymond about first so she left a note for Raul and then snuck out before it had even got light.

Le Paname didn't open until six-thirty so Margot waited outside, smoking her first cigarette of the day. Ten minutes later, the feeble bleat of a low-powered engine preceded the arrival of a moped into the square. Its wheels bounced up onto the kerb beside her and the rider hoicked it up onto its centre stand. Seeing that it was Margot waiting by the café door, Raymond quickly removed his helmet.

"Good morning, Margot," he said, a little bit red in the face. The leather jacket he was wearing was a little too big for him and he didn't look anywhere near as cool as he probably imagined, poor thing. "We don't normally see you here so early."

"I couldn't sleep."

"I was sorry to hear about your house."

"Thank you."

"Do you need any help fixing things up?"

Margot shook her head. "That's very kind but it's all taken care of."

They stood in silence for a moment, face to face in the café doorway. Margot fixed him with a winning smile. "There is something else you can help me with though."

"Oh?"

"I wanted to pick your brains."

The young man's eyes widened. Margot touched his arm reassuringly. "Don't worry, it's an English expression. It means I want to ask your advice."

"What about?"

The café door opened just at that moment and the owner looked out, mumbling a bonjour. He grumbled on to himself as he went back inside.

"Is there somewhere private we can talk?"

"There's the yard at the back."

"Okay."

Raymond led her through three interconnecting rooms to a storage area at the rear of the café where he quickly stowed his helmet and jacket. He tilted his head and opened a dusty glazed door. "Sorry about the smell." He wrinkled his nose as they stepped into the courtyard. The odour coming off the overflowing bins was pretty foul.

Margot passed him a cigarette and struck a match. She lit his first and then managed to light one for herself before the dying flame nipped her fingertips. She dropped the match onto the concrete. "You're good with technology, aren't you?"

"I'm okay, why?"

The back door was still open so she reached across to close it, checking first that no one was listening. She turned back to Raymond and moved a step closer. "Do you know of any eaves-dropping devices that are easy to get hold of?"

"*Eaves*dropping devices?"

"You know – a bug."

His eyes widened. "Why do you want a bug?"

"It's better you don't know. But with all the wonderful tech around nowadays there must be something people use."

Raymond filled his lungs with smoke while he gave the question some thought. "There's the bugE."

"The what?"

"It's basically a flash-drive with a microphone built in."

"How does it work?"

"It picks up sound and then stores them as files on the flash-drive. The files gets transferred to a server and then transmitted to your phone. All you need is a 4G signal and an app."

"How big is it?"

He shrugged. "The size of a button."

"And can you buy them around here?"

He raised his eyebrows. "My friend works in an electronics shop. He could probably get one."

Holding the cigarette between the centre of her lips, Margot reached into her bag. She took out her purse and then removed the cigarette. "If I gave you some money do you think you could buy one for me?"

He shuffled his feet. "I suppose so."

She pulled out some cash. "Will this be enough?"

His eyes lit up. "That's far too much. They'll be no more than a hundred."

Margot pressed it into his hand anyway, and then leaned forward conspiratorially. "This is just between you and me, okay?" She winked.

Raymond blushed. "I'll go in my break."

"Text me when you've got it."

———

It was eight-thirty when she got back from her swim. There was no sign of movement from Raul's cabin so she had a quick shower, put on some clean clothes and went straight back out.

She spent an hour wondering around the museum and then went down to the bench at the end of the promenade to watch the children play on the swings. Raul phoned at ten.

"Is everything okay?"

"I'm just running some errands. I'll be back soon." She wasn't going to tell him about the bug. He would only try to talk her out of it.

"Could you do me a favour while you're out?"

"Depends what it is."

"Could you pick up a couple of bottles of perry? I'm cooking pork chops and morcilla for dinner. I thought a dry white perry would go nicely with it."

Margot rolled her eyes. He'd only just got up and already he was thinking about dinner? The pork chops did sound rather nice, though.

"Anything else?"

"No. That will do. Just be careful."

"I will."

Raymond texted at eleven-thirty – *its ready*

———

He was outside, serving tables, when Margot entered the square. He quickly finished seeing to the customer he was with and then nipped inside, gesturing for her to follow. Margot stood waiting while he saw to another customer, and then, when the coast was clear, went with him into the yard. Raymond closed the door quietly behind them and then drew a small plastic bag from the front pocket of his apron. Margot opened the bag without speaking; inside was a small white cube-shaped box. Inside that, the bugE was packaged up with the finesse of a product that had been designed in California. Raising her eyes, she found Raymond looking on in anticipation.

"These are legal, aren't they?"

"I think so."

"I wouldn't want your friend to get into any trouble."

"He won't."

Margot released the little black button from its clip and balanced it on the tip of her index finger. It was amazing that so much technology could be packed into such a small space. "What's its range?"

"It depends on the environment, but at least ten metres. You can adjust the sensitivity in the app."

"How do I get the app?"

He took out his phone. "Here's a link." He tapped and swiped. "Download it. The first time you open the app you'll have to pair it with the device. Then just follow the instructions onscreen."

"And what do I do when I want to listen?"

"Just open the app. It doesn't have to be live at the time. The files will stay on the server until you're ready to download."

"And my phone will download them automatically?"

Raymond nodded. "You won't miss a thing."

"How long will the battery last?"

"A few months."

A tingle of excitement passed through her. She wasn't entirely sure what she was going to do with it yet, but the possibilities seemed endless. She clamped an arm around his neck. "You're a genius. *Muah.*" She gave him a big wet kiss on the forehead. "I owe you one."

The poor boy blushed as red as a strawberry.

Back on the yacht, Raul was in the deck salon, polishing the table with a soft white cloth. "I was about to send out a search party."

"Sorry. I got waylaid." Margot kept her hand in her pocket, fingers wrapped around her little white box. When he looked at her, she smiled innocently.

They went below and Raul retreated to the galley where a pot was simmering. She was surprised to see that the table had already been laid for dinner.

"Did you get the perry?"

She clamped shut her eyes. "Damn!" She was such an idiot. "Sorry. I completely forgot."

Raul looked so disappointed that she instantly offered to go back. But he arrested her by the shoulders. "Sit down. I'll fetch it myself."

———

Margot sank deep into her cushions. Night-time had settled upon the harbour and she could happily have dozed for an hour, but she still felt bad about forgetting the perry so once they'd finished eating, she cleared up all the dirty crockery and carried it down to the dishwasher, leaving Raul to put his feet up. While she was down there, she rootled through his booze cupboard for something special: he had some rather nice

Spanish wines hiding at the back; a bottle of rum and toffee liqueur that was tempting; a scarlet Aperitivo she'd never even heard of. She sorted through the collection of brandies and smiled wickedly as she pulled out a bottle of Cognac Grande Champagne. He had such good taste it would be criminal to make him drink it alone.

Up on deck, Raul had lit candles and lined them up along the centre of the table. Margot placed the bottle between them and then re-made her nest of cushions. Raul, relaxing on the other side, heaved a sigh of deep satisfaction. "That was an excellent meal, even though I do say so myself."

Margot flopped down. "You're a very good cook. If I owned a boat like this I'd hire you as my chef."

"Thank you."

"Have you had any training?"

"No. I'm self-taught. But don't all farmers love their food?"

She raised her head to look across. "I had no idea you were a farmer."

"We used to have a cherry farm. My family owned three thousand trees in the valley de Jerte."

"That's an awful lot of cherries."

"We grew Picotas. The blossom in spring was beautiful. People would come from miles around."

Margot sat up to the table. She uncorked the bottle of cognac and poured out two good measures. She could picture him as a farmer; tending to his trees in the blazing Spanish sun, an old straw hat on his head. "Why did you sell it?"

"My daughters didn't want to take it on. I don't blame them. It's a hard life. And when my wife died things were never the same."

He seemed happy to linger in his thoughts so she regarded him for a while without speaking. She'd often imagined herself and Hugo running a business together: a quaint B&B by the seaside, a boutique hotel in the centre of a grand old European capital. They'd been the kind of couple who would have worked well together, though hospitality was unlikely to have suited Hugo. He'd been a policeman through and through. She had a sip of her cognac.

"Raul?"

"Mm-hmm."

"Do you think we could go sailing tomorrow?"

He slowly emerged from his reverie and moved into a seated position. When he looked over, his cynicism was clear to see.

"Suddenly you're keen to go sailing. I wonder why."

Margot regarded him from over the top of her glass. "You know why."

"Yes, and I like my life just the way it is, thank you very much."

"Oh, come on – where's your sense of adventure?"

"I've grown too old for adventure."

"Really? You're the one who's sailing solo around the world."

He opened his mouth to speak but failed to form any words. She had him there. He reached for his glass and had a good sip.

"It's not just about that house," Margot went on. "Someone's been watching me. It's making me really uncomfortable."

"You don't think you're reading too much into it?"

"No. It's Enzo. He's got someone keeping an eye on me. I'm sure of it. I can barely go into town without thinking I'm being followed."

Margot gave him a moment, but he still wasn't swayed. She shrugged nonchalantly, and then drank the rest of her brandy.

"If you don't take me I can always find someone who will."

He held her stare for a few long moments and then let out a weary sigh. He pinched shut his eyes and rubbed his face. "All right. You win. I'll sail you down the coast, we'll look at the drug dealer's house; I'll say, 'oh my, what a lovely big house he has there,' and then we'll come straight back. Understood?"

Margot made a movement with her head, vague enough to be mistaken for a nod.

25

For once Raul rose early and Margot had only just come out of the shower when she heard him clattering around in the galley. Outside it was barely light. She put on a striped sailor shirt and a pair of white jeans and went out.

"A sea dog never sets sail on an empty stomach," Raul said, shifting pans on the gimbal with seemingly half a dozen dishes on the go at once. "And in honour of your English roots, I'm cooking eggs, bacon, sausage, fried tomatoes, mushrooms, and —" the microwave pinged "—good old-fashioned English baked beans."

Margot puffed out her cheeks. "I hope those pills work."

He dismissed her pessimism with a wave of his hand. "You'll be fine. The weather forecast says light wind. At this rate we'll be rowing there."

After breakfast they prepared the boat for departure. Raul uncoupled the shore power cable and untied the mooring ropes while Margot made sure everything below deck was secure. He attached the Spanish flag to the pole at the stern and then rolled back the canopy on the deck salon. Two identical consoles stood side-by-side, each with a big chrome steering wheel, and Margot sat on the right and watched Raul tap away at a touchscreen. When the engine fired up, he carefully manoeuvred *Carpe Diem* out of its berth, the steering wheel in front of her turning in tandem with the one he was controlling. They approached the turret at the mouth of the harbour and then headed out into open water. A tingle went down Margot's spine as the sea opened up to them. There was something both noble and visceral about going to sea in a boat like this.

They motored out for a couple of kilometres before Raul killed the engine. The boat began to pitch and roll, now in the hands of the mighty body of water. When Margot looked back to shore, Argents had been reduced to a toy-town nestled at the base of the craggy green hills. Raul handed her a yachting cap with the word CREW embroidered on the front.

"You'll need to wear this."

Margot gave it a dubious look but did as he said. "I'm not calling you skipper."

"You'll be keel-hauled if you don't."

"What's my first job?"

"The first job is to raise the mainsail. Would you like to do that?"

Margot studied the mainmast, rising twenty metres into the air above them. It looked quite complicated with bundles of ropes strung left, right and centre but she nodded. "Shall I winch it up?"

Raul seemed surprised. "You can if you like."

Margot rubbed her hands together, ready for the challenge. She gingerly worked her way around to the base of the mast where a small handle was hooked up next to a winch. "Is this the one?"

"That is the winch for the mainsail, yes."

She bent over and inserted the handle. It took an awful lot of turns to move the sail just a small way, but she gripped the handle with both hands and gave it her all, determined not to be beaten.

"Have you ever been sailing before?" Raul called out from his console.

"Only once," Margot called back. She paused for a breather, wiping the sweat from her brow. "On a loch in Scotland. Though it wasn't actually a sailboat."

"Well, all I can say is you're doing a wonderful job."

"Thank you."

"I mean, you can carry on raising it from there, if you like, and I'm sure if you put your back into it you'll manage to get it all the way up to the top. Or—" He waited until she was looking at him and then made a show of reaching for a button at the base of his console. "I could just do this."

An electric motor started to whir, raising the sail effortlessly. Margot's jaw dropped. When she turned back to Raul she found him grinning mischievously. Eyes narrowed, she pulled the handle out of the winch and held it upright. "Next time I'll find somewhere else to insert this."

He laughed heartily.

Raul spun the wheel. The boom swung out and the boat leaned sharply, turning on a sixpence. High above them, the sail began to inflate and *Carpe Diem* transformed into a completely different beast. Soon they were clipping along at a brisk pace, the only sound the hiss and splash of the hull cutting smoothly through the waves. Raul smiled happily, seeming in his element, while Margot installed herself in the tandem seat and held tightly onto the grab rail.

"If you look at the screen in front of you," Raul said, "you can see readings for the wind direction, our current speed, the depth sounder."

"How fast can it go?"

"Fifteen knots on a good day."

At the moment they were only doing seven but the proximity of the water made it feel a whole lot faster.

"If the wind picks up I'll open the staysail. Let's put it on autopilot for now."

"Autopilot?" she queried.

He tapped some buttons on the touchscreen and then took his hands off the wheel. Margot was amazed when both steering wheels then moved under neither of their control, the computer keeping them on course. She gave him a peeved look.

"I thought you said sailing was difficult?"

"Someone has to be here to press all the buttons." He grinned. "Come on, let's go up to the bow."

He led her along the narrow walkway at the boat's edge, explaining the function of the various ropes and pulleys along the way. A stainless-steel guard wire was all that separated them from the sea, and with the boat leaning Margot had to concentrate hard to stay on her feet. Raul paused at the front of the cockpit and pointed to a pair of sun loungers at the base of the mast. "This is the sunbathing area," he said. "Clothes optional."

Margot rolled her eyes. "Keep dreaming."

The anchor controls were next, and then the guard wires came together at the prow. Raul gestured for her to stand out there – it seemed a bit theatrical but Margot wedged herself into the space.

"Isn't it wonderful?" Raul called out.

It certainly was invigorating. Leaning out, face tingling in the wind; if she didn't look sideways Margot could almost convince herself it was just her and the water and the salty sea air. Like she was flying. And the thrust of the powerful boat behind her, pushing them onwards, stirred something quite elemental. A couple of minutes may have passed before she found herself stepping back to Raul, her cheeks glowing, brimming with good feeling, the incident with the winch now completely forgotten.

———

The wind stiffened as they sailed past the lighthouse at the tip of Cap Béar. Their speed increased to ten knots so Raul switched off the autopilot and took back the controls. He pushed another button to unfurl the staysail and seconds later the boat was moving along at a cracking speed, riding the waves in choppier water. Margot remained fixed to her seat, watching the numbers on the screen creep up, while Raul stayed busy at the wheel. *Carpe Diem* had gone from a luxury cruiser to a full-blow racing yacht.

But the constant up and down motion soon made her feel queasy. Pitching and rolling, rising and falling; she closed her eyes and worked on keeping her head still. It wasn't long before she was re-tasting her breakfast. Raul gave her a concerned look.

"Are you okay?"

"I don't think those pills work."

"Why don't you go below? Have a lie down."

Margot opened her eyes and breathed in deeply through her nose. If she focussed on the horizon then hopefully she would be okay. "Is it much further?"

"It's not far. I'll move in closer to land. It should be a little calmer."

He pushed the button to furl the staysail and the boat slowed down. A few taps on the touchscreen altered their course and the boat turned towards the craggy red cliffs of the Côte Vermeille. Raul took them in until they were only a few hundred metres offshore and then tacked again, changing their bearing due south. They rounded a headland and the water became calmer. A little further on they sighted a cove and headed straight for it. The horrible rolling motion finally petered out.

"Feeling better?"

Margot took a deep breath. She nodded. "A little."

They entered the mouth of the cove and Margot took off her sunglasses to gaze up at the cliffs. A few small houses were perched on green strips right up at the top, but there was nothing that resembled the architectural marvel she'd seen on the internet.

"There's a whole series of coves running along this stretch," Raul said, busily tying up ropes. "I'm sure it was hiding in one of them."

He came back to the wheel and they continued under power of the engine. They hugged the coastline, never straying more than a couple of hundred metres offshore. Jagged cliffs and sandy coves unfolded before them, and there were few signs of life. Occasionally they spotted a house, nestled on a ledge or clinging to a promontory, but mostly it was uninhabited.

A few kilometres on they came to a cove that was so secluded they very nearly missed it. From its narrow mouth the cove opened up into a teardrop shape. And there, staring straight back at them from a sheer red cliff, was the structure they'd been looking for. Raul cut the engine and let the boat drift.

If anything, the house was more even impressive than it had appeared in the photos. It looked like a spaceship had made a mistake with its transport device and materialised halfway into the landmass. Trees shaded its uppermost levels, while garden terraces stepped down the slope like paddy fields on a hillside in Asia. The swimming pool was an amazing feat of engineering: a blue glass box jutting out the rockface. Margot couldn't help feeling envious as she took it all in.

"There," Raul said. "You've seen it. Can we go now?"

Margot finally drew her eyes away from the incredible spectacle. She didn't give him an answer but the look on her face was easily understood.

They'd drifted in a little too close for comfort so Raul fired up the engine and moved them further out to sea. He dropped anchor around a kilometre offshore and from there they still had a clear view of the house through the mouth of the cove. He fetched a pair of binoculars and handed them to Margot who sat down on the edge of the boat, feet dangling over the side. She tried to focus on the house, but with the boat moving so much it was difficult to keep it in view. When she finally got it sharp, the detail was quite good. She could see the huge walls of glass, the bronze ring sculptures, some sun loungers lined up on the terrace. A small private beach lay at the base of the cliff with a walkway on one side leading to an empty jetty. At first it appeared the beach was accessible only by sea, but when Margot looked more closely she saw that the rockface was punctuated by a series of wooden staircases. In places they disappeared behind rock, but they must have linked up to create a continuous route down from the house. And vice versa.

A swell came in, making the boat roll uncomfortably. The queasiness came back with a vengeance and Margot was forced to get up. She pushed the binoculars into Raul's chest. "Here. You have a look." She retreated into the shade of the deck salon where she buried her face in a cushion. Why hadn't the human body been designed for sea travel?

When she next looked up, Raul was leaning with his elbows on the cockpit roof, binoculars pointed at the cove.

"Is anything happening?"

"A rather splendid Cormorant is sunning itself on the rocks over there."

Margot exhaled. "I meant in the house."

"Oh, okay. Well, it's hard to tell. I mean, I see a lot of moving rock. Somewhere in the middle of it all is a big glass house."

Margot hissed in frustration and pushed her face back into the cushion. Raul peered down under the canopy.

"What?"

"Can you see any people?"

"Not right now, no."

He seemed indignant but looked again. After a few moments he sighed. "I see a garden, I see a swimming pool. The doors in the glass wall are open but I can't see anyone inside." He lowered the binoculars with another defeated sigh and this time came down into the deck salon. He sat close beside her. "Margot, what are we doing here?"

"It's called surveillance," she said, her voice still muffled by the cushion.

"You're making yourself ill and we're both getting grumpy. Is it really worth it?"

A shard of pain pierced her brain. Margot was tempted to give in. Perhaps she should just forget the whole idea, accept she wasn't cut out for this and go back home. But no. She wasn't a quitter. She took the cushion away from her face. "Keep watching. I'm going for a lie down."

After making her way gingerly down the companionway steps she hurried into her cabin. A green-gilled version of herself briefly flashed back from the bathroom mirror before a clench from her stomach shot bile into her throat. Face down in the toilet bowl, Margot longed for the moment she next laid foot on dry land.

———

Margot dozed on her bed. When she came to, the queasiness had abated and her headache eased. She actually felt hungry, and thirsty. It was eleven-forty-five and the sun was dazzling.

She went into the galley and dropped two slices of bread into the toaster. She downed half a glass of water from the jug. When the toast popped, she spread it thickly with butter and wolfed it down in less than two minutes. After washing her hands and face in cold water she went up on deck, feeling a little more human.

To his credit, Raul was still leaning on the canopy, watching the house through the binoculars. Margot donned her yachting cap and picked up his sunhat and then went to his side. "Have I missed anything?"

"You look better."

"Thank you."

She handed him his hat but he placed it on the canopy. He raised the binoculars back to his eyes.

"Some people have come out onto the terrace. A man and a woman."

"How old?"

"The woman is a brunette. Mid-forties. The man is shortish. Salt and pepper hair. Around the same age as myself but not nearly as handsome."

Margot rolled her eyes.

"What are they doing?"

"The woman is lying on a sun lounger. The man is sitting at a table at the opposite end of the terrace. They look like they're ignoring each other so I'm guessing they're husband and wife."

"Will you please take this seriously."

"I am taking this seriously." He passed her the binoculars. "I assume that's Enzo?"

Margot had a quick look. It was Enzo, all right. She nodded, and quickly handed them back. "Keep watching."

"Are we going to be doing this all day?"

"Until something interesting happens, yes."

"Wonderful," Raul said flatly and went back to the surveillance.

They didn't speak for a while and Margot drifted off into thought. She wondered whether to bring him on board with her plan – she hadn't yet said anything about her listening device – but then she wasn't decided on what she intended on doing with it yet. If she could somehow get into the house and plant it in the right place all they would have to do was sit back and listen. He would surely incriminate himself at some point.

"The man has just got up," Raul continued. "He's walking along the terrace to another set of doors. He's going inside. It looks like an office. He's—oh my!"

"What?"

"There's another woman in there. This one's blonde and *very* attractive. She's wearing a short yellow dress and her legs go on, and on, and—"

Margot thumped his arm. "You're not meant to be enjoying this."

Raul gave her a peeved look. "You told me to describe what I see."

"Stick to the facts."

"The facts? Okay, well, the facts are Enzo and the young woman are still in the office. No, wait a minute ... maybe I'm wrong. This one could be his wife."

"What do you mean? What's going on?"

"He and the woman in the yellow dress have just kissed on the lips. Now they're fooling around on the terrace. The other woman has seen them but she's doing nothing about it. You don't think—" He suddenly lowered the binoculars and gave Margot a confused look. "Maybe they're having a ménage à trois."

"Given what else he's been up to I'd say that's the least of his sins."

"You don't seem shocked."

"Why? Are you?"

Now it was Raul's turn to *tut*. "You French."

"I'm half English, remember?"

"Oh, yes. So how does that work – you sleep with two men and then blush over your cups of tea the next morning?"

Margot thumped his arm again. "You're meant to be watching the house."

"So I am. But will you please stop hitting me?"

They narrowed their eyes at each other before Raul went back to the surveillance.

He was quiet for a few minutes. The sun was hot on their backs and Margot got distracted when she gazed down into the water. It looked so cool and inviting she was tempted to jump in. There was surely some wonderful diving to be had around here.

"Oh, here we go." Raul shuffled his feet, growing excited.

Margot leaned in to his side. "Here we go what?"

"Enzo and the young woman are back in the office, only I don't think it's work they have in mind. They're smooching on the desk. Enzo's slipping his hands around her waist. They're kissing. Hot lips running up and down each other's necks. She reaches behind to unzip her dress. It slides to the floor. Now she's taking off her bra while Enzo hooks his thumbs into the sides of her—Oh, my." He tore his eyes away from the binoculars, apparently struck dumb.

"What?" Margot snapped in frustration. "Why have you stopped?"

Raul looked at her most solemnly. "Because I'm a gentleman, not a Peeping Tom."

Margot hissed. "Give them to me!"

She tore the binoculars out of his hand and leaned with her elbows on the cockpit roof. She focussed, located the woman on the sun lounger, swung across the terrace to the open doors. There was Enzo, and the woman in the yellow dress, but all they were doing was sitting in the office working at a desk.

What the ...? She turned sharply to Raul. "They're not doing anything!"

He smirked. "You seem disappointed."

Her blood boiled. "You swine!" This time she thumped him hard.

———

Margot stormed off down the companionway steps, closing the hatch doors firmly behind her. She stood in the salon for a few moments, grinding her teeth in anger. If there was one thing she hated it was being wound up. When she'd calmed down, she moved to the navigation console and punched the button to switch on the screen.

A few minutes passed before the hatch doors reopened. Raul's voice came down through the gap. "Are you still angry with me?"

"Yes!"

"Oh."

He didn't come down. When Margot twisted round, she could see him hovering at the top of the steps, looking sheepish.

"Would it help if I said I'm sorry?"

"No," she snapped. "It would help if you jumped in the sea."

"Oh."

Margot sighed. She couldn't stay mad at him for long.

"Don't worry. I'll be getting my own back."

Raul smiled.

Forgiven, he came down the steps and fetched the open bottle of wine from the fridge. He began to pour out two glasses, but Margot stayed his hand. She wanted to keep a clear head. He poured himself a large one instead and then joined her at the navigation table, peering at the screen from over her shoulder.

"So what's the plan now?"

"Shush. I'm thinking."

He gulped some wine. "Okay. Well, I don't wish to be rude, but could you think a little more quickly? If someone sees us hanging around out here they might get suspicious."

Margot propped her chin on her hand and studied their position on the chart. There was a whole series of coves stretching away to the south and from what she could see on the map the area was sparsely populated. She sat back, and folded her arms.

"Let's go a little further south and then come back after dark." She tilted her eyes to his. "Maybe they'll put on a better show for you when the lights go out."

————

If anything, the coast became even more idyllic – the cliffs more craggy, the beaches more isolated. They came upon a perfect half-moon bay with a wide sandy beach nestled at the base of a sheer wall of rock. Raul dropped anchor in water so calm and blue it could have come straight from a holiday brochure.

As the sun climbed higher in the sky the air grew hot. The cliffs trapped in the heat, making every metal surface painful to touch. After they'd eaten a lunch of sautéed tomatoes and fried olive bread, Raul declared it was time for a siesta and he took off his shirt and lay flat on his back on one of the loungers. "Coming to join me?"

Margot stayed under the cover of the canopy, for once preferring the shade. "No thanks."

She looked at his bare hairy chest as he settled himself down. He could do with shedding a few pounds though he didn't carry it too badly. "I hope you're wearing sunscreen."

"I'm Spanish. I was born under a baking sun."

"It won't stop you getting skin cancer."

"Said the lady who smokes like a chimney."

Touché. Margot put on her sunglasses and lay down on the bench instead. With her head propped on a cushion she could see past the guard wire to the empty beach. Tame white waves washed up the smooth golden sands. It was tempting to swim over, go for a little exploration, see if there was any way of climbing that cliff. In many respects life on board a yacht suited her perfectly – being able to just dive over the side and swim in open water whenever she liked.

She turned onto her other side and raised her head with an additional cushion, too keyed up to settle. There was a small opening at the front of the canopy and through it she could see Raul's upper torso, his oily brown skin sizzling in the heat. It was good of him to do all of this for her, especially as she'd not really given him anything in return. Margot reached across the table for her bottle of water.

"Are you still awake, old man?"

"Do I look like I'm still awake?"

She dripped some water onto her fingertips and flicked it at him. If he noticed he didn't show it. She dried her hand and then lit a cigarette.

"I bet when you planned your hedonistic retirement you never imagined you'd be doing something like this."

"Lying on a sun-lounger – yes. Spying on a gangster – no."

When the time came for her to retire Margot doubted she would be happy spending her days on a sun lounger. Her boredom threshold was far too low; she would have to have something to do. When so much in life had already passed her by she was determined to make the most of every day that remained. She took a long draw on her cigarette.

"Do you miss being a cherry farmer?"

Raul flexed his shoulders, adjusting his position. "I miss the harvest. And doing things on the farm with my wife. What about you – do you miss being a lawyer?"

"No."

He turned onto his front so that he could look back at her through the gap. "That was very succinct."

"I was a lawyer in Paris for five years but it was never my ambition. I wanted to be a judge, like my father."

"What made you change your mind?"

"I trained to be a barrister in London but I had a little setback."

"What kind of setback?"

Margot gazed out to sea. A small flock of gulls was diving down into the water, feeding on something that was floating on the surface. When she didn't answer Raul went on,

"How many years did you spend training?"

"Three years for the law degree, a year for the Bar course, another year doing pupillage."

He raised his eyebrows. "It must have been a pretty big setback to give up on all of that."

Margot inhaled a lungful of smoke and blew it slowly out through her nose. "I got pregnant halfway through my pupillage. But the baby died. A cot death."

She turned back to Raul and watched his face go through a series of emotions, from stunned surprise to aching sympathy. He slowly drew himself up into a seated position. His Adam's apple seemed to double in size when he tried to swallow. "Oh, Margot. That's terrible."

She nodded.

"Was it a boy or a girl?"

"A little boy. I was going to call him Ralph, after my grandfather."

For a little while neither of them spoke. Margot tried to keep herself anchored in the present, concentrate on things close by:

the table in front of her, the cushions beneath her, the sound of the water sloshing against the side of the hull, but her mind kept drifting. She stared into space as she thought back to those darker days. Some memories never lost their impact, no matter how deeply you tried to bury them.

"One morning I went over to his cot and there he was, just lying there. I picked him up, held him in my arms. The poor little thing looked so peaceful."

"Oh, Margot."

"It shouldn't have been such a surprise. He'd been poorly from the start. He was born at thirty-one weeks. He'd only been out of the hospital for fourteen days." Barely enough time to make a scratch on the world.

"I can't begin to imagine how that must have felt. For you or Hugo."

Margot's eyes snapped back to his. "Hugo wasn't the father."

"Sorry. I just assumed—"

She shook her head. "It was a boy in chambers. We were way too naïve. We thought we could have it all. I was going to have the baby, take a couple of months off work and then get on with my career. I thought I could take it all in my stride, but when the baby died everything changed."

"We all think we're invincible when we're young."

"I couldn't face going back to chambers so I hopped on a train and went travelling in Europe instead. I walked from town to town a lot of the time. And then I had a little breakdown. It wasn't pretty." She opened her ashtray and collected the ash from her cigarette. "But I picked myself up. And then, about a year later, I was in a club in Montmartre and there was Hugo, sitting at the bar with one of his colleagues." Margot smiled as she recalled the scene. "He had this twinkle in his eye when he looked at me."

"I saw your wedding photographs. He was a handsome man."

"It was love at first sight."

Raul smiled.

She paused to take another draw on her cigarette. "Two weeks after that my money ran out. My only option was to go back to England. But then we stood on the platform at the Gard du Nord and he asked me to marry him."

"How romantic."

"Two months after that I moved into his apartment. Hugo had inherited some money and already paid off his mortgage so I didn't need to work. Then ten years ago I re-trained in French law."

"So all that education didn't go to waste after all."

She shrugged. "I worked as a lawyer in Paris for a few years but it didn't work out. We were both so busy we rarely saw each other and that wasn't what I wanted. Perhaps I was a little too reliant on him. I never thought how I'd cope on my own."

Raul got up from the lounger and came to sit close by her side. His warm hand settled upon hers, and when she turned to look at him his pearly blue eyes were smiling fondly.

"You know, when I first saw you, I wouldn't have put you down as either a housewife or a lawyer."

Margot smiled, suddenly intrigued. She stubbed out her cigarette and closed the lid of her ashtray. "Really? So what did you have me down as?"

"An international jewel thief."

She tossed back her head and laughed. "You've got a wild imagination."

"Or a writer moving to the seaside in search of inspiration for her next great novel."

"I wish."

He was on a roll. "An interior designer, bored with her life in

Paris, looking to make a new start with a handsome widower who owns a sailboat."

She laughed again. In a previous life maybe. "Anything else?"

He squeezed her hand and looked more deeply into her eyes. "A long-distance swimmer who's lost her way?"

And just as abruptly her good humour evaporated. Margot pulled her hand free. How is it that some words can cut straight to the bone?

———

The hum and thwack of a powerboat moving at speed rudely disturbed the peace. Margot looked up from the bench where she'd been dozing and scanned out to sea. The boat was a few kilometres out, moving in an arcing trajectory, seemingly on course to join them in the bay. She alerted Raul who was snoozing on the sun lounger and then slid her feet into her sandals. The boat slowed as it neared the shore and promptly changed course, causing a wake to spread out. When the waves reached the bay, *Carpe Diem* rocked gently from side to side. Margot lowered herself in the seat, not wanting to be seen, but the powerboat didn't seem interested and headed north at a more modest pace.

The sun disappeared behind some clouds so Raul put on his shirt and went below to make something to eat. While he was busy doing that, Margot went for a shower. On the way back, she nipped through the door opposite her cabin and had another look at the wetsuits. They were all very modern, and there was a nice sleeveless one that looked like it would fit. She held it up against herself, but then Raul called her name so she quickly went out.

They ate a goat cheese salad with fig and arugula and by the time they'd finished darkness was creeping in. An hour later the sun had completely gone down so they retraced their route back to the cove. Raul turned out all the lights and they motored cautiously through the darkness, the landmass to their left now reduced to a series of shifting grey shapes. As they neared the entrance to Enzo's cove Raul altered course and steered them further out to sea. Bright lights shone out from the house, making it look even more like a spaceship.

They dropped anchor around fifteen hundred metres offshore, the sea around them a featureless black void.

"I hope we're not in any shipping lanes," Margot said, for some reason feeling the need to lower her voice. On the horizon, beacons from distant ships were the only lights to prick the darkness.

"Hopefully they'll honk before they hit us."

The swell had increased in the past few hours and *Carpe Diem* pitched and rolled uncomfortably. Raul fetched the binoculars and looked out from his seat at the console, but with the boat moving so much he struggled to keep a steady view.

"Can you see anything?" Margot asked eagerly.

He tutted. "Not really. There's a light on by the jetty. And a boat moored up. I think it's that powerboat we saw earlier."

"Couldn't we move a bit closer?"

"It's too risky. If anyone sees us with our lights out they'll know we're up to no good." He tore the binoculars away from his eyes and blinked deeply. "Now it's making *me* feel sick."

Margot sighed in frustration. "This is no good."

"Just give me a minute."

She shook her head. "No. We need to get closer."

"It's too dangerous."

"Then I'll just have to swim."

"What?"

Margot swallowed. "I'm going to swim over to the house."

Raul flinched. "Have you lost your mind?"

"It's not that far. And you've got some wetsuits."

He seemed at a loss. "And what are you going to do when you get there?"

Margot hesitated, her thoughts beginning to race. "Plant a listening device in his office."

"A *listening* device. You mean a bug?"

She nodded.

Raul scoffed. "And how will you get it into his office – sneak in and hope no one notices?"

"Pretty much."

He stepped away from the console and clapped a hand to his forehead, trying to keep a hold on his emotions. "Margot, this is insane."

"No it's not. I've thought it all through."

"You can't keep putting yourself in danger like this."

"That's for me to decide."

He squared up to her and took hold of her by the shoulders. "Look. I get why you're angry. Someone killed your husband, took away the life you loved, and now you want revenge. But it wasn't Enzo who killed Hugo."

"That's not what this is about?"

"Isn't it?"

Margot shook herself free. "You don't understand me at all."

Raul's face hardened. "So this has been your plan all along, I take it?"

"More or less."

"And you waited until now to tell me?"

"You wouldn't have brought me otherwise."

"Well, thank you for that vote of confidence."

He turned away. Margot felt bad for hurting his feelings but she wasn't backing down. The silence grew. When it turned into something uncomfortable she turned on her heel and went below.

————

It was too risky to switch on a light so Margot squeezed herself into the wetsuit by the light of a torch. It fit as snugly as she'd imagined. She packed her float bag with the bug, a penlight, a bottle of water and a quick-dry towel and then went back up. It was a relief to see that Raul had gone back to the surveillance, and the moment he noticed her he put down the binoculars and looked at her with calmer eyes.

"I'm sorry," he said. "What I said, that was out of line."

Margot nodded. "And I'm sorry I didn't tell you sooner." She put on her bathing cap and tucked in her hair.

"You're sure you won't reconsider?"

Margot shook her head. "I've made up my mind. I'll swim over to the beach and then hide in the garden until they've gone to bed."

"How will you get in?"

"I was married to a policeman for twenty years. I know a few tricks."

"The powerboat left a few minutes ago. I couldn't see who was onboard."

"Okay."

"If there's any sign of trouble you get the hell out of there."

"Don't worry. I will."

"I'll keep an eye on you through the binoculars. As soon as I see you heading back I'll throw out a buoy."

"Good thinking."

She handed him her phone. "Could you look after this for me, please? The bug sends files to an app and I don't want to risk losing it."

Raul put it in his pocket. "It will be safe with me."

"Right." She was all set to go but delayed a few moments. She didn't like leaving with the thought he might still be angry with her.

"At least wait a little longer," he said. "It's barely ten o'clock. Gangsters never go to bed before midnight."

Margot smiled. "Is that a fact?"

"It's the first thing they teach you at police academy."

He was so sweet. But Margot straightened her back, bucking herself up. "The moon will be up at eleven-o-three. I need to go now."

"You've accounted for everything."

"Perfect planning and all that. Plus, the swim will take me half an hour." She put on her goggles and nose cap. "Wish me luck."

He blew her a kiss.

She adjusted the strap on her float bag and went to the steps at the stern.

"Oh, Margot."

She looked back. "Yes?"

"Take care."

"I will."

Margot loosened her shoulders, drew in a deep breath, and then jumped soundlessly into the water.

26

Despite her show of bravado, Margot tensed rigid as her body rushed down through the water. She'd never swum in the sea at night and panic seized her the moment she resurfaced. She swam around to the bow of *Carpe Diem* and held onto the anchor chain for a while, regaining her bearings. In daytime it would have been an easy enough task, but the enveloping darkness was really quite disorientating. She focussed on the lights from Enzo's house while she tried to steady her breathing. When her confidence came back, she took a deep breath and ducked under. She thought she heard Raul call out, but his words were lost in bubbles as she quickly got into her stroke.

But it was difficult to find a rhythm. The sea was a roiling dark monster, fighting her for every stroke, and the current seemed determined to push her off course. After ten minutes, Margot paused to tread water. Looking back, she was surprised to find that *Carpe Diem* had already been lost in the dark. Even if she wanted to go back it was too late now. In the opposite direction the coast was a band of blurry grey shapes, but the bright lights of the house at least gave her a target to aim for. She settled her nerves, took control of her breathing, and then got back into her stroke.

Slowly but surely the mouth of the cove came closer. Once past the cliffs, the water became calmer and her target seemed easily within reach. At the first touch of sand, Margot hauled herself to her feet and trundled up to the top of the beach, breathing in relief.

She tore off her goggles and bathing cap and sat down on the soft wet sand. The cove was pitch black and there was nothing to indicate the presence of *Carpe Diem*. At least that meant they wouldn't have been seen from the house. Margot raised a hand to make an A-okay sign, just in case Raul was watching through the binoculars.

She tilted her head to the cliff, looming high above her. From this angle, nothing of the house could be seen other than a cloud of hazy white light reaching out from the terrace. She sucked thirstily from her water bottle and then dried her face with the towel. With the penlight gripped between her front teeth, she carefully extracted the bug from its box and then tucked it safely into a pocket. After one last look out to sea, Margot set off.

A short wooden ladder led to a walkway. Wide timber boards had been fixed to the rock with pitons and steel wire with the left-hand route leading straight to the jetty. But Margot turned right and followed the walkway to the first of the wooden staircases. Miniature lanterns on bendy poles lit the way and she ascended the first few flights at speed, her bare footsteps silent on the smooth wooden treads. The staircases twisted and turned around crags in the rockface making it impossible to see more than a few metres ahead. She kept her head cranked upwards, on the lookout for trouble as she turned every corner. As fatigue crept in her pace slowed, but she reminded herself there was no need to rush.

The staircases went on and on. She'd scaled at least ten individual flights before she reached the first of the garden levels, the sizzle of the sea now a long way below. An immaculate rectangular lawn stretched out before her, bounded by ornate green shrubs, and Margot's feet sank into cool soft grass as she crossed to the next set of steps. Ten metres up, the air was glowing with white light spilling out from the terrace. Away to one side, a corner of the swimming pool jutted out into mid-air, a delicate glass box filled with so much water it boggled her mind. She ascended another flight of steps, these ones made out of stone, and then followed a short path to a viewpoint where a summer house crowned a small promontory. From there she could see the upper levels of the house. If anything, it seemed even larger now than it had from at sea.

Margot checked the time. It was 22:46. Her pulse was drumming in her ears, but she was confident no one was nearby. From the summer house, a path weaved through a shrubbery and then into the main part of the garden where the row of bronze rings was situated. Another rectangular lawn hosted a line of sun loungers, but the path led her up the side of the property and into another shrubbery, this one packed with semi-tropical plants, many of them taller than she was. A woody slope rose up to a bank of tall trees that extended around the front of the property. When the path finally emerged from the bushes, Margot found herself on the edge of the terrace, looking along its length to the swimming pool. Lights were on, but there were no signs of life.

She hunkered down in the cover of the shrubs. Most of the rear of the house was visible from here, but she spotted no cameras, counted only two lights on in rooms higher up. One set of doors was still open and through it she could see into the kitchen. Some low-level lights were on in there, but there didn't appear to be anyone around. With the door wide open and the office almost in sight, Margot was tempted to sneak straight in, but she quickly dismissed that thought. It was far too risky.

Instead, she moved some of the foliage out of her way and sat down on a smooth flat rock, settling herself in for a wait.

———

One by one lights blinked off around the property. At 23:03, a man came into the kitchen, and although the interior was dimly-lit, the figure Margot saw was too tall to be Enzo. The glass doors started to slide shut and blinds came down, turning the wall to black. When the pool lights went out, all that remained was the row of tiny lanterns running along the edge of the terrace. Margot waited fifteen more minutes, and then came out from her hiding place.

She felt like an actor taking to the stage as she trod quietly across the terrace. She imagined Raul watching the performance from the comfort of the yacht, cheering her on. It looked like several sets of doors were integrated into the glass wall, but the joints were so seamless there was no obvious way of opening them from outside. When she reached the door to the office there was nothing resembling a handle.

The end of the terrace was in line with the side of the house and when Margot turned the corner she found yet more steps leading up. This elevation was clad in metal, and with no windows in sight she risked turning on her penlight. It revealed one small window, quite high up, and her heart gave a flutter of excitement when she saw that it was open. It was too high to reach unaided, but the edge of a planter made a perfect step up. She hooked her fingers onto the frame, and with one determined heave managed to feed her head through. The rest of her body followed suit and Margot dropped down onto a tiled floor.

She paused, hunkered down. She was in some kind of utility

room. An array of electrical boxes covered one wall, complete with a huge bank of controls for the lighting. On the opposite side, Margot's penlight picked out two large washing machines, an industrial sized dryer, a huge chest freezer. It was tempting to have a peek inside – what would a man like Enzo keep in his freezer? – but she kept her mind on the job in hand.

The room had only one door. Easing it open she found a short blank corridor. She stepped out, carefully closed the door behind her, and then moved to the nearest corner. Now she was in the stairwell – one flight leading up, another going down. If she'd visualised the layout of the house correctly then Enzo's office would be down one level and around to her left so she took the stairs down. It landed on a balcony from where a handrail separated her from the vaulted ceiling of the living room. Beyond it, the wall of glass was a magnificent thing to behold.

Margot paused again. If anyone found her here like this there would be no way out, no phoning Pierre, no way to alert Raul, not even Captain Bouchard to intervene. But she wasn't turning back. She checked for cameras and alarm sensors – there didn't appear to be any. Either they were very well concealed or Enzo was confident his reputation alone was enough to deter potential intruders.

She crept down to the living area. Nightlights built into the skirting gave her enough light to see by so she switched off her penlight. A trio of huge white sofas occupied the main space with a dining table off to the right, the kitchen some distance beyond. To her left was a single door which she assumed lead to the office. Margot was so tense she was afraid her lungs might seize, but she held her nerve and crossed to the office door. Pausing with a hand on the handle, she cast one last look back, and then quietly went in.

She left the door open. In contrast to the modern style of the rest of the house, the furniture in the office belonged to an earlier century – an antique partners' desk sat squarely in the centre while oak bookcases dominated two of the four walls. An old clock on the shelf ticked noisily. She might have been entering a bank manager's office, or a gentleman's study – not what she'd imagined for the lair of a crime boss. Margot paused at the edge of the desk, wondering what things had gone on in this room, what decisions made, what deals done. Strands of carpet crept between her bare toes as she rounded the desk and looked down at the overstuffed leather armchair. Was this where he'd sat when he'd given the order to firebomb her house? Heat rose to her cheeks when she spotted the lighter on his desk. How easy it would be to set fire to a piece of paper, casually drop it on the floor, retreat to a safe distance and watch this place burn down. Destroy something that was precious to him.

Margot refocussed. That's not what she was here for. Despite what Raul had said, this was about justice not revenge.

She searched for a place to hide the bug. A cigar box on the desk, a pot plant in the corner ... a dozen locations immediately suggested themselves. It had to be close enough to the desk to pick up the sound of his voice but not too close that it was likely to be found. She got down on her knees to look under the desk, and then somewhere nearby a door opened.

Margot looked up so abruptly her head caught the underside of the drawer. Pain shot through her skull but she gritted her teeth and choked any sound.

Someone was coming down the stairs. Quickly moving footsteps, heavy enough to suggest they belonged to a man. Margot got to her feet and hid behind the open door.

In contrast to the urgency with which they'd descended the stairs whoever it was now appeared to be in no hurry. Quiet footsteps approached from the direction of the living room. Margot's heart was beating so wildly she feared the sound would give her away, but she held her breath and didn't make a sound. Through the gap between the door and the frame she watched a man move cautiously into the room. She got ready to slam the door in his face, make a dash for the terrace, go back down the wooden staircases and hurl herself into the sea.

But the man didn't appear to have noticed her. He remained stationary on the other side of the door, little more than five centimetres of timber separating them. Margot could hardly believe he couldn't sense she was there. It wasn't Enzo; when her eyes switched focus to a shadow on the wall she had the strongest suspicion it was Paolo.

He sniffed the air. Any moment now he was sure to snatch back the door and confront her. Margot considered striking first, lash out while she had the element of surprise, but after a few more seconds Paolo turned on his heel and retreated into the living room. Receding footsteps sounded on the stairs.

Margot blinked. It was hard to believe she'd got away with it, but now she needed to get out. She peeled some sticky tape from the dispenser, formed it into a loop, and then stuck the bugE to the underside of the desk. A delicate close of the door, and then she quietly made her escape.

————

Fighting the urge to look back, Margot crossed the terrace with her head down. No alarms had gone off; no lights come on. She raced through the shrubbery and ran across the lawn, face glistening with sweat. She bolted down the staircases, three steps at a time, amazed she didn't trip up. It seemed too good to be true, but the farther she got from the house the more she allowed herself to believe it. By the time she reached the beach she was mildly euphoric.

Even so, she didn't relax. She grabbed her bag from behind

the rock and quickly put on her cap and goggles. She secured the float bag while she was wading into the water, and after one final glance back, threw herself onto the waves.

Boosted by adrenaline, Margot swam the first two hundred metres in next to no time. As the elation wore off and fatigue crept in, she paused to tread water, the black sea rolling around her. The house had been reduced to a blur in her steamed-up goggles, but she was certain no one had come after her. In her haste to get away, however, she'd neglected to check what time she'd left the beach. The journey in had taken her thirty-eight minutes; when she lifted her goggles to look at her watch the time was 23:56. She must have been swimming for at least twenty minutes, but there was no sign of a buoy. She pivoted, checking her orientation, making sure the house was still directly behind her. Satisfied she was on the right course, she swam on for another fifteen minutes. Still there was no sign of a buoy.

Margot paused again. She looked all around, twisting her body through a full 360. Where was the boat? All that surrounded her was dark open sea.

"Raul!" she called out.

A shudder passed through her. She hadn't veered off course.

The boat had gone.

And so had Raul.

27

A *beep-beep* pulled Enzo from a light sleep. Hand roving the bedside table, he located the phone and brought the screen right up to his face.

Message from Mutt: need 2cu.

He closed his eyes and groaned. It was almost one a.m., and he needed his beauty sleep.

In the bed on the other side of the room, Marielle made some grunting sounds but didn't wake up.

Mutt was waiting just outside the door.

"What?" Enzo whisper-snapped.

"Sorry, Boss. That yacht's just turned up. The one we were watching in Argents."

"Turned up where?"

"Outside the cove. It was just anchored there, lights out. Mule spotted it from the powerboat."

Enzo fixed him with a baffled frown. "What the hell were they up to?"

Mutt shrugged.

"How long have they been out there?" He turned to look out to sea but there were no windows in this part of the corridor.

"We don't know. Mule's taken it down to Nazaire. He wants you to call him."

Enzo screwed shut his eyes, finding this hard to get his head around. "Was that woman on board?"

"He didn't say."

Jesus! Why was she still interfering? Had she got a death wish or something?

"All right." He calmed down and then went downstairs to make the call on an encrypted phone. He raised the blind on his office window while he waited for an answer. If she'd been out there spying on him she was going to regret it. Mule picked up.

"Boss?"

"What's happening?"

"I've got that guy from the yacht. I've put him in the Old Customs House, but what do you want me to do with him?"

"Was anyone with him?"

"No. But both cabins had been slept in."

"So where the hell is she?"

"The guy won't say."

Enzo clenched his fist. "Then persuade him, for god's sake."

"Okay."

He almost tapped the call end button but quickly had second thoughts. "Wait a minute. Don't do anything yet. I'll come down and deal with it myself."

Enzo took the elevator up to the second level and strode down the corridor to Paolo's room. He knocked lightly, and opened it before receiving an answer. The lights were out, but his brother was still up, sitting at the window, still in his outdoor clothes. Enzo frowned.

"You okay?"

Paolo slowly turned his head. "Just thinking."

Enzo nodded, though was none the wiser.

"Listen. I've got a job for you. Meet me down in the hall in five minutes."

———

The car wound its way along the narrow coastal road. In the back seat, Enzo and Paolo lurched from side to side as Mutt swung the Mercedes through a series of tight bends. The lummox always drove like his favourite fast-food joint was about to close.

"Hey, Mutt, slow down, will you? You're making my brother get car sick."

Paolo remained slumped in the seat beside him, hands pushed into his coat pockets. He'd not said a word in the five minutes since they'd left the house, and Enzo hadn't tried to make smalltalk. Marielle's words echoed inside his head: *He hates you and everything you represent* ... Maybe that was true, but he could be turned. Everyone could. All you had to do was find the right buttons to press.

"Where're going?" Paolo finally piped up.

"Not far."

Enzo looked at the side of his brother's face and gave him a playful nudge. "What do you think of Crystal?"

Paolo shrugged.

"You couldn't take your eyes off her, you dog."

"You get what you pay for, I suppose."

Enzo widened his eyes. "You think I pay her?"

"I doubt she's attracted by your looks."

"I pay her as a PA, yes. Everything else comes of her own volition."

Paolo smirked, slowly nodding his head, and then turned to look out the window. "Right."

"It's true. And do you want to know why?"

"I'm sure you'll tell me."

"Women are attracted to power, not looks. I could have a dozen like her every day of the week if I wanted to and it wouldn't cost me a bean. And so could you."

Paolo didn't turn away from the window, but Enzo sensed him tense up. It was just a matter of planting the right seeds, getting him thinking, leading him in the right direction.

"Everything in life is about power," Enzo went on. "That's what we all want, isn't it? The ability to make other people do things they otherwise wouldn't. Work for you, have sex with you, be so afraid of you that all you have to do is click your fingers and they'll come running."

"You brought me out here to talk philosophy?"

"No. I brought you out here to give you a taste of power. Once you've felt it you won't want to go back."

The car slowed down as they came into Nazaire. Mutt turned off the main drag and took the access road into the harbour. He steered his way between potholes, and pulled up in front a chain strung between bollards. Mutt got out to unhook it, and then drove up to a pair of tall wooden gates where a big white sign read: CONDEMENED – KEEP OUT. The Old Customs House was a three-storey lump that looked like it had been built to withstand a nuclear blast. Enzo had bought it a while back with the intention of turning it into swanky apartments, but in the past few years the town had gone steadily downhill. The harbour was too shallow to accommodate the bigger ships, and the town had got bypassed in favour of the more developed ports to the north and south. It was little more than a ghost-town these days, a curio for those taking the old road down to Spain, but it did have its uses.

Mutt got out to open the gates and then drove into a cobbled courtyard. When he turned off the ignition, the air was so quiet you could have heard a mouse sneeze.

"Hey, Mutt – give us a minute."

For the third time the big lummox hauled his weary ass up out of the driver's seat.

Enzo waited for the door to shut and then lit a cigar. He lowered the window a touch and emptied his lungs before turning to face his brother. "Remember that kid in school who used to bully you?"

Paolo narrowed his eyes.

"The lanky one with the greasy hair," Enzo prompted.

"What about him?"

"Remember how I taught him a lesson?"

"You smashed his hand with a hammer. Broke every bone up to his wrist."

Enzo chuckled. It had been thirty-five years but he remembered it clearly: the snot running down the kid's face, the terror in his eyes. He'd been nine years old at the time, maybe ten. Ended up so traumatised people thought he'd gone mute. "Got me out of school, though, didn't it?'

Paolo wasn't amused. Enzo sucked his cigar while he went on chuckling to himself. Truth was he liked hurting people, got a kick out of it. Cigarette burns were probably his favourite. You could have someone binning their granny with a few well-placed stubs on the inside of the forearm. He'd lied. It wasn't just about power. But that was a confession that belonged to another day.

"The point is, if I hadn't taught him a lesson he'd still be pushing you around right now, wouldn't he? Instead, he was scared of you. You were the one with power. All you had to do was whisper a few choice words in his ear and he'd have dropped his pants in front of the whole class. That's a good feeling to have, don't you think?"

Paolo sighed wearily. "Is this going anywhere?"

Enzo gave him a long hard look. "Inside that building is

someone who needs to be taught a lesson. You and I are the ones who are going to do that."

"What's he done?"

"He's been spying on me. Sticking his nose where it doesn't belong."

Enzo rolled the cigar between his fingertips, studying his brother's reaction. The cool detachment had left him and he was looking a little uncomfortable. Violence had never come naturally to Paolo. He could hit out in anger and frustration, but not sit down and calmly pull the wings off a fly. It was time he learned.

"There'll be no comeback," Enzo went on. "We can do whatever we want to him in there, no one'll hear. But now you're in with me, you'll need to do everything I say. You got that?"

Paolo got the seriousness in his tone. He nodded.

"Good." Enzo raised a fist; Paolo reluctantly bumped it.

The three men crossed the moonlit courtyard, shoes clicking on cobbles. Mutt unlocked the back door and they went in through a storeroom, then a kitchen, then a hall. The windows were shuttered so they switched on the light and breathed in air that felt like it hadn't seen the inside of a lung in fifty years. Stacks of dusty old furniture had been pushed to the walls; cobwebs the size of arachnid cities smothered the once-grand light fittings. Mutt halted next to a door under the stairs and took a single large key from his pocket. He opened it, reached inside to flick on the lights, and then stood aside to let Enzo and Paolo go first.

A steep narrow staircase led down to the basement. The air at the bottom must have been five degrees cooler and was laden with a dampness that betrayed their proximity to the sea. Puddles filled the sunken patches in the old stone flags. This room was also crowded with packing crates, but in the centre of it all was a cleared space where a man sat on a chair, arms tied behind his back, mouth sealed with tape.

The three men took up their positions. The man's eyes widened to circles and he let out a whimper like a dog that had just disgraced itself. A bruise on his forehead had started to swell.

"We found his ID on the yacht," Mutt said. "His name's Raul Pérez."

"Spanish?"

"That's what it says on his passport."

Enzo nodded thoughtfully. That kid he'd beaten up at school had been Spanish. Strange how these things came around.

"You brought the hammer?"

Mutt reached into his coat.

"Okay. Let's see what else he can tell us."

Enzo took off his jacket and carefully rolled up his shirt-sleeves. He didn't want the silk to get spoiled.

28

Margot turned in the water, scanning around desperately. Where on earth had he gone? He wouldn't have abandoned her, surely. She suddenly felt very alone.

"Raul!" she cried out, even though she was now certain no one was there to hear.

The moon was rising. Clouds on the horizon filtered its light to a pale milky glow spreading out across the empty sea. Margot could feel the energy seeping out of her, her feet starting to cramp, her hands gnarling up. She couldn't stay out much longer. Unless Raul materialised soon she would have to swim back to the beach, though she wasn't sure she could manage another one-and-a-half k, not on top of everything she'd already been through. She carried on treading water, yearning to see *Carpe Diem* appear over the next batch of waves, just like when she'd first encountered it. But it soon became obvious she was waiting in vain. Squealing in frustration, Margot set off back to shore.

By some small miracle she made it. She trudged up the wet sand, legs as heavy as tree trunks, and dropped down next to the very same rock. She snapped off her bathing cap, hardly believing what had happened. Had she misjudged him? She thought back over the things they'd said in the past few days and tried to imagine a reason why he might have done this. She remembered how pissed off he'd been about the danger she was putting herself in, the risks she was taking, but it was hardly a reason to abandon her. Margot shook her head, refusing to believe it. There had to be another explanation.

Whatever the reason, it was imperative she find the yacht. Her phone was still onboard, and without it she would have no way of listening to the bugE. But in the midst of her despair came an idea: if she could access a computer she could use the find-my-phone app. The idea came laced with trepidation, however. Margot tilted her head to look up at the cliff. The nearest computer was up there, in Enzo's office.

———

Margot ascended the staircases more slowly this time, feeling the strain on every step. The moon had come out from behind the clouds and she barely needed the light from the lanterns. She crossed the lawn and followed the path through the shrubbery, the tangled branches now an eerie sight. Again, she paused on the edge of the terrace, struck by a feeling of déjà vu. A light was on in the office. The time was 01:12.

Margot crouched. From this angle she couldn't quite see in. A window higher up was also lit and the hum of an extractor fan was coming from somewhere. A shadow moved inside; she thought she saw someone hurry down a staircase. Then lights went on in the trees behind her and Margot turned her head to hear a car starting around the front of the house. Quickly, she scrambled up the wooded slope. A fence barred the way, but it wasn't high and she easily climbed over. Dropping down onto a footpath she immediately took cover in some bushes. She found herself on the edge of a gravel drive, ten metres away from the front porch where a familiar black Mercedes was parked.

A few minutes passed before Enzo and Paolo came out of the house, stooping to get into the back of the car. A light went on at the top of the drive, and through the bushes Margot could see an electric gate opening. She ducked as the car drove by, and then watched it loop up and go out onto the road. When the gates closed behind it everything went quiet.

Her mind raced. It was 01:30. There were bound to be others in the house, but this was her chance. She climbed back over the fence, eased her way down the wooded slope, and then ran across the terrace.

The utility room window was just as she'd left it. Two minutes later Margot was sneaking into Enzo's office for the second time that night. She switched on his computer without sitting down and logged into her Cloud account. The find-my-phone app was on a go-slow and it seemed to take forever to settle upon a location, but finally a little red circle appeared. Margot looked closely at the screen. According to the map, her phone was in the harbour at Nazaire, five kilometres away. What on earth was he doing there?

She logged out, deleted the entry from the browser history, and then switched off the computer. After checking to make sure everything was exactly as she'd found it, Margot quietly left the office.

She paused in the utility room, a basket of clean laundry catching her eye. If she was going to Nazaire on foot she would need some clothes. She pulled out a thin white jacket that looked like it would fit. Digging down further she found a pair of wide-leg trousers also in her size (when she looked at the label she was delighted to see they were both Isabel Marant. Far too tempting). She took off her wetsuit and stuffed it into a bag, and then put on the clothes and slipped on a pair of pumps she found on the shelf below.

An escape from the front door was far too risky so she retraced her route back to the terrace. She scrambled up the wooded slope, climbed the fence, took a shortcut over a lawn to reach the electric gates. A big green button let her out onto the road, and then all that lay ahead of her was a ribbon of empty black tarmac. Margot stashed the bag with the wetsuit behind a rock and then set off in the direction of Nazaire.

The road was steep in places, rising and falling as it wound its way along the coast. She jogged the downhill sections, dug in hard when the gradient turned uphill. The only time she had to pause was on the final stretch where the road rounded a promontory before snaking down into the harbour. Sweating and fatigued, Margot sat down on a rock. Perhaps two dozen buildings made up the settlement, the streets so dark and empty it looked like a plague had hit. A motley assortment of boats was moored up in the harbour, but she was too far away to tell if *Carpe Diem* was amongst them.

Margot completed the final stretch at a more leisurely pace. She followed the access road into the harbour and set off along the jetty. A long line of boats stretched out along the boardwalk, and her heart rose in relief when she spotted *Carpe Diem* right at the end, its smooth white lines contrasting sharply with the tatty old fishing boats.

But something was not right. Her sixth sense urged caution as she approached the stern. The mooring ropes were untidily secured as if they'd been done in a hurry. Margot switched on her penlight as she silently climbed aboard. Cushions were scattered across the floor in the deck salon; the lid on the under-seat storage locker had been opened. The doors to the companionway were ajar, and when Margot moved closer she saw that the wood on one side was splintered, the lock hanging loose.

She peered down through the hatch, scanning with her penlight.

"Raul?"

No sound came back.

Margot descended through the companionway, dreading what she was about to find. A flick of the light-switch confirmed her worst fears. Books and cushions were strewn across the floor, the wall cupboards emptied. A bottle had been smashed on the table, the beautiful smooth oak horribly scratched. The boat felt like its soul had been torn out. Margot moved quickly through to the guest suite and switched on the light – her eyes went straight to the bedside cabinet where the drawer had been upended. She dropped to her knees and searched for her phone, but it wasn't there. She rocked back onto her haunches and closed her eyes in disbelief. What on earth had gone on here?

The scene inside Raul's cabin was even worse: they'd smashed his guitar, torn down his photos, slashed the bed linen. His beautiful boat was trashed, and it was all her fault. Margot wandered back into the salon, her mind awhirl. She had to call the police, own up to what she'd done, accept the consequences even though this time it would be more than just a slap on the wrist. She pinched shut her eyes and forced herself to think. She needed to calm down, pull together some kind of plan.

Her mouth was horribly dry so she grabbed a bottle of water from the fridge and gulped half of it down. Her thoughts began to clear. This was where her Cloud account had pinpointed her phone; there could be no mistake. And it had taken her less than an hour to get here from Enzo's office so the phone can't have been gone long. A thought pinged into her brain – she hadn't checked the safe.

She snapped a fingernail in her haste to lift up the seat on the navigator's chair, punched in the combination without even thinking. 1066. Would he have had time to hide it? The green light came on and she snatched open the door, and breathed in relief when she saw her phone.

Margot switched it on and opened the bugE app. Surprisingly, two notifications popped up. She tapped on the download button and held the phone to her ear: the first recording was timecoded at 01:08, the second at 01:38. The second file was five seconds long and consisted of some muffled sounds, a door being opened, taps on a keyboard ... she groaned when she realised it was a recording of herself entering the office just a little while ago. The other recording was Enzo: a one-sided conversation, presumably speaking on the phone, but it revealed nothing.

A noise came from outside. Cocking an ear, Margot heard the sound of footsteps on the boardwalk. Her eyes darted left and right; realising she'd got all the lights switched on she cursed. The yacht must have been standing out like a flare. She scurried around, flicking every switch, and then moved through the darkness to poke her head up through the companionway. And there she froze.

A man was approaching purposefully along the jetty.

29

The man spotted her and immediately broke into a run. Margot shot up the companionway and jumped onto one of the console seats. Her fingertips scanned the controls, desperately trying to bring life to the screen, but the slot where the ignition key should have been was empty. She thumped the console in frustration. Snatching a glance over her shoulder, she saw that the man was now only twenty metres away. There was only one option – swim for it.

Margot ran for the bow. Even fully clothed she was confident she could outswim him, but as she crossed the deck she slipped on a skylight and fell heavily onto her side, catching her hip on something hard. Despite the pain, she quickly got back on her feet. She dashed for the guard wire, preparing to jump straight in, but the man was closing fast. He lunged for her leg and caught hold of an ankle, and they both went down. Margot flipped onto her back and kicked him hard in the face with the heel of her foot. As she scrambled away she dared to believe she might make it, but then something hard and heavy came crashing down on the back of her head and everything went dark.

Long hazy seconds drifted by. When Margot came to her senses she found her arm being pulled, a tearing pain in her shoulder. After dragging her to the rear of the boat, the man lifted her up onto his shoulder and then carried her down to the boardwalk, her face swaying into the back of his trousers. The boards turned to concrete, then cobbles. The thought of what might be coming fired an urge to escape and Margot tried to free her arms, but pain cut through her wrists from where her hands had been bound. The fear she was about to be sick stopped her from crying out.

They came to a halt, somewhere dark and clammy. Margot managed to raise her head high enough to see that they'd crossed a small courtyard and were outside a door. Her head hit the door jamb as the man clumsily carried her through. She bucked violently, but his grip was so tight it felt like her thighs were clamped in a vice.

They moved through a series of darkened rooms and into a hallway that smelled of old furniture. All Margot could see were dark and dusty floorboards until they moved into a tight passage and down a narrow flight of stairs. The air grew cooler as they entered a room that was lit with bright white light. When the man released his grip, Margot slid down his back like a bag of meat and crumpled into a heap on a cold stone floor.

"Margot?"

Raul's voice sharpened her senses. With her hands still bound it was a struggle to right herself, but with a determined effort Margot wriggled into a seated position. The scene that confronted her was the stuff of nightmares: Raul tied to a chair, his face bloodied and beaten; and standing in front of him, two men looking at her with a mixture of curiosity and bemusement – the brothers, Enzo and Paolo Bellucci.

———

The fog began to clear from Margot's brain. The goon who'd brought her in had dropped her in a puddle and foul-smelling water was leaking in through the thin fabric of her trousers. Instinctively, she tried to scrabble to her feet, but the goon swooped in and lifted her into the air as if she were nothing more than a ragdoll. In the next moment, Margot was being held in a chair while someone tied her up with rope. She struggled, but they were far too strong.

"Well, isn't this a scene?" Enzo stepped forward, hands on his hips.

Margot desperately tried to take it all in. She turned to her side where Raul was slumped pitifully in the chair, his shirt torn, his lips swollen. She could hardly bear to look at him.

"I'm sorry, Margot," he muttered wearily. "I didn't—"

"Zip it," Enzo snapped. "You'll speak only when I say you can speak. You got that?"

Margot turned to their captor and observed the blood on his knuckles. Heat flashed through her and without even thinking she spat straight at him. "Bastard!"

It missed his leg by a few centimetres, but Enzo's face darkened. He clicked his fingers, and the next thing Margot registered was a blur of movement followed by a dizzying shot of pain in the back of her skull. She reeled, then turned her head to the goon who'd hit her. A heavyset man with a no.1 buzz cut – she recognised him instantly. Raul exploded into life and tried to buck his chair towards them, but the other man kicked him full in the chest, toppling him like a bowling pin. When they righted him, Raul looked totally done in.

"Are we all settled now?"

Enzo took a handkerchief from his pocket and wiped the blood from his knuckles. Beyond his shoulder, Margot spotted Paolo lurking in the shadows.

"She was carrying this." The goon with the buzz cut tossed a phone through the air. Margot betrayed herself with a look of alarm, and Enzo grinned as he caught it. He switched it on but didn't get very far.

"Looks like we'll need your thumbprint." He tossed the phone back to the goon. "There's two ways of doing it, of course. You can either cooperate and unlock it for me, or I can have one of my boys fetch the snippers from the car."

She didn't think he was bluffing.

The goon lowered the phone behind the chair to where Margot's hands were tied. She didn't protest as he twisted her thumb and pressed it onto the home button. He handed the unlocked phone back to his boss and the basement stayed quiet while Enzo swiped through. Margot had hidden the app in an anonymous folder and it was unlikely he would find it without knowing what he was looking for. She kept her face straight, trying to give him no reason to suspect how valuable the phone was to her. She looked across at Raul, and his eyes slowly crept up to meet hers. Her heart went out to him.

"I can see you've been reading up on me."

Enzo swiped back and forth through the screens. She hadn't erased her browsing history but she'd been careful not to look up anything relating to the bugE. Seemingly satisfied, he tossed the phone back to the goon with the buzz cut who dropped it into his trouser pocket.

"You're an amateur. Why am I wasting my time on you?"

"Is that why you tried to burn down my house?"

Enzo didn't react. "I had you checked out. You have no family. No one who's going to mourn or miss you. I could kill you right now and no one would give a damn."

"So what's stopping you?"

"Why have you been spying on me? I've been trying to get it

out of your friend here but he wasn't in the mood for talking. Now you've shown up perhaps he'll be a little more cooperative."

He approached her chair and leaned down, eyes on the same level. At a stretch, Margot reckoned she might just headbutt his nose, but she resisted the temptation.

"Where have you been for the past few hours, huh? You weren't at home. You weren't on the yacht. And then all of a sudden you turn up here. So how did you know where to come?"

Margot returned a steely-eyed look. At least he hadn't recognised the clothes she was wearing. How ironic that she was sitting here in either his wife's or his mistress's high-end designer trousers. The silence grew as Enzo stood waiting.

"Well? Are either of you going to talk to me? I really wish you would. Because if you don't, things will get very unpleasant."

Margot desperately tried to think of something to say, to find a way out of this, but her mind was still reeling. Enzo's patience suddenly ran out and he stepped away.

"Give me the hammer." He clicked his fingers at the goon to his side who retrieved a claw hammer from the top of a packing crate. Enzo snatched it from him in his eagerness to get on.

"Now here's my dilemma: do I use this on you, hoping it'll persuade your friend to talk, or do I use it on him hoping it'll loosen your tongue? Which of you would crack soonest, I wonder?"

His eyes flicked back and forth between the two of them. Margot had never felt so powerless. Despite the adrenaline coursing through her veins she was still at a loss. After a little deliberation, Enzo made up his mind and stepped over to Raul. Margot watched in alarm as the goons untied one of his hands and wrestled his arm flat against the arm of the chair. They secured it with tape while Enzo laid the hammer on top of his knuckles. Addressing Margot, he said,

"Tell me what I want to know or this guy never plays the guitar again."

Margot very nearly cried out, but at the last moment held onto her emotions. Suddenly she saw with clarity what she needed to do. A cold hand wrapped around her heart as she looked back into Enzo's eyes. "Go ahead."

"What?"

"Hit him."

He grinned. "You're bluffing."

"He means nothing to me."

"You expect me to fall for that old trick?"

Margot held his stare. Despite his apparent self-assuredness Enzo wavered. He spent a long time thinking about his next move, and then stepped back towards Margot.

"You know what, I believe you. Not that he means nothing to you but that you would have sat there and watched me mutilate him and still not said a word. There's a coldness in you. I can feel it."

Margot kept her head held high. The only coldness inside her was a determination not to be defeated. Nothing he could say would injure her.

"But I guess you've made it easy for me. I doubt your friend will be so callous as to let you suffer. I'm guessing he'll sing like a canary rather than see that pretty face of yours get messed up." He weighed the hammer in his hand. "But not with this." He handed it back to the goon. "I've got something special lined up for you."

He turned his head and clicked his fingers. Paolo stepped out of the shadows.

"I believe you two have met."

Margot and Paolo locked eyes. He wore the same blank expression as when she'd met him in the garage that day, unblinking eyes staring straight through her.

"My brother here's got a score to settle. You're the reason his best friend's in jail."

"That's not true!" Margot blurted out. "Etienne's not a murderer and you both know it."

"Suddenly she wants to talk."

"I know you planted the wrench in his hut. The only reason you would do that was to save your own skin. Or his!"

The cockiness drained from Enzo's face. He clearly hadn't realised she knew so much. He leaned in to his brother's side. "It sounds like she's accusing one of us of murder. I think it's about time we shut her up, don't you?"

Paolo balled his fists. Margot braced herself as he moved a step closer. She'd never been hit since her school days, and then she'd given as good as she'd got. But she wasn't afraid. She would tell them nothing.

"Go on, Paolo – hit her."

Raul cried out, but one of the goons kicked his chair and toppled him for a second time. This time they left him on the floor.

"You can do whatever you want to her," Enzo went on. "No one'll find out."

Paolo shuffled his feet, limbs rigid, jaw set tight. Margot bared her teeth, ready to take what was to come. She recalled the pictures she'd found in his garage: the women tied to chairs, strung up from chains. This must have been a dream come true for him and he was going to enjoy every last second. It seemed like every pair of eyes in the room was on the younger brother, waiting to see what he would do. But the seconds slowly passed, his arms stayed locked. His eyes seemed to lose focus as he looked back at them all. Enzo shuffled his feet, growing impatient.

"Come on, Paolo. If she hadn't stuck her nose in none of this would have happened. It's all down to her. Teach her a lesson she won't forget."

Despite Enzo's goading, Paolo's feet remained rooted to the spot. He lowered his eyes and unclenched his jaw. Margot remembered him standing on the other side of the door when she'd been in Enzo's office, just a few hours earlier. He'd surely known she was there and yet had said nothing. Whatever conflict was going on inside him she could only be grateful. Enzo exhaled angrily.

"Look. She's all tied up, just how you like them. Shall we strip her for you? Would that help?"

Enzo cocked his chin to the two goons who readied themselves. But then his mood changed and he seemed to find something funny.

"Maybe we should have brought you a camera. Then you could have taken some pictures." He directed his joke at the other two men who joined in with the amusement.

But Paolo wasn't laughing. His face contorted into a look of pure hatred and in one swift movement he spun round and punched his brother full in the face.

Enzo staggered back. His head had taken the full force of the blow and blood dripped from his nose. The goons tensed, unsure how to respond. Paolo glared at his brother, face still full of fury, while Enzo stood there, head turned away, dazed and confused. He rubbed his jaw; ran an exploratory tongue over his front teeth. Everyone in the room waited for the inevitable response. But Enzo merely straightened his back, took the handkerchief from his pocket, and wiped the blood from his face. He stepped back into the light and, ignoring his brother completely, unrolled his shirtsleeves.

"Get him out of here," he said. The goons promptly escorted Paolo up the stairs.

The basement fell silent. Enzo seemed uncharacteristically

lost for words and when he'd finished fussing with his shirt he faced Margot with a look of contempt. He sniffed.

"Don't think this is the end of it. We'll see how you're feeling after two days down here."

He spat on the floor, narrowly missing her leg, and then charged off up the stairs.

30

A flick of the light switch plunged the basement into darkness. It was like they'd exited a negative nightmare – light and horror replaced by darkness and relief, the pungent smell of old seawater a clear signal that this world was the real one.

"Margot – are you all right?"

Raul's hoarse voice came from somewhere close to her right. Margot couldn't see him, but she had a clear image of him lying on the ground, still tied to the chair, his face a beaten-up mess. She felt awful. "Oh, Raul. I'm so sorry."

"Don't be."

"It's all my fault."

"We can argue about that later. Let's just get out of here before he changes his mind and comes back."

Margot pinched shut her eyes to try and clear her head. She wriggled her arms inside the bindings, but every small movement caused the ropes to dig deeper. Her waist and thighs were bound to the chair with a separate length of rope. The only parts of her body she could move freely were the bottom halves of her legs; with a little careful coordination she managed to hop the chair backwards, one small fraction at a time.

"How badly hurt are you?" she asked.

"I'll live, though I'd say my dancing days are over."

"Is anything broken?"

"Only my pride."

"Stay where you are. I'm going to topple over and lie down beside you."

As her eyes adjusted to the dark, Margot made out his lumpy outline spread across the floor. She gave a firm push with her feet; the chair slid jerkily backwards until one of the legs got stuck on a low-lying slab. Pushing with her right foot, she tilted the chair onto its side and then let it unbalance. Her shoulder took the brunt of the impact, acting like a pivot and swinging her head onto the slabs.

"Ow!"

"You okay?"

She gritted her teeth. "Fine. Shuffle closer."

They both shimmied until they were back to back. Margot felt his fingertips roving over her hands, exploring up her wrists. "Can you reach the knots?"

"I think so."

He started to undo them.

"You know, Margot, I never imagined the first time we laid down together it would be like this."

"I'm sorry to disappoint you."

"I thought I'd at least get dinner and a movie first."

"When this is all over I'll buy you dinner at the Georges V. Now hurry up and get these knots undone."

It took several minutes but Raul finally managed to pick apart one of the knots. Margot loosened her arms, and with a little more wriggling slackened it enough to open her shoulders.

"Almost there."

He freed her hands and she quickly untied the rest, rubbing her arms to get the blood to circulate. A minute later they were both untied. She righted his chair and then helped him feel his way into it. It was a relief not to be able to see what they'd done to his face.

"You sure you're okay?" she asked.

"Just turn on the lights."

Margot felt her way to the bottom of the stairs and then cautiously ascended. She flicked on the light and tried the door handle, unsurprised to find it locked. She pressed an ear to the woodwork, but there was no sign of anyone still out there.

Raul was still slumped in the chair when Margot went back. Her heart sank in despair. The flesh on his face looked so tender she didn't dare touch it. "Oh, Raul. I'm so sorry."

"At least you came to rescue me."

"You're not rescued yet. I promise they won't get away with this."

Raul wearily shook his head. "Just get me back on my boat. That's all I ask."

If only she could.

Margot stepped back and surveyed the space they were in. The basement was much larger than it had initially seemed and the ceiling was quite high. The only way out appeared to be the staircase, until Margot spotted a small, half-moon window high up on one side.

"Do you think you could climb out of there?" She pointed.

Raul twisted his neck. "If the only way out of here was to climb Mount Everest I'd do it." He groaned as he got to his feet. "We'll need something to stand on."

There were plenty of crates. Margot shifted some of the furniture out of the way to make space and together they dragged two of the packing crates across to the window. It wasn't quite high enough, but with a coffee table on top Margot managed to reach. She cleaned a circle in the grime with the sleeve of her coat and peered through. The window looked onto the courtyard, the shiny cobbles now bathed in moonlight. Her eyes were almost level with the ground so it would be easy to climb out, but as she looked more closely Margot realised the window was just a glazed panel with no obvious means of opening it.

"I'll have to break the glass."

"Is anyone out there?"

"There's a car. A dark blue BMW. I don't think anyone's inside."

She waited a few moments, scanning intensively, just to be sure. Then she looked back down and searched for something to break the glass. "Hand me that poker."

Beside him was a galvanised bucket with a hefty black poker sticking out. He passed it up and Margot turned back to the window. The glass was only thin, but if anyone was still in the building there was a good chance they would hear. "Once we climb out we'll need to get a move on."

"Margot."

A hand on her elbow caused Margot to turn sharply. She was surprised to find that Raul had climbed up beside her. "What?"

"You wouldn't really have let them hit me with the hammer, would you?"

He looked at her with puppy-dog's eyes. Margot softened. He had no idea how guilty she already felt. "I was bluffing."

"You were very convincing."

"I used to play cards."

Raul gave a measured nod of his head, apparently reassured. "Remind me never to play strip poker with you."

Despite the circumstances, Margot smiled. "That's a promise."

She turned back to the window: one sharp tap with the head of the poker and the glass shattered. It broke messily, leaving jagged fragments still stuck in the frame. Margot carefully removed them all and then hauled herself through. She turned, crab-like on the cobbles, and reached back to give Raul a hand, but he brushed her aside and climbed out to join her like a man who thought he had something to prove. They rose to their feet and faced the courtyard as one, ready to take on the world. But the place was lifeless, their foes disappeared. If anyone was still inside they certainly hadn't heard.

"This way," Raul whisper-shouted.

Margot turned to see him running towards the gates. She quickly caught up and joined him at the wall, hunkered down like a pair of commandos. The gates were unlocked and one leaf was ajar. Margot opened it a little more and stuck her head through the gap. The harbour was right there in front of them, beyond it an expanse of moonlit sea. The jetty was no more than a hundred metres away, but when she leaned further out she spotted the goon with the buzz cut, smoking by the wall. There was no way of getting to the jetty without him seeing. She jerked back, almost bumping heads with Raul.

"What is it?"

Margot held a finger to her lips. With the utmost care they both leaned out. The man was at least ten metres away but he was swinging his foot at something on the ground, looking bored.

"I'll try and distract him," Raul said. "You make a run for it."

But Margot grabbed his arm. "We need him to come in. He's got my phone."

"We'll have to leave it."

"We can't!"

"Mar—"

"Rattle the gate and then get behind me."

"And then what?"

"I'll hit him with this." Margot raised the poker she still held in her hand. But Raul shook his head.

"No. Give it to me." He brusquely took it out of her hand. "I'm not a violent man, but after what those bastards did to me ..."

"Don't do anything stupid."

"Too late for that."

He ushered Margot behind him and then gently rattled the bolts.

The timber was too thick to hear any footsteps, but he must have heard. Margot's pulse quickened as the seconds ticked by. Instinct had her clutching Raul's arm, though when she realised what she was doing she immediately let go. Ten seconds passed, maybe twenty. Margot began to fear he'd twigged what was going on and would find another way in, but then a shadow crossed the gap. A hand reached in. Raul raised the poker, and the moment the goon appeared brought it down hard and heavy on the top of his head. The man dropped in an instant.

They dragged him inside. Margot got down on her knees and searched his pockets – two iPhones, one of which, she was relieved to see, was her own.

"Watch out, he's coming round." Raul stepped back, gripping the poker. "Shall I hit him again?" He readied himself for a second attempt.

But Margot stayed his hand. "Let's just get out of here, shall we?"

They ran through the gates and into the harbour. Margot threw the poker into the water as they turned the corner onto the boardwalk and was fizzing with relief as they raced up the steps onto *Carpe Diem*.

"They've taken the key." She showed him the empty slot.

"Don't worry – there's a spare."

Raul blundered around below deck for a few short seconds and then emerged, breathless but brandishing a key. He slid it into the slot and started the engine, but then stepped away from the console. Crouching next to one of the deck lockers, he started rummaging through; Margot was alarmed when he pulled out a fearsome-looking dive knife. "Wait here," he said and went back down onto the boardwalk.

"Where are you going?"

Margot feared the bloodlust had got to him and he was about to do something foolish, but instead he halted just a few metres away where a large powerboat was moored up. He forced the cover on the outboard motors and then hacked at the wires inside. Pleased with his handiwork, he came back grinning.

"That was the boat they used to board me," he explained. "Let's see them come after us now."

Raul opened up the throttle and *Carpe Diem* moved steadily out to sea.

31

They motored directly out to sea and didn't stop for several hours. When they finally weighed anchor, the navigation console showed their position at around sixty kilometres off the coast of Spain. But there was nothing, not even the faraway blink of lights, to signify dry land.

Raul was horrified by the mess they'd made of his boat and as soon as they went below he started tidying up. Margot grasped his arm.

"We can sort it all out in the morning. You really need to lie down."

His left eye had swollen to the size of a tennis ball.

The effects of the beating must have caught up on him because he didn't protest. Margot led him through to his cabin, made him take co-codamol and then dressed his wounds as best she could.

"You really need to go to a hospital."

"Please don't fuss."

She fetched a packet of frozen peas from the freezer and wrapped it in a tea towel. Raul groaned when he lay down on the bed with the packet on his face, but slowly he began to settle.

"Margot."

His left arm swung droopily over the side and he emitted a strange kind of groan. Clearly the painkillers were starting to kick in. "Did I ever tell you that you're a very ... very .... beautiful woman?"

Margot folded his arm back onto his chest. "*Shush*," she said, and kissed him softly on the forehead. And she stayed with him for a few minutes. If only she could have been there for Hugo when he lain in the alley, breathing his final few breaths.

———

Several hours passed. When Margot next opened her eyes she thought she was dreaming: a blazing white disc shone from a perfect blue sky. *Carpe Diem* rocked on the calmest of seas. Littering the space around her were crumpled cushions, a screwed-up jumper, a few dirty plates; she quickly realised she'd fallen asleep in the deck salon. She had no idea what time it was; perhaps mid-morning judging by the position of the sun. Pain sliced through her neck when she eased herself out of her bed of cushions, and every joint ached. She moved to the stern and stood with a flattened palm to her brow, scanning the horizon, but there was no land in sight. Apart from a far-off container ship she might have been the only person left alive on Earth.

The tranquillity was a tonic to her frayed nerves but she went below to check on Raul. Peering into his cabin, she was relieved to find him still zonked out. She left him there while she tidied up the salon, and when she'd got it looking a little more presentable she retired to her cabin. Checking her phone, she was dismayed to find there was still no signal.

Two hours later Raul woke up shouting. Margot hurried to his bedside and found him sitting bolt upright, panting like an animal, gazing around the cabin in a state of confusion.

"It's all right. It was just a bad dream. Go back to sleep."

She tried to settle him down but he was determined to get up. He fought past the pillows she tried to plump up for him and hauled himself out of the bed. He staggered into the salon where he dropped heavily onto the sofa, head in his hands. "Have I died and gone to hell?" he groaned.

Margot trailed along and sat down beside him. She couldn't help feeling awkward. Bedside manners had never been her strong point. "Can I get you anything?"

"Yes, a gun, so I can shoot myself."

At least the swelling in his eye had gone down, though his bruises had thickened and darkened somewhat. He turned to give her a phlegmatic look.

"I'll be all right, don't worry. Just so long as I haven't lost my good looks."

Margot smiled. "I'm sure they'll come back. One day."

She cooked him a breakfast of bacon on toast and brewed a fresh pot of coffee. She had no appetite herself and was content to sit and watch him eat, although every chew had him cringing in pain.

Afterwards, she helped him up into the deck salon and had him lie down in the shade. Like a good nursemaid, she made up another cold pack with a flannel and ice. When she'd finally got him comfortable, Margot crashed on the opposite side, and as the excitement of the past few days finally caught up on her she fell into a deep exhausted sleep.

———

When she next came to, Raul was staring at her from his sick bed, their eyes level across the top of the table.

"Is your bug working?"

She pulled herself upright. He must have been up whilst she'd been asleep because two bottles of water had appeared on the table. She took one and drank thirstily. "There's not a good enough signal out here."

She waited, hoping he might suggest they move closer to the coast, but he said nothing. She wasn't going to push.

"Can you believe Paolo reacted the way he did?" she said.

"I wouldn't like to be a guest in their house right now. Can you imagine the atmosphere at breakfast?"

Margot smiled.

"There was nothing I could do," Raul said, taking a more serious tone.

She looked at him enquiringly. "When?"

"When they came alongside. There were two of them. They had guns."

"You weren't to blame. And thank God you hid my phone."

"I saw you make it to the beach. After that I couldn't keep track; the boat was moving around too much. I was afraid they'd found you."

"They very nearly did."

She gave him a brief recap of events at the house and how she'd hidden behind the door when Paolo had come into the office. "He must have known I was there. Yet he obviously didn't tell his brother."

"I hope you're not feeling any sympathy for him."

Margot looked away. No, she had no sympathy for him. He was the one who'd killed Aswan's father, yet exactly how it had happened was something they would probably never know. She looked back at Raul. "I couldn't believe it when I swam back and found you'd gone."

A glimmer returned to his eye. "Did you think I'd deserted you?"

"Just for a moment."

He smiled warmly. He sat up on the cushions and reached across the table for her hand. Margot leaned out to let him hold it.

"I would never willingly have left you, Margot."

A tingle passed through her, the likes of which Margot had not experienced for some time. It was nice to know she could still feel that way.

————

In the afternoon, Margot fussed around below deck – tidying things that had already been tidied, cleaning things that had already been cleaned – and then went back up and did a circuit of the deck. She sat down in the cockpit salon and folded her arms, sighing heavily. The contrary side of her wasn't sorry when her blundering around made Raul wake up.

"What's the matter with you?" he said, cranking open his eyelids.

"Bastards stole my smokes."

"What?"

"When they boarded the boat. I left them in my drawer."

He pulled himself up and had an old man's chuckle. "I'm sorry. I can't help you with that."

"Hmm," Margot said and stared miserably into the distance. She'd been smoking since the age of sixteen and right now didn't regret a single one of the little white coffin nails.

"Perhaps this would be a good time to quit."

"This would be the worst possible time to quit, trust me." She became conscious of her foot tapping the floor and made herself stop.

Unable to go back to sleep, Raul got up and tidied his sick bed. When he faced her across the table he looked a little more human.

"So, what do you want to do now?"

"How long can we stay out here?"

He shrugged. "Pretty much as long as we like. The freezers are fully stocked, the water-making system just keeps going. *Carpe Diem* was designed for crossing oceans."

"We need a phone signal."

"Shouldn't we just go to the police?"

Margot shook her head. "We need to catch them in the act. If we find out when their shipment's coming in I can call Pierre. He can have the drugs brigade waiting."

"Enzo's hardly likely to just blurt it out."

"Maybe not, but my bug's the only hope we have."

The look on Raul's face betrayed his scepticism, but he moved to one of the consoles and sat down at the wheel. He spent a few minutes tapping away on the touchscreen. "We could go down to Menorca. There'll be a phone signal there."

"Won't it be busy?"

"Not on the northern side. The coastline's pretty rocky."

Margot joined him at the console and looked at the chart. "How far is it?"

"Seventy kilometres. If we set off now we could be there by dusk."

It seemed a good idea, though the only problem was it meant moving further away from Marseilles which was where Enzo's shipment was most likely to come in. But if it meant she could listen to her bug it would at least be progress. She retrieved her yachting cap and pulled it onto her head.

"Very well, skipper. Let's go to Menorca."

———

They set off under power of the engines. When the wind did pick up, Raul raised the mainsail and *Carpe Diem* moved along at a steady four knots. Within three hours they sighted land. Raul altered course, tacking through a patch of choppier water, and then steered them towards the island from the east. Green-topped craggy white cliffs came into view and the island steadily grew larger. They furled the sail and steered into a bay where the water was as clear as crystal.

Two other yachts had already staked out a claimed so they moved on. The next bay was deserted, but Raul passed it in favour of their third option which turned out to be a perfect U-shaped inlet, perhaps fifty metres wide at its mouth. Rocky headlands screened it from the sea, and the sandy beach was so pristine it looked like it had not once suffered the trample of human feet. When they dropped anchor in the middle of the bay, the rest of the world seemed very far away.

"I've heard there are some particularly good nudist beaches along this stretch," Raul said when he'd finished securing the ropes. "It would an excellent place to go skinny-dipping, don't you think?"

Margot rolled her eyes. "I take it someone's feeling better." She gave him a haughty look and they went below.

Her phone signal had crept up to three bars. She opened the app and was stunned to see *sixteen* notifications pop up. Raul came into the salon and sat down beside her.

"Any good?"

Margot showed him the phone while the files were down-loading. When it was ready, she put it on speaker. Most of the recordings were one-sided conversations – Enzo on the phone, making what sounded like routine calls to his shipping company. Another was the tail end of an argument he was having with someone, presumably his wife. Another started off as a jumble of muffled sounds which quickly developed into noisy love-making. Squirming, Margot fast-forwarded. In the final recording he appeared to be talking to himself, grumbling about something or other. But there was no mention of anything relating to the shipment.

Margot switched off the phone in disappointment.

It was starting to get dark so Raul closed the canopy and they turned on the lights. He seared some salmon fillets for dinner, and with her appetite restored, Margot ate greedily and cleared her plate before Raul was even halfway through.

"My, you were hungry."

"Withdrawal symptoms."

As soon as he'd finished, she cleared away all the dishes.

"It's a good job they didn't take any of the wine," she said as she went for a raid on the booze cupboard.

"They were barbarians. They wouldn't have known a good bottle of wine if you'd hit them over the head with it."

She chose a bottle of Côtes de Thongue and poured herself a large one. When Raul went to take a shower, Margot went up on deck with the bottle for company and sat at the table, peeling an orange. Her hands had to have something to do.

Ten minutes later Raul joined her, towel-drying his hair. "Are you going to eat that?" He indicated the naked orange she'd left on the table.

"No. I just like peeling them." Margot started on another.

He took it away and came back a few minutes later with two bowls of fruit salad. He'd segmented the orange, added some kiwi and pineapple, drowned it all in Limoncello – Margot was pleased to see he'd brought the rest of the bottle for good measure.

When they'd finished eating, they turned off all the lights and went to relax on the sun loungers. The sky turned from indigo to black, and they gazed in awe as a million stars came out. The darkness was so encompassing they could have been part of the void themselves, though the alcohol had gone straight to Margot's head and the 'firmament' seemed a poor choice of word for what they were looking at. More and more pinpricks of light kept appearing, filling in the black spaces.

"So many stars," she said dreamily.

"My wife was into astronomy," Raul said, inches away on other side of the mast. "I bought her a telescope for her birthday one year. We used to go up into the mountains and look at the Milky Way."

"That's nice."

For a long while they enjoyed a companionable silence. The warm Balearic air was so soporific Margot could have happily fallen asleep.

"Did you and Hugo ever try for a baby?"

Margot's brain slowly retuned. She turned her head to face him, though it appeared he was still looking up at the sky. "Yes, but it never happened. The doctors never really found out why."

"I'm sorry."

"Maybe it was a blessing. I might have been a lousy mother."

"I don't believe that."

That was nice of him, but maybe some people weren't cut out to be parents. "What about you? Do you think you've been a good father?"

"It might sound big-headed but yes, I do. Of course, my kids might not agree."

"Maybe I'll ask them one day."

"I would need to forewarn them first."

Margot smiled.

"How old were they when your wife died?"

He cocked his head as he worked it out. "Eleven, twelve and fifteen."

"And you've brought them up on your own since then?"

"We all helped out. My eldest became like a mother to the other two."

"And you're still close?"

"Yes. Very."

"That's nice."

A shooting star flashed by, closely followed by another. Weren't you supposed to make a wish? Trust in the gods to make it all good again? Instead, Margot felt an aching sadness. Some things could never be repaired, no matter how hard you tried. But she drew in a deep breath and propped herself on one elbow, determined not to fall into melancholy. "Did you bring the Limoncello?"

"I left it on the table."

"Be a lamb and fetch it, would you?"

He tutted. "What did your last slave die of?"

"Insubordination."

He rolled off the lounger with a groan and a wheeze. Margot felt guilty and went after him, and they both stumbled along in the dark which perhaps was not such a good idea given they'd drunk so much and were surrounded by ropes and guard-wires, any one of which could have caused them trip and fall into the sea. But with a little comical fumbling they made it to the safety of the deck salon where they crashed down on the benches. Raul switched on the lights while Margot reached for the Limoncello.

"You know," he said, smiling like a drunken old man, "when I was growing up on the farm, my grandparents were our rock, the centre of everything. In those days we all lived together in one big house. But when Grandad died I got very upset. I was only a boy. I couldn't see how we could ever be happy again. But as time went by things got better. My father took over the farm; he showed me how to look after the trees. Eventually I couldn't even remember how things were in Grandad's day, but we were just as happy."

"And your point being?"

"My mother used to say that life is like a snow-globe. Most of the time everything is settled and the world looks fine. Then once in a while someone comes along and shakes it all up. When you're in the middle of the snowstorm you think your world is utterly destroyed. But then everything settles back down. It's not the same as it was before but it can be just as good."

Margot thought about that for a while. Then something struck her funny bone and she spluttered with laughter. "That's a terrible analogy."

Raul took a moment to catch up, but then he spluttered, too. "It is, isn't it?"

They both fell about laughing, and in the confusion the Limoncello got knocked from the table. They stooped in unison to pick it up, and then somehow Raul's face was moving steadily towards hers. Margot froze, eyes on his lips, but then quickly turned away. When they came back up, all they shared was an embarrassed smile.

———

The next morning Margot delayed getting up. She stayed in bed for an hour after she'd woken, listening to the sound of water lapping against the hull. She checked her phone and refreshed the app, but no new notifications came through. Bright sunlight shone onto her window, and when she looked out she saw that it was another serenely beautiful morning. She put on her Speedo and went out.

There was no sign of life from Raul's cabin so she went up on deck to find him sitting at the stern, a huge fishing pole in his hand. Margot retrieved his sunhat from where he'd left it on the bench and placed it on top of his head.

"Morning, skipper," she said brightly.

"Good morning," he replied flatly.

She could tell by the way he merely glanced at her that they were not going to talk about the attempted kiss. She wasn't cross it had happened, but neither was she going to be the one to bring it up.

The silence continued so Margot stepped up to the guard wire and gazed out to sea. The bay was bathed in bright golden light and there was barely a breath of wind. She scanned the green-topped cliffs, looked across at the sandy beach; nowhere could she see a single human being. It was bliss. She moved back to the stern.

"How are your bruises?"

"Better, thanks. What about you?"

"I had a bit of a headache but I'm fine now."

"Are you going for a swim?"

"No. I dress like this when I'm doing the housework."

Margot hoped it might coax a smile out of him but he wouldn't play ball. She moved a little closer, her bare thighs level with his head. His desire to turn and look was almost palpable, but he somehow found the strength to resist.

"What are you hoping to catch?"

"According to the fish-finder there's a shoal of bass nearby."

"Fish-finder?" Margot queried.

Raul nodded. "It's an app on the radar. You're not the only one who knows how to use technology."

She looked down into the water. It was so clear there was hardly any need for radar; if a shoal of fish swam by he'd surely have spotted it with his naked eye. "Isn't that rather like cheating?"

Raul twitched his shoulders. "I suppose you're going to quote Samuel Johnson at me."

Margot frowned. "Am I?"

"A fishing rod: 'a stick with a hook at one end and a fool at the other.'"

She smiled. "That's not what I was thinking." Though it was rather apt.

"How long have you been sitting there?"

"An hour, maybe."

"Don't you get bored?"

"What's the matter – have you run out of oranges to peel?"

Margot regarded him in consternation. Did he think she'd rebuffed him? Was that what this was about? She filled the silence by putting on her swimming cap. "You could come swimming with me."

Now he turned his head. Margot watched his gaze travel slowly up over her middle and settle somewhere short of her neck. She didn't mind him looking, but he still wasn't smiling.

"No thanks," he said.

"You can swim, can't you?"

"Of course I can swim."

She planted a hand on her hip and exhaled. "Then what's your problem?"

He turned sulkily back to the fishing pole. "You're so graceful in the water," he muttered. "Next to you I would be like a walrus."

"Now who's feeling sorry for themselves?"

He didn't respond at all this time and Margot's patience ran out. "Fine. Suit yourself."

She made her way round to the prow and then dived in over the handrail.

———

He'd cheered up by dinner time. He'd managed to catch three decent sized bass and seemed pleased with his efforts. Margot left him filleting them in the galley while she went for a shower.

Her mind was on other things and when she stepped out of the cubicle it didn't occur to her that she'd left the cabin door wide open. She didn't bother to close it when she crossed to the chest of drawers. Getting dressed in front of the mirror, it took her a few moments to realise that Raul's reflection was also looking back at her. He was still in the galley, but the way the mirror was aligned meant he had a straight-line view. And from the look on his face Margot could tell he'd been watching.

She swallowed. The moment became a bubble in time, both of them aware the other could see and doing nothing about it. But then Margot unfroze her limbs. She carried on dressing, and when she was done, calmly closed the door.

———

The conversation at dinner was stilted. Margot sensed he felt guilty and was looking for a way to apologise, but when he did try to bring up the subject something compelled her to steer the conversation away. When he cleared away the dishes, she couldn't help staring at his hands. A farmer's hands, broad and muscular. An image of him caressing her flitted into her mind where it lingered, in danger of turning into something more.

They drained the bottle of wine and Raul rose from his seat. "Shall I open another?"

Margot shook her head. "I'm quite tired, actually. I might have an early night."

"Me too. I'll wash up first."

Margot paused, not quite sure what had just been communicated, but then rose from her seat and went to her cabin. She halted just inside the door, hand on the handle. Nine months since she'd buried her husband. Sometimes it seemed much longer. Hugo was the last person who would have expected her to abstain, but was this too soon? Grieving could be so exhausting. Was it asking too much for a little fun to come back into her life?

Margot switched on the beside light and perched on the edge of the mattress. This time, she intentionally left the door ajar.

———

32

Marielle was doing a poor job hiding her amusement. When she laid the plate of chops on the table in front of him and took in Enzo's disgruntled reaction, her whole upper body quivered in a state of suppressed laughter. Enzo rubbed his aching jaw. Since Mutt had let slip what had happened in the Old Customs House she'd hardly been able to keep a straight face. She leaned in, pouting like a mother to her child.

"Does pumpkin want me to cut it into iddy-biddy pieces for him?"

She tried to pinch his cheek, but Enzo flapped her away. He slid the plate across the table and grabbed a nectarine from the fruit bowl instead. "Funny how you have a habit of putting me off my food."

"Same with you and sex."

He sneered. Maybe one of these days he might not let her have the last laugh. He got out of the seat and retreated to his office.

The doors were still open so he stood on the terrace, looking down at the empty cove while he bit into the nectarine. It was eight p.m. and the sky was darkening. Mule had been out patrolling all day and had sent word to the nearby ports, but there had been no further sightings of the yacht. Enzo wasn't especially worried. The moment they showed up on land their days would be numbered, and if they chose to go to the police it would be their word against his. He'd already had the basement cleansed. And he had plenty of eyes and ears in the local police stations if they wanted to go down that route. Besides, he had bigger fish to fry. His shipment was due in tomorrow.

He lobbed the nectarine stone over the cliff and then took the elevator to the second level. He strode to Paolo's door and knocked loudly. He wasn't expecting an answer, but he waited. Through the woodwork, he said, "We need to talk. Can I come in?"

There was a sound he took as a yes.

Paolo was lying on the bed, dressed in his outdoor clothes. He'd been looking at his phone, but he tossed it to one side and then got up and went to the window. It was like stepping back thirty years; all those times Enzo had gone into the kid's room to try and pick up the pieces after one bust-up or another.

Enzo kept his distance, hands in his pockets, waiting to be acknowledged. This was his house, for god's sake. He deserved at least that much respect.

"You hungry? Marielle's cooked chops."

Paolo shook his head, eyes on the window. Enzo balled his fists.

"Look. I've said I've forgiven you. What more do you want?"

"Maybe I haven't forgiven you."

"If anyone else had done what you did I'd have thrown them off the cliff by now."

"Aren't I the lucky one?"

Enzo bit his tongue. Sometimes he just wanted to punch him so hard. He made himself calm down.

"Look. What I said about the camera, it was no big deal. I

was just trying to gee you up. I didn't mean to hurt your feelings."

Paolo nodded his head, though not like he was convinced. Enzo gave him a few more moments.

"So?"

"So what?"

"Are we good?"

"I'm still here, aren't I?"

Enzo breathed out wearily. At least that was something. He joined him at the window but ignored the view.

"We'll be leaving in a couple of hours. I don't want any more fooling around. If this all goes to plan there'll be fifty grand in your pocket by the end of the week. Just think about that."

Paolo adjusted his position, straightening his back and rubbing his chin. Enzo relaxed a little. Pushing the right buttons, that's what it was about.

"And there'll be plenty more to come if you behave yourself. Okay?"

Paolo moved his head. Where his brother was concerned that was as good as a yes.

33

Margot could sense Raul on the other side of the half-open door: hear the slight wheeze in his breathing, smell the sandalwood in his cologne. She pictured him frozen like a statue, poised, ready to make his move.

The seconds ticked by and Margot continued to wait.

Without making a sound, she stretched to the switch and turned off the ceiling light, leaving only the bedside lamp. It was 9:15 p.m.. Timbers creaked as *Carpe Diem* rocked on gentle waves.

And yet he still didn't make a move. Margot frowned. What was stopping him? She wasn't just imagining him being out there? She hadn't misinterpreted the signs, been too cool with him? Her hand moved to the door handle, tempted to open it fully and end the stalemate, but then a *beep* from her phone made her heart jump into her mouth.

It was the tone she'd assigned to the bugE. She couldn't ignore it. Margot snatched the phone from the far side of the bed and opened the app. One file was waiting to be downloaded, recorded an hour ago. She tapped the button and held the phone to her ear. Two voices, Enzo and Paolo:

"*You ready?*"

"*I guess so.*"

There was the sound of a door closing, followed by the metallic scrape of a drawer being opened. Margot remembered the filing cabinet she'd seen in his office.

"*What's this?*"

"*Take it.*"

"*You expecting trouble?*"

"*Not especially. But I want you ready, just in case.*"

Margot pressed the phone closer to her ear. There was a series of clicking noises, metal on metal, like a gun being checked. Then a series of muffled sounds she couldn't make sense of. Neither of the two men said anything for a few moments and Margot thought that might be the end of the recording, but a glance at the time code showed fifty seconds still to go. She put the phone back to her ear.

Enzo: "*Why the sudden interest in my office?*"

A pause, then Paolo said, "*Just looking.*"

Another pause. It was far from clear what was going on but the atmosphere seemed to have changed. Paolo's voice had a slightly higher pitch when he said,

"*What time's the ship coming in?*"

"*Four.*"

"*In the morning?*"

"*Of course.*"

"*Marseilles?*"

"*Naturally.*"

"*Where, exactly?*"

There was a longer period of silence. Margot held her breath. Would Enzo really give him an answer? It seemed too good to be true. She visualised the two of them, face to face in that office, just like when she'd overheard them talking in Paolo's garage. What unspoken communication was passing between them right now? Part of her no longer cared; all she wanted was to hear the right words come out of Paolo's mouth. Enzo drew in a breath.

"*The* Valdez. *Dock 14*."

And Margot's stomach flipped.

The recording ended and she put down the phone, nerves tingling. This was it. She would call Pierre right away; have the police waiting on the dock, ready to catch them in the act. There was plenty of time. But first her eyes shifted to the door. A feeling of regret swept through her. Whatever moment had been awaiting them was gone.

"Raul," she said quietly.

He didn't acknowledge her at first, reluctant perhaps to admit he'd been out there, and Margot had to go to the door and pull it open. There he was, just as she'd imagined, apart from his eyes now heavy with disappointment. She gave him a sorrowful look, and then switched on the lights.

"Come and have a listen to this."

34

Seated in the windowless office on the edge of the port, Enzo rubbed his tired eyes. It was five a.m. and he'd been staring at the row of small screens for over an hour. Out on the dock, the *Valdez* was safely moored up, slowly giving up its cargo. He switched to another camera, this one a view from the gantry crane. The hook and spreader moved in and out of the ship's hold, pulling out containers with millimetre precision, adding them one by one to the stack on the yard. It was mesmerising to watch.

Naturally, everything was controlled by computer these days, the process ninety per cent automated. A ship the size of the *Valdez* could be unloaded and loaded again with the assistance of a mere handful of dock workers. And the computer never erred, of course. If it so happened that two containers were moved to one particular spot on the quay and all trace of them on the manifest got deleted then no one would think anything of it. As far as the data trail was concerned the containers had never even existed.

Enzo flicked to the camera on the lorry park and zoomed in. Both his trucks were ready and waiting. Thirteen minutes from now the first container would come out of the hold and be placed on the edge of the stack; three minutes and two seconds after that the second container would follow. Fourteen minutes would pass before a glitch in the software summoned the yard crane, and one of his men would be waiting with the forklift, ready to move the containers onto the trucks. Two minutes after that the trucks would be on their way: one to an industrial estate on the outskirts of the city, the other to Paris. Sometimes it seemed too easy a way to make a million euros.

Enzo checked his watch for the hundredth time. Just ten minutes to go now before the first container came out. Despite having done a dozen similar shipments over the past few years, this part always made him nervous.

Mutt came in through the door at the end of the office, two paper cups in his hand. He passed one to Enzo and then leaned to the monitor. "How's he doing?"

Enzo switched to the motorised camera and panned the quayside in search of his brother. The place was pretty much deserted at this time of day, but his keen eye picked out two figures moving stealthily between the arc lights. There in the shadows on the edge of the lorry park was Paolo, keeping watch on the access road.

"He's good," Enzo said, and his heart swelled a little bit with pride.

Mutt leaned closer. "What's that?" His fat finger pointed to a blotch on the screen.

Enzo moved the joystick. A black SUV was parked by the barrier at the entrance to the access road. The interior light had briefly been on and it had looked like someone was inside. He picked up the walkie-talkie.

"Hey, Mule – check out that SUV over by the barrier."

Enzo did a quick flick through the cameras. Everything appeared to be in order: the crane was still moving, the stack growing bigger. Eight minutes to go before his first container came out. He clicked back to the SUV; zoomed out and panned. Mule was approaching from the bottom righthand corner of the screen, but he was going the wrong way. Enzo jabbed the walkie-talkie button.

"Mule – the other side, you dimwit."

Mule looked round in confusion before spotting it. Enzo moved the camera back to Paolo who was a little further back, maybe a hundred metres from the SUV. When Enzo asked, he said he hadn't spotted anything. Back on Mule: he was heading the right way now, but ten metres from the barrier he slowed, seeming to grow wary. On the screen Enzo could see him raise his walkie-talkie.

"Boss?"

"What?"

There was no need for a reply. Before either of them could speak again, the lights came on in the SUV and four men burst out. Enzo watched in stunned disbelief as they charged up to Mule, machine guns aloft. He was face down on the tarmac in no seconds flat. Then the fireworks really kicked off – cars began streaming in from left, right and centre. Enzo got up so sharply his chair toppled back. What the hell?

He punched through the camera channels. Back at the ship, the crane was still working. Just two minutes and thirty seconds to go now. For the briefest moment Enzo dared to think there might still be time, but then an armoured police truck burst through the barrier and he knew it was all over. He panned frantically with the joystick, searching for Paolo, and spotted him wandering towards the unfolding chaos, looking oblivious. Enzo jabbed the walkie-talkie button.

"Paolo! Abort. Get the hell out of there!"

A vein throbbed in Enzo's temple as two cars raced towards him. Paolo was still walking towards the blue and red circus.

They were right there in front of him; couldn't he see, for Christ's sake? He jabbed the button once more.

"Paolo! Run, goddammit!"

But Paolo had turned into a zombie. Enzo zoomed in on his face. Had he taken leave of his senses? He was a dead man walking.

Mutt strode to the office door and looked out. "Boss, there's a car coming. We need to get out."

Enzo's eyes flicked from the screen to the door and back again. He was going nowhere. Not without his brother. Paolo was taking the gun out of his pocket and laying it down on the ground. He could have escaped; he'd had the chance, but he was putting his hands up in surrender. Enzo's brain seized. His mind went back to the two kids playing in the snow, that time school had been shut. They'd thrown snowballs at this old guy's windows, shattered the glass in his porch. The kids had all ran, but Paolo had slowed down at the end of the street, let the old guy catch up, grab him by the shirt collar and give him an earful. He could have outrun them all yet he'd stayed there and carried the can. Enzo had looked on and done nothing.

"Boss!"

Enzo blinked. Mutt was waiting for him by the door, shooting anxious looks. In the space of just minutes the whole operation had collapsed in front of his eyes and Enzo couldn't believe it. He picked up the walkie-talkie for one last try, but it was too late. The police had got Paolo surrounded.

"Boss! We need to go."

Mutt strode forward and tried to grab his arm, but Enzo snatched it away. He would go down there and drag his brother out with his bare hands if he had to, and to hell with anyone who got in his way. He made a move for the door, but Mutt blocked him. The two men faced off.

"He's made his choice. Don't go down with him."

The pressure of Mutt's hand in his chest brought Enzo back to his senses. He blinked again, and refocussed. What had got into him? The only thing that mattered was saving his own skin, looking after *numero uno*, just like it had always been.

On the monitor, Paolo was face down on the tarmac, being barked at by cops with machine guns. Leaving another small piece of his heart behind, Enzo tugged his shirt-cuffs and followed Mutt down to the car.

35

Three weeks later.

Chapelle Saint-Marc stood at the top of a small green hill, its graveyard split across two distinct plateaus: one overlooking Argents, the other facing the sea. Standing alone in her widow's weeds, Margot stared down at the two rectangular holes in the ground, one of them half the size of the other. Fitting, perhaps, that the final resting place of Aswan and his father be so close to the water.

She'd had to twist a few arms to get everything organised at such short notice. Fortunately, she'd found a sympathetic ear in Pere Chevalier who for years had campaigned on the issue of rights for migrants and had gone out of his way to help. He'd bent a few ears, and by some small miracle had managed to find this small corner in the crowded graveyard.

Pierre and Camille were on their way down. Pierre had finally agreed to have some time off work and they'd left Paris in the early hours. They were bringing the baby, and afterwards had promised to stay for the weekend – they both certainly needed the break. Margot had spent all of yesterday sprucing up the house. All the repairs were now finished and the place looked like new. Gone was that terrible stench of soot and smoke; now the rooms smelled of fresh paint. On either side of her fireplace stood replicas of her bookcases, albeit empty versions for now. Replacing Hugo's records and her books would be a rather more difficult task.

Margot's phone buzzed inside her bag: a text from Pierre to say they'd finally arrived. She walked round to the front of the church and looked out from the gate. They'd had to park a long way down the street, and when they did appear were hurrying towards her, Pierre carrying a bundle, Camille with an armful of baby paraphernalia.

"Sorry we're so late," Camille said, kissing Margot on both cheeks. "The traffic was a nightmare."

"Not at all. Thank you both for coming."

Pierre showed off his precious cargo. He peeled back a corner of the lacy white gown to reveal a chubby white face. Noémie was even cuter than she'd looked in the photos. He smiled proudly.

"Would you like to hold her?"

Margot bit her bottom lip. The child was fast asleep, as serene as an angel. It would have been nice, but Margot shook her head. "Maybe later. I think the priest is waiting."

It was a brief but touching ceremony. A dozen or so locals turned up to pay their respects. As a finale, Pere Chevalier looked to a wider audience and, voice slightly raised, quoted from Deuteronomy:

"Cursed is he who withholds justice from the foreigner, the fatherless or the widow."

"Amen," said Margot emphatically.

She choked back a tear as the pallbearers lowered Aswan's miniature coffin into the ground. She'd wanted to bury his back-pack with him but it was being treated as evidence and the police wouldn't release it. She folded up a replica football shirt and dropped that onto the coffin instead. The three of them thanked the priest and they warmly shook hands.

Noémie woke up grisly so Camille took her for a little walk while Margot and Pierre strolled back to the car.

"I don't suppose I could bum a smoke?" Pierre asked. "Being cooped up in the back of the car's given me cabin fever."

"Sorry," Margot said. "I haven't had a cigarette in eighteen days."

Pierre's face brightened. "You've quit?"

"Trying to."

He took hold of her hand and gave it a squeeze. "Good for you."

"Not so good for my hips," Margot said, patting her side. "The amount of chocolate I've been eating instead."

They walked out through the arch and set off down the street. Margot peeled off her black lace gloves and pushed them to the bottom of her purse. Twice in one year; she hoped she never saw the horrid things again.

"Any news from Marseilles?"

"They've seized two containers. There was fifty kilos of heroin hidden in a shipment of rugs from India. And they've arrested a dozen people at the port where it was loaded. It's a major haul." Pierre leaned in. "You ignored every warning I gave but I'm glad you persisted."

Margot allowed herself a small smile of satisfaction. It could all have ended very differently and she felt lucky to have come out of it unscathed, suffering no more than a few cuts and bruises. "I just wanted justice for Aswan."

"I know."

"Any sign of Enzo?"

"No. They raided his house and his office in the docks, but

he was long gone. But don't worry, he'll be back, and when he does we'll be waiting."

Paolo had confessed. He'd given them a detailed account of what had happened on the night Aswan and his father had lost their lives, how he'd killed Aswan's father in the heat of the moment and dumped the body down by the fort. His account of what had happened to Aswan seemed plausible. He'd owned up to a dozen other smuggling offences and to forging passports, though claimed he made little or no money out of it. His motives were altruistic, he'd said, though the fact he'd been happy to let his friend take the blame did him no favours.

As far as Enzo was concerned, however, Paolo had refused to comment. His desire for absolution didn't extend as far as implicating family, it seemed.

"Oh, I've got something for you." An air of suppressed excitement took hold of Pierre when they reached the car. "Wait there."

Margot stood on the pavement while he nipped round to the passenger side and reached in through the door. When he came back, he was holding a brown paper bag which he presented to Margot with great care. "I found it last week."

Margot gave him an enquiring look. She opened the bag and peered inside. It was an LP, that much was obvious, but when she pulled it out and caught sight of the sleeve she let out a little gasp of excitement. *Yesterday and Today* by The Beatles. She beamed.

"Where on earth did you find this?"

"I have my sources."

"Oh, Pierre."

"It's not got the original sleeve but it is an early one."

"It's wonderful."

Pierre's eyes turned a little bit glassy. He swallowed, struggling to shift a lump in his throat. "I was thinking I could bring one with me every time I came to visit," he said, voice cracking. "We could restore the collection one by one."

A wave of raw emotion swept up through Margot's body and it took her a moment to compose herself. She inhaled deeply.

"I think I like that idea very much," she said, and pulled him in for a hug.

36

Raul was cleaning the deck of *Carpe Diem* with a broom and a hosepipe when Margot approached along the jetty. He was so involved in the task that he didn't spot her immediately and she slowed, remembering the day she'd first encountered him on this jetty. How she'd cursed him.

"Ahoy there, skipper!"

Raul looked up in surprise. Realising who had accosted him, he turned off the hosepipe and put down his brush. "You startled me."

"Permission to come aboard?"

"Margot, have you ever needed my permission to do anything?"

She smiled away his comment and bounded up the steps at the stern. It had been a week since they'd last seen each other and the time had dragged. Last week he'd been in Madrid, visiting his daughter, and he'd been unable to get back in time for the funeral. In honour of the small reunion, Margot had squeezed into an old pair of blue jeans – she'd always looked good in them, though they appeared to have shrunk. She slid through the gap between the two consoles and sat down in the deck salon, happy to be back. It was surprising how much she'd missed it. *Carpe Diem* had become like a second home.

The harbour was alive with activity and gaggles of tourists were meandering along the jetty, casting appreciative eyes over the yachts. Elderly men in baseball caps, women eating ice creams; speculating, no doubt, about the great adventures their owners must have. And it had been an adventure, a shame it had had to end. Margot closed her eyes and tilted her face to the sun, blissfully soaking up the heat. In her idle moments she'd entertained ideas of following Raul's lead and setting off on a journey of her own, maybe even join him on his lap around the world if he asked her to.

It occurred to her that he hadn't spoken for a few minutes and she opened her eyes. He'd abandoned the hosepipe in favour of a soft white cloth and was now absorbed in polishing some of the chrome-work. Margot stared at him until he raised his head, then tried to coax a smile out of him.

"It's looking rather splendid."

"Thank you."

"To look at her you'd have no idea what she's been through."

He carried on polishing, seeming determined to get out its maximum shine.

"Did you get the scratch out?"

"Pardon?'

"The scratch. On the table in the salon."

"Oh, yes. Go down and see."

Margot did just that. The table looked as good as new. Indeed, everything was back to how it had been on the day she'd first climbed aboard. When she went back up, Raul was still busy polishing. She went to stand by his side and leaned against one of the wheels, thumbs hooked into the front pockets of her jeans. He smiled politely and Margot smiled back.

"Are you taking her out today?"

"I thought I might sail across to Sardinia."

"That sounds nice."

"There are some extraordinary sea caves over there. I've always wanted to check them out."

"Mm-hm." Margot nodded her head like one of those dashboard dogs. She hoped he might elaborate, perhaps invite her to go with him, but he remained silent. "How long will it take?"

He shrugged.

"A day?" she prompted.

"Maybe a few days."

"You'll be back for the weekend, though, won't you?"

He paused. A couple of moments went by before he put down his cloth and faced her properly. And when he did, the look on his face told Margot everything she needed to know. She took her thumbs out of her pockets and straightened her spine. Her good mood drained like someone had pulled a plug.

"I see."

Raul gave her a sad sorry look. "I thought it was time to move on. There's so much to explore."

"Of course. Wherever the wind takes you and all that."

"Italy was always going to be next on my itinerary."

"I'm sure it will be lovely there."

Margot nodded again. She worked on hiding her disappointment but it wasn't easy. For a while she couldn't even bring herself to look at him. How quickly some people can permeate your life; how wrenching their departure can feel. She gathered her emotions and produced a smile. "Well, the wind brought you to Argents-sur-Mer and I'm glad it did." She extended her arm for a handshake.

Raul looked down at her hand but didn't shake it. The corners of his mouth crept up ever so slightly and the twinkle returned to his eye. "You could always come with me."

"And sail around the world together?"

"Why not?"

Margot retracted her arm. Less than a minute ago she'd entertained that very idea but now it seemed ridiculous. It would never happen. Happy little visions like that belonged to other people, or the world of fantasy.

"I don't think I could handle the seasickness."

"We could stock up on pills."

Margot shook her head. She glanced around the deck of *Carpe Diem* one final time, remembering with fondness the good times they'd shared, and then moved towards the steps at the rear. Raul followed like a shadow.

"I guess this is goodbye."

"I suppose it is." Margot reached for the handrail.

"Margot."

She turned back. "Yes."

"I hope you find it."

"Find what?"

He paused. "Whatever it is that will make you happy."

She had that image again: of jumping in just as the tide was going out. When she leaned back and kissed him on the cheek, Raul held onto her elbow, perhaps wanting more, and for a moment Margot thought she might crumble and give in. But the feeling quickly passed.

As soon as she got home she took off the jeans and threw them in the bin.

———

Margot was snoozing in the courtyard when her phone juddered on the wrought-iron table. Her eyes were slow to focus and she couldn't quite read the number.

"Hello?"

"Madame Renard?"

"Yes."

"This is Captain Bouchard of the Gendarmerie de Argents-sur-Mer."

Margot rolled her eyes. She swung her legs over the side of the sun lounger, her bare feet connecting with an empty champagne bottle that had somehow managed to get down there. She picked it up and returned it to the table. "What is it?"

"Judge Deveraux asked me to call. She would like to see you at four o'clock."

"Why?"

"She didn't say."

Margot checked the time: it was two p.m.. She removed her sunglasses and rubbed some life into her eyes. "Very well."

"I'll meet you at the *Palais de Justice* at four p.m. sharp."

Margot sobered up with two cups of strong black coffee. Most of her clothes were in the wash, and she still hadn't replaced those that had been lost in the fire. The only decent outfit she had in her wardrobe was the jacket and pants she'd taken from Enzo's laundry room so she put those on.

This time, the receptionist greeted her with a friendly smile and sent her straight up. Captain Bouchard was already waiting in the vestibule, fidgeting with annoyance. As Margot closed in on him, he raised his wrist and pointedly stared at his watch.

"It is four-o-six, Madame."

Margot breezed by with her head held high before knocking sharply on the door. She flicked him a conquering look as her hand turned the handle

Judge Deveraux came out from behind her desk and intercepted them en route. "How lovely to see you, Madame Renard."

"It's nice to see you, too."

"And thank you for coming."

"Not at all."

They warmly shook hands. Anyone would think they were old friends.

The judge indicated seats on the nearside of the desk as the secretary brought in coffee. The judge remained standing while she filled the china cups and added milk and sugar – none for Margot, three lumps for the captain. She carefully handed them their cups before retreating to her side of the desk.

"I hear you've moved back into your house."

"Yes. They've finished all the repairs."

"I'm glad to hear it. Biscuit?"

She offered them a plate. Margot declined, Captain Bouchard took two. They each had a sip of their coffee before the judge returned her cup to the tray. Her eyes were sparkling and she seemed quite buoyant.

"I imagine you're wondering why I asked you here."

"The captain was very cryptic."

The judge smiled. "The first reason was to formally thank you. The fact we apprehended the smugglers and foiled a substantial drugs plot is largely down to you. Your determination is to be admired."

Margot gave a small nod of her head.

"I understand you also paid for a funeral for the boy and his father."

"It was the least they deserved."

"How commendable." The judge smiled wistfully and the office fell silent. She was looking Margot directly in the eye and Margot flushed, not quite understanding her interest. After a few moments, the judge came back and shifted her gaze.

"Which brings me to the second reason."

"Yes."

"I was hoping I might enlist you." She said 'enlist' in a conspiratorial way.

Margot frowned. "Enlist me, for what?"

Judge Deveraux shuffled some papers. "I've been looking into your background; I hope you don't mind. But I see your father was a judge in England and that you trained as a lawyer in both London and Paris."

"It was a long time ago."

"Nevertheless, it would be a shame to let such talents go to waste. You've proved what a diligent investigator you can be. You could be a real asset to my office."

"That's very kind of you but—"

The judge raised a hand. "Please don't be modest. You're a compassionate, intelligent woman and it's important we stand up for ourselves in this patriarchal world." Neither of them looked at the captain but the judge's words were enough to stick pins in him. Judge Deveraux continued, "We always have a number of cases where, for whatever reason, the investigation reached a dead end or failed to result in a prosecution. Our 'cold cases', if you like. I've always felt it would be useful to have a fresh pair of eyes look over them."

Margot straightened in her seat, beginning to see where this might be heading.

"I was wondering if you would be interested in working for me. You would remain in a civilian capacity, of course. The cases you would be given would be at my discretion and you would take a purely advisory role. But, in principle, is that something that might interest you?"

Margot was flummoxed and didn't know how to respond. She clasped her hands around her knee, and when she opened her mouth to speak the words evaporated on her tongue.

"You would need to liaise with Captain Bouchard, of course. I trust that won't be a problem."

Margot brightened. Suddenly the proposition took on a whole new dimension and she saw the potential. A sly smile warmed her face. "I'm game if the captain is," she said.

And this time they both turned to the man at her side. Captain Bouchard gave a begrudging nod of his head, looking as if he'd just swallowed a fly.

THE END

WHAT NEXT?

Margot Renard will return in:

Five Dead Men

For updates, visit: www.rachelgreenauthor.com

PLEASE REVIEW THIS BOOK!

Please don't underestimate the importance of reviews to authors, particularly independent authors who don't have the backing of a huge marketing machine. If you enjoyed BODY ON THE ROCKS please consider leaving a review online, at either Amazon or Goodreads—it would be greatly appreciated.

FOLLOW:

https://twitter.com/AuthorRachelG
https://www.instagram.com/authorrachelg/
https://www.facebook.com/AuthorRachelG
https://www.bookbub.com/authors/rachel-green?follow=true